TWO DEAD HEROES

Ian McCollum

Published in 2020 by FeedARead.com Publishing

A CIP catalogue record for this title is available from the British Library.

Cover design by *Bec Smith*

Millthorpe is a real, rather delightful village seven miles west of Chesterfield town centre. Millthorpe Hall is, however, fictional. All the other places named in this book are in North Derbyshire.
All characters and events in this publication are fictitious and any resemblance to real persons, living or dead, is purely coincidental.

Any mistakes in police procedures or equipment are mine alone –
it's just a story and I hope you enjoy it.

Home matters…

It should have been a wonderful family day out in the school summer break. A trip to Matlock, ice cream, paddling pool, boating lake, fish and chips and laughter, lots of laughter. It was a huge breakthrough and the parents were gloriously happy.

Home – and a movie all snuggled up together on the sofa. Popcorn and the 'once-a-week' glass of diet cola. An appeal from the girls for a second film, first rejected then allowed – they could have a lie-in tomorrow - everything was going just right.

Until…

…the younger girl wanted a drink of water. Dad told her to go to the kitchen and help herself because neither adult had paid attention to what was happening outside; the light had faded.

The girl walked into the dark kitchen and the awful memories came rushing back. She screamed. When her parents arrived five seconds later, the girl was lying on the floor and shaking violently.

She was rushed to bed and cuddled until she slept but, from that moment on, Sophie refused to enter the kitchen.

The Day family had a serious problem.

Prologue

The three young men on the train were perhaps being a little too raucous to be considerate to those around them.

Nobody complained – for three reasons: their banter was lively but good-humoured; the table between them was covered in documents and empty cans - and they were the toughest looking trio it was possible to imagine.

The men were in civvies but it didn't take a genius to work out they were military. Nicknamed the 'Chezzies' by their comrades in 40 Commando, Royal Marines, Gary 'Shiner' Martin, Stephen 'Red' Hamilton and Tahir 'Chalky' Abbas were men on a mission. But there was no violence in their plans – it was love and potential change of career that was leading them all home.

Shiner was big and so bald his suntanned scalp looked polished – despite the myriad of tiny white scars.

Red was smaller and rather better looking. His equally suntanned, scarred face was topped by lush auburn hair with distinctive ginger flecks.

The final member of the trio had much darker skin. Some people would have guessed correctly that Chalky was of Pakistani origin but no one in their right mind would have even considered calling him 'Paki' to his face.

Had the other passengers studied the group more carefully they would have been relieved to see all the empty cans were alcohol-free and the papers were complex business documents.

As the train rolled into Chesterfield, the paperwork was bundled into Chalky's briefcase. They shook hands. They high-fived. They each shouted "Agreed!" They laughed. Passengers around them joined in the laughter – three happy blokes preparing for something unknown – but obviously something very exciting.

Outside the station, waiting illegally next to the statue of locomotive wielding George Stephenson, was a black Mercedes. Chalky waved to his friends, climbed in and was gone.

Shiner looked at Red and uttered a single word, "Beer!"

Both were still laughing at their need for Dutch Courage as they walked up the hill into the town centre.

-

It was perhaps a coincidence that, almost exactly 48 hours before, two passengers had arrived at Chesterfield Station and were picked up by an almost identical black Mercedes. The couple, in their forties, were met by their son, Robert (not his real name) who recognised them from a photo he'd received an hour before. Mr and Mrs Jones (not their real names) were a rather nondescript pair; they liked it that way. Robert drove them to a rented holiday cottage in Barlow but they didn't stay long. The Jones family mission required quite a significant amount of preparation and they were strangers in town.

PART ONE
Chapter One
Day's DAY 1

Wednesday:

Their first night out together for two months was ruined.

Sophie had been the catalyst; her recovery after the move to the new house had been dramatic. She walked into the kitchen and calmly announced that she and Alice were perfectly alright and it was time for mum and dad to go out on a date night. The only condition was that 'Uncle' Andy would agree to babysit. Acting Detective Sergeant Andy Grainger had become a regular visitor to the Day household since the kidnap incident and had worked hard to earn that esteemed title. Andy had asked if he could bring along Dipa Sindhu; Jess agreed, recognising the first tentative steps in a relationship.

And so, that Wednesday evening, Derek and Jessica Day had taken a taxi to the Pomegranate Theatre to watch a movie. They had planned to go for a drink at the Pig & Pump afterwards but, within five seconds of leaving the auditorium, DCI Day knew that wasn't going to happen. The foyer was filled with the reflection of blue flashing lights – too many for a simple street fight.

His first impression was confirmed by the presence of PC Rouse by the main door.

"Mr Rouse, what an unexpected pleasure!" Day's tone suggested otherwise.

"Sorry sir; sorry Mrs Day," whispered the constable, "we've found a body just across the road in the churchyard."

"A drunk?"

"Definitely not, sir." Rouse's flat reply activated Day's alarm bells.

He looked into his wife's eyes and uttered the same apology he had made a thousand times before. She smiled and nodded. Day melted; what had he done to find such an understanding woman?

"Take Mrs Day home, please Mr Rouse and bring DS Grainger back with you – he's babysitting. I'll walk across."

"Will do, sir."

They walked outside and the PC opened the front door of his car for Mrs Day. As soon as the door was closed, Rouse whispered again to the DCI, "Didn't want to cause your lady any distress; it's not a body – it's just a head!"

-

It was a mild night for late September as Day strode across the zebra crossing towards the young PC guarding the tape across the bottom of the churchyard steps.

"Evening, Mr Dawson, where's the action?"

Dawson gave a grim smile, lifted the tape and pointed upwards. Day looked up at the magnificent Crooked Spire of St Mary and All Saints and was temporarily transported back to the heartbreak of his grandfather's funeral.

Three flights up, DC Kamil Malysz was waving in Day's direction.

"Sir," he said simply.

"Just a head, Kam?"

"Yes sir." The young Polish detective was a man of few words.

"Where is it?" asked Day.

"Round the other side of church, near big bee." Everyone in Chesterfield knew all about the controversial Bee Sculpture.

"Okay, lead the way." As they began to walk the length of the churchyard, Day couldn't resist asking, "Just as a matter of interest, Kam, how did you know where to find me?"

"DS Sharp told us, sir."

"She's not been hanging around the station while I've been on leave, has she?"

"Sir."

"Heck! I told her to keep away until her convalescence is over – she's at least another two weeks to go."

Kamil just nodded.

What was now puzzling Day was how Sharp knew he and Jess were at the Pomegranate. What he didn't know was that his wife's strategy was based on the 'keep your friends close and your enemies closer' adage. While Jess didn't regard Mandy Sharp as an enemy, she certainly saw her as a potential rival. During the detective's prolonged recovery, Jess had made a point of getting involved.

"Who found it, Kam?"

"Some kids found it half hour ago behind sculpture, they're at church door with PC Ainsworth."

"Kids?"

"Teens, sir. Three boys."

As they turned the corner of the impressive building, there were the boys - looking sheepish. Day nodded to them. "Thanks for sticking around lads, be with you in a minute."

The two detectives walked the remaining few yards towards the bee sculpture. The shiny wooden insect was looking sinister in the distant streetlights. Day asked, "Okay, Kam, what have you observed so far?"

"Youngish male, head shaved, not clean cut."

"Right, let's have a look."

From a discreet distance, using his colleague's torch, Day was able to see the head resting on a bed of autumn leaves in a dip in the soil behind the sculpture. An instant of recognition hit his memory then vanished. "Must have been unloaded from a bag… after dark… someone wanted it found… but not this quickly… how come the boys spotted it here, in the shadows?"

"They was playing soccer, sir. Lost the ball over here. They expecting bollocking for playing in churchyard!"

"It was still daylight when we went into the Pomegranate. Boys found it around nine so it must have been dumped in the ninety minutes or so before that. Useful for CCTV!"

The initial impressions firmly recorded in his brain; Day instructed the SOCOs to carry on setting up the tent. Two photographers were taking pictures of everything in sight. Police tape was now blocking every entrance to the churchyard.

Day looked at his watch. "Just over half an hour ago? Good, someone's been working hard getting the troops here so fast!".

8

"Good job a quiet night until this, sir. And I learn a lot from watching DS Pug, also." Kamil was taking the credit without making a fuss.

Day smiled inwardly; the young DC was definitely a quick learner but hadn't yet discovered that using his superiors' nicknames didn't go down too well with some. Pug Davies would be arriving soon, hopefully in a good mood.

"Let's have a quick chat with these lads then send 'em home, shall we?"

As the two detectives made their way to the church main door, there was a fuss on the path behind them. A woman was trying to force her way past another young constable. The black mini dress, high heels and unsteady gait said it all.

"Sorry madam," said the PC with exaggerated patience, "the churchyard is closed to the public; there's been a police incident!"

"Public! Public! I'll give you public! Don't you recognise a senior officer when you see one?" The voice was steady enough.

The constable almost melted into the paving stones. "Oh shit! Sorry ma'am," he whined.

Detective Superintendent Halfpenny spotted DCI Day and called over. "There you are, Derek. Everything under control?" She took off her stilettos and handed them to the PC before walking, rather more steadily, towards her second in command.

Day was almost as shocked as the unfortunate PC but managed to reply, "Yes, ma'am, the troops are all arriving now."

"Excellent, I'm glad they found you. I know you're supposed to be on leave but are you able to stay and take charge? I've just got a cab up from Casa and I'd like to get back. I'm on a date with a bloke who might be a keeper. He's already bought me a slap-up meal and a sixty quid bottle of plonk!"

Day had no idea how to cope with his boss in this sort of situation so he blurted out, "Everything is getting sorted,

9

ma'am. Feel free to get back to the hotel." It was the best place around and Day thought Halfpenny deserved a treat.

"Great! I'll just have a quick look at the corpse before I go; where is it?"

Day led her back towards a suitable viewing point not too close to the bee sculpture.

"Poor bugger!" was all she said before wandering back to a very forlorn constable to retrieve her shoes. She struggled to put them on for a few moments then gave up and set off back towards her waiting taxi. She turned and called to Day, "See you in the morning, Derek – I'll be in early!"

Day just had time to think 'doubt it' before a laughing Pug Davies arrived by his side.

"Bloody hell," he said, "Jill's on form tonight!"

Day made no comment; he knew Pug and the Detective Superintendent had been colleagues for more than twenty years.

The arrival of his friend made Day feel much better. "Hi, Pug. Will you do your magic and check the perimeter while I have a chat to the lads who found the… it?"

"No problem, I'll sort it." And Day knew it would be sorted.

On his way to talk to the boys, Day took a short detour to speak to the constable who'd fallen foul of Jill Halfpenny. "Don't panic, Mr McKillop, the Superintendent rarely bears grudges. I doubt she'll even remember!"

The PC gave a pathetically grateful nod to acknowledge the reassurance.

"I've got all their details, sir," said PC Ainsworth as Day approached the group by the church door. "This is Tom, Zack and Mark, they found the err… body."

Day looked at the football under the arm of the tallest boy and correctly guessed they were expecting to receive a serious telling off for kicking a ball around the churchyard at nine o'clock on a Wednesday night. "First of all, lads you're not in any bother for playing footy in the churchyard," he said. "In fact, we're very grateful you did the right thing and phoned the police then stuck around to help." He studied the three faces. "It must have been a terrible shock?"

"Fuckin' 'ell yes!" said the tall one, apparently named Zack. All bravado. "Any chance of a reward?"

Day tried to hide his recoil at the use of the ubiquitous word. "I'll see what I can do. First question – was anyone else in the churchyard when you arrived?"

"No, we wouldn't have had a kick around if there was," replied the boy introduced as Tom.

Disappointing. "Okay, I'm going to organise lifts home for all of you in a few minutes but first, just tell me which entrance you used and what happened."

Zack described the events in creditable detail until he got to the bit where Tom kicked the ball and it went behind the bee sculpture. "Mark went to get it and we heard him shout 'shit'. We went to have a look and there it was."

Day turned towards Mark, who hadn't yet said a word and was now looking decidedly unwell at the prospect of reliving the memory.

In his most gentle voice, Day said, "Tell me exactly what you saw, Mark."

The boy swallowed and began. "The ball was next to it. It was pretty dark back there and, at first, I thought it was one of them bald dummies you see in shops, then I touched its forehead." He held up his right index finger and looked at it in disgust. "It was all warm and soft."

Mark looked ready to faint so Day asked Ainsworth to take them to her car and see if she could find all three some drinks. As the group walked away, Day was mightily relieved to see Acting DS Andy Grainger approaching.

"Where do you want me, sir?" he asked.

"Hi Andy. Girls alright?"

"Alright? I'm glad of the excuse to escape, it's not good for my self-esteem being thrashed at Rumikub by a couple of kids!"

Day forced a grin. He'd had a similar experience. "Go after those lads, Andy. Ainsworth can drive them home; you go with her and see if you can get anything useful out of them. Tell the parents their boys have been really helpful so far and book appointments for them all to come into the station early

11

tomorrow. First thing preferably. Ask all three lots if they think their boys might need counselling – particularly the little lad called Mark."

"Will do boss."

As Grainger jogged off, a Jaguar followed by two vans swept into the turning circle between the Tourist Information Centre and the shopping area.

Doctor Smythe stepped out of the Jag and eyed the contents of the vans suspiciously. As he turned to inspect the churchyard, he spotted Day immediately. A constable held the tape for him to pass.

"What ho, chiefy!" he said with exaggerated politeness. "The press didn't take long to find you, did they? I've been told you've only got a bit of a body for me this time!"

Day looked over the doctor's shoulder at the three reporters who had been stopped at the barrier.

"Anything to tell us yet, DCI Day?" one shouted.

"Crikey, they get to crimes quicker every time," whispered Day. "They'll be here before me next."

The doctor picked up his mood and made an offer. "I'll go and speak to them, shall I? I could tell them you've found body parts. In a churchyard! Body parts in a churchyard – get it?"

Day got the joke but wasn't particularly amused. "Walk this way, doc, the bit you want to see is behind the bee sculpture."

As the two made the short walk, Doctor Smythe asked, "Seen anything of young Sharpy?"

"Too much, I'm afraid, doc. She can't keep away from the station and I keep sending her away. I owe her so much but I daren't be responsible for prolonging her recovery; she's got another two weeks before they'll even consider letting her return. At least Jess has been keeping an eye on her while I've been taking a couple of days off."

"I know what you mean but I don't agree. I saw her weekend before last; body's made a good recovery but she's not got enough to occupy her mind. In my esteemed medical opinion, she'd be better at work right away!" Doctor Smythe

12

was never shy about offering opinions – medical or otherwise.

"I could do with her. Everything about this situation shouts complications." DCI Day was just about to find out how complex his next few days would be. While Doc Smythe was having his first tentative look at the head, Day's mobile rang.

It was PC Walters, manning the front office at Beetwell Street Station. "Sir," he said, "I think I might know who your head belongs to!"

Chapter Two

Afghanistan

The three Royal Marines were following the squad of Afghan soldiers they had been helping train for more than a month. This was the new recruits' first, hopefully straightforward test. The village they were approaching was thought to have been cleared of Taliban fighters but, in this bizarre war, nothing was certain.

The local trainee soldiers were good lads, enthusiastic and fit. Their lieutenant was inexperienced but a bright, quick learner.

The main road into the village was the perfect setting for a trap. It was little more than a narrow lane between two rows of severely damaged dwellings. Half way down was a burnt-out car.

The lieutenant signalled his men to get down and they all took up defensive firing positions as they had been trained.

'So far, so good!' thought Corporal Gary 'Shiner' Martin. 'Red' Hamilton to his left and 'Chalky' Abbas on the right thought the same.

Suddenly, there was movement at the far end of the lane. Six kids emerged. They wandered into the open looking very confused – as though they'd been ordered to walk out there but not told what to do when they arrived.

"Trap!" mouthed Shiner to his colleagues. Both nodded.

The children were looking around when one noticed the platoon of Afghan soldiers lying in the dirt at the far end of the lane. He waved. A shot came from nowhere and the boy's head disintegrated. The children scattered.

'Don't!' thought Shiner.

The Afghan lieutenant gave an anguished cry and stood up.

"Don't!" said Shiner under his breath.

The lieutenant waved his men to their feet and signalled them forward.

"No sir! Stay down, sir!" yelled Shiner.

The officer didn't hear or chose to ignore the shout. He led his men in two wary columns down either side of the street towards the panicking children.

Shiner signalled his two comrades to hold their positions. It was a good decision; as the Afghan soldiers began to pass the wrecked car, it exploded with colossal force. When the smoke cleared, the marines could see half of the young recruits had been blown to a bloody pulp. Most of those that still resembled people were already dead but a few soldiers and children were crawling and calling out in pain.

Shiner waved the 'stay down' signal.

A full minute passed before there was more significant movement at the far end of the street. Two black-clad figures emerged and began to saunter through the carnage. A young soldier tried to rise and appeal for help but received only a sharp kick and a single shot to the head.

It was the execution of one of the injured children that caused the marines to act. Shiner looked to his left and signalled, 'enemy left, take out in three'.

The two shots were simultaneous. Both Taliban fighters fell dead. The marines expected massive and immediate retaliation but there was none. If any other enemies were around, they must have assumed it was their comrades finishing off more victims.

Red radioed for an evacuation but knew it wouldn't be quick; their training mission had been to enter the town covertly and they'd left their transport three miles behind.

Taking advantage of every bit of cover, the marines crept forward checking for survivors. They found two children and the young lieutenant still alive but all were in desperate condition. As they began to carry the victims into the shelter of an abandoned house, a dozen or more Taliban fighters emerged from the far end of the street.

The new arrivals were surprised to see foreign soldiers attempting a rescue. They had believed the few shots they heard were from their comrades completing their successful IED ambush. The split-second delay saved the three marines and their burdens. The house would provide flimsy cover but it was enough to offer just a chance of survival.

Chapter Three

"We had a call at 5.13pm. A young woman told us her boyfriend had phoned to say he was on his way and he'd be with her in a half hour. An hour later he hadn't arrived and wasn't answering his phone. Of course, we told her not to panic – he'd probably met some friends and was having a couple of pints. She did leave some details. His name's Gary Martin and he's a marine just returned from duty in Afghanistan. Sir, his nickname's 'Shiner' – he's completely bald!" PC Walters was obviously embarrassed.

Day didn't respond immediately. 'A soldier? Afghanistan? Beheaded? Hell's bells – this is going to be complicated! Hang on, that's the recognition!' he thought. About six months before there'd been an article in the Derbyshire Times about three Chesterfield lads getting wounded in Afghanistan. It wasn't a large photo of three men in uniform but it was enough for Day's legendary memory. "Okay Mr Walters, don't panic. Text me the girlfriend's details. I'll go and see her; she bound to have a decent photo handy. The sooner we can confirm it's this poor lad the better. Is there a spare response car around or is everyone tied up here?"

"Sorry sir, but you're right. Everyone on duty is at the churchyard," replied Walters.

"Right, I'll improvise." Day had a good idea where his favourite driver would still be. He was right - and five seconds after his call, she abandoned the pot of tea she was sharing with Jess and set off to pick him up.

10.30pm
PC Dipa Sindhu drove to the girlfriend's address at Old Whittington. It was a pleasant little bungalow at the top end of the village.

The door was opened immediately after the first ring. It was a man in his thirties; very muscular and with a bleached blonde brush cut that gave him the look of an American Football quarter-back.

"Oh," he said. "Who are…" Then he noticed Day's warrant card. "Police?"

"DCI Day and PC Sindhu, sir. We're looking for Ms Gina Thomson, is she in?"

"Oh shit; you're a Chief Inspector, this isn't good. What's happened?"

"We need to talk to Ms Thomson. Is she in?" Day repeated.

"Sorry, yes, of course. Come in. I'm Will, her brother." The big man offered his hand.

Day shook it as he squeezed past.

Gina Thomson was seated on a sofa next to another woman who could have been her twin if she hadn't been twenty years older. The younger woman was crying and the older was in full comforting mode.

"Police, Gina. Mum, this is DCI Day and Constable…?"

"Sindhu," added Dipa helpfully.

Day nodded hello but he already had his answer from his first glance around the room. Above the fireplace was a portrait of a stunning young woman accompanied by the head he had seen in the churchyard.

Gina Thomson didn't look so stunning now. The announcement of Day's rank caused the same reaction as her brother's.

"What's happened?" she stammered.

"Please sit down, Inspector," interrupted the older woman.

The two officers sat on a matching sofa opposite before Day began. "You phoned in to report your boyfriend, Gary Martin missing at 5.13 this evening?"

The younger woman nodded. "We've phoned everyone who knows him, no one's seen him since he left Wetherspoons."

"Do you have a recent photo of Gary?" asked Day.

"Of course." She pointed to the wall and then reached over towards a bookcase and handed Day a picture of a smart young marine corporal standing outside what was obviously Buckingham Palace. "That's the most recent I have. I took it myself when I went with him to collect his medal six months ago. That's the last time I saw him." A faraway look came into her eyes.

18

Day studied the picture. Total confirmation. "A Conspicuous Gallantry Cross? You must have been very proud?"

Gina didn't answer but her brother intervened. "Come on, Inspector, what's happened? I've just been into town to look round the pubs for Gary. There were a lot of sirens and blue lights as I was leaving. Big fight?"

Day didn't deny it but then Gina came back into the conversation. "Gary doesn't fight! I know it sounds daft for a marine but he's really gentle at home... with me!" She looked down at her feet and counted to ten before steeling herself. "Is he dead?"

The question was brutal and Day sought the best way of giving a not too brutal response. "A body has been found but it's too early to confirm the identity. However, I think you should prepare yourself for the worst news." Day's quiet voice didn't soften the blow and Gina dissolved into more tears.

PC Sindhu edged forward ready to offer support but she was held back by a glare from the girl's mother.

"I'm so sorry to ask questions at a time like this but I need to know one or two things really urgently. When did Gary set off to town and who with?"

Will Thomson, recognising his sister's severe distress, answered for her. "He didn't leave from here, Inspector. He came in by train. We were expecting him around lunchtime but, obviously, he didn't show. It's a pretty easy guess who he was with. The two lads who got medals with him are both from Chesterfield and they stick together like glue."

There was a quiet snort from the mother but Will continued quickly. "They're good lads, Inspector."

Gina added, "They were coming up together. Gary said he had a couple of questions to ask me and his mates were going to ask their girls, too. An offer I couldn't refuse, he said. I'm sure he was going to propose." She sobbed then seemed to steady herself. She walked out of the room and returned just moments later carrying a small plastic box. "Gary cut the last of his hair off six years ago. The sample in there might help with DNA, I suppose?"

Day was almost lost for words. "Thank you. Do you have the names, phones and addresses of Gary's colleagues, please? I could do with details of his parents, too."

"We know Red's address, we've been to his house, haven't we pet?" said Will. "But we don't know Chalky so well – he likes to keep to himself. I'm sure Red'll know it though."

The information was exchanged and recorded in Sindhu's notebook.

"Thank you for that, all of you. You have my word, as soon as we know anything for definite, you will be informed immediately." Day stood to leave.

"I'll see you out, Inspector," offered Will.

As soon as they were outside, Will went straight to the point. "You've been a little cagey, Inspector – is it Gary you've found?"

"Near enough certain, I'm afraid. Your sister's going to have her heart broken!"

Will's response startled Day. "Yes, but she'll recover – she's a lot tougher than she looks. I reckon you have to be tough to be a military girlfriend. Very determined lass is our Gina. You know, she was offered all sorts of modelling contracts in her teens but all she wanted to do was be a bloody physiotherapist – for as long as I can remember. She's so focused it scares me sometimes."

"It's good she's got you to look out for her; she'll certainly need you in the coming months."

"Always," Will replied. "Let me know if there's anything I can do to help. I run my own business so I'm in and out all day but if you need me this'll do the trick." Day was handed a business card. 'THE COMPUTER SHOP', Chatsworth Road. Day had seen the blandly named enterprise in passing.

"Thanks," Day said as he brushed past a motorbike parked on the drive. It was still warm. "Nice bike."

"Oh, that's just my runabout. My proper, proper bike is locked in the garage; would you like to see it?"

Day was surprised by the offer but Dipa Sindhu couldn't help herself; she was an enthusiast. "What have you got?" she asked.

Will Thomson was obviously very proud of his possession and began what could have been a lengthy description: "Vincent Black Shadow, '55 model…"

Day wasn't in the mood for a technical lecture. "Thanks again, Mr Thomson. Keep your sister safe; I'm sure we'll be in touch first thing in the morning. I wish I could be optimistic."

As the two police officers climbed into Sindhu's car, Day asked. "What do you make of all that, Dipa?"

"A Vincent? If it's in good nick, it'll be worth a fortune!"

"Not the bike… the family?"

The tall PC shuffled uncomfortably in her seat for a few moments. "Strange dynamics!" she stated.

"Hmm, I thought so, too. Gina's reaction seemed genuine but the brother was rather casual about the situation. Mother was just plain weird…"

"Racist!" said Sindhu bluntly. "She wasn't happy about my presence in her house."

"Ah, I wasn't going to say anything but that's what I picked up, too. It must have been uncomfortable for you?"

"Not as much as it was for her, I'm glad to say!" Sindhu even managed a little chuckle.

"I can't begin to imagine what it's like to be on the receiving end of prejudice; do you ever get used to it?"

"I learned how to deal with after I'd been called a 'Paki' the first couple of hundred times. It cheers me up to think that people who call me that are seriously thick. At least it amuses my Pakistani friends when I tell 'em!"

Day sat in the passenger seat shaking his head.

"Where to, boss?" asked Sindhu, breaking his stupor.

"I'll phone ahead then it's off to the parents' house, please. Just for a few moments then I really need to see this 'Red' character – before we have a very popular team meeting at 2am!"

Chapter 4

Afghanistan

Five hours of hell awaited the three marines!

Gunfire and grenades came through every window as they dragged their burdens from room to room in the large, ruined building.

Medic 'Chalky' did as much first aid as was humanly possible while his two comrades carried the injured to the next area of temporary safety before taking up guard positions.

At two to three-minute intervals a new, small group of fighters would charge in through a random opening – but they were dealing with the best of the best. Every intruder was shot within seconds of appearing inside. Piled bodies began to block some of the access points.

The Taliban fighters realised they were up against a formidable enemy and resorted to using RPGs to blast out the foreigners. Shrapnel rained down and, two hours into their ordeal, each of the marines had many minor wounds. A radio message said help was on the way but no definite timeline was possible. They discussed calling for US air support but decided that would place them at greater risk. Despite Chalky's best efforts, one of the children died.

Thinking all those inside were dead or disabled, the fighters launched another, more determined incursion. Most were killed and the others retreated. The assault with grenades resumed.

Then silence.

A massive explosion was followed by the unmistakeable sound of tank tracks on hard ground. Heavy machine guns spat. Shiner risked a look outside and was rewarded with a phenomenal sight – three American Abrams tanks – weapons the Taliban had virtually no defence against. Within minutes, the area was cleared of opposition and their patrol's original transport team entered the building accompanied by an American colonel.

"Bloody hell, Shiner, you've had a bit of bother here, mate!" said the marine sergeant who'd just arrived.

"You took your fucking time!" was the response but there was gratitude in his eyes.

"Yeah, once we realised you walked into hundreds of the bastards, we knew we'd have no chance until help arrived. Luckily these yank tankers were on exercise down in the next village and came straight away. That is Colonel Adamson – you've got him to thank."

The US colonel had been wandering around the building but returned to the survivors at the mention of his name. "Jeez, corporal, you've done some good work here; I've counted thirty-three of the bastards. You guys can come and work for me anytime. Sorry you got hurt; we would have been quicker but we had to refuel – our babies are real thirsty!"

"You were in the nick of time, sir. We're very grateful," offered Chalky.

The colonel, apparently noticing him for the first time, looked him up and down before replying, "You're welcome…"

That was the end of the pleasantries; the three marines and their two survivors from the IED explosion were hustled into a Humvee. Next stop, hospital.

None of their wounds were life-threatening but several weeks of painful treatment followed. Eventually, the three marines were sent for by their CO.

They weren't expecting any thanks and, at first, they didn't get any. "You allowed your patrol to walk into an obvious trap!" The CO wasn't one to mince words.

Red and Chalky knew that wasn't strictly fair – they had both heard Shiner tell the young lieutenant to stay put - but corporals can't give officers orders.

"My fault, sir. I accept full responsibility," offered Shiner.

"Agreed! When the silly young bugger stood up and charged down the street you should have shot him – at least that would have saved some of his men!"

The three chastened marines couldn't believe their ears, the Major was working up to a serious rant. Then they found out why. "Of course, it had to be a bloody yank colonel who came to your rescue, didn't it? Those buggers are so easily impressed; he thought you were heroes, told me you should all get medals! I told him you'd be lucky to keep your stripes, Corporal Martin! But then, it got bloody worse. That daft lieutenant you kept alive is only the son of a government fucking minister! And now the whole Afghan government thinks you're heroes, too, God help us!" The CO paused for breath. "Our allies think you're heroes, so heroes you are and you're going to get medals. I can't fucking believe it!

-

Home matters…
The family had been in a dreadful panic about Sophie's relapse. There was plenty of advice and support on offer but nothing seemed to help. The girl simply would not go into the kitchen.
"We'll have to move house!" said Derek to Jess at a midnight conference.
"I'm sorry to say I agree with you. Trouble is, it takes ages – not to mention the expense."
"Sophie's mental health comes first. I can't see an alternative."
"Okay, I'm going to talk to some estate agents tomorrow. We'll get this on sale and then we can start looking. It'll probably take until Christmas – if we're lucky." Derek wasn't at all optimistic.
But - a real stroke of luck was on the horizon.
The following Friday it was Jimmy Hammond's retirement 'do' at the Rose and Crown. Derek had always liked Jimmy and he allowed Jess to persuade him to go along to show his face.
It was pretty lively when Derek arrived but he managed to get to the bar and order a half of his favourite beer, 'Golden Bud'. That was to be his only quiet moment; Jimmy spotted him and came over.
"Good to see you, sir. Glad you could come!" he stated just a little too loudly.

24

"Less of the 'sir', Jimmy. We're well beyond that stage! How are you – having a good time?"

"Brilliant, every time I put my glass down someone swaps it for a full 'un." He turned suddenly serious. "How's the family?"

"Not good, Jimmy. Sophie's got really bad feelings about being in the house; we've started to think about moving but it's obvious it's going to take ages."

To Day's surprise, Jimmy Hammond turned and walked away without comment. 'Oh well,' he thought, 'Jim must be more drunk than I thought.'

After talking to three more colleagues, Derek felt a tug on his arm; it was Jimmy again but he wasn't alone.

"Derek," he said, in a rather embarrassed tone, "you know Sally, the wife, don't you?"

"Of course, I do." He took her hand. "Good to see you, Sally, it's been too long."

"You too, Mr Day. Jimmy says you've got a house problem?"

"True, but there's no way I'm going to let it spoil Jimmy's party!"

She smiled and said, "It's actually helped make Jimmy's party even better, Mr Day. We're off to Australia next week to see the grandkids. We've never seen two of 'em so hope to be away at least six months and we were a bit nervous about leaving the house empty over the winter. You wouldn't like to house-sit would you?"

Day was gobsmacked! He had an idea that the Hammonds lived in a newish detached house in Upper Newbold and, when the shock subsided, realised the offer was certainly worthy of consideration. "That's incredibly kind, Sally, Jim. I hardly know what say."

"Talk to Mrs Day and, if she's keen come and have a look. No obligation – and you really would be doing us a favour," offered Jim.

Derek doubted their reasoning but was overwhelmed by the generosity of the Hammonds' offer. "Thank you so much, can I ring you over the weekend about it?"

"Course you can," said Jimmy, "but preferably not first thing tomorrow morning!"

And so it was settled. A viewing took place; terms were agreed; the Day family house was put up for sale; furniture in storage; personal items were transferred by an enthusiastic bunch of police volunteers - and four happy people moved into a house on Holme Park Avenue just a week later.

Chapter Five

Gary 'Shiner' Martin's parents were an interesting pair. When the father, in his pyjamas, opened the front door, Day immediately thought of an expression he'd heard his colleagues use - but one of which he didn't really approve. (MTTT = 'more tattoos than teeth.)

The mother, in total contrast, was fully dressed and apparently much more refined although it was obvious she'd been crying.

There was nothing more to learn from this mismatched couple. Gary had told them he would be arriving in Chesterfield around lunchtime and spending the afternoon with Gina. They hadn't been expecting him at home until 8pm but Gina had phoned and told them he was unaccounted for long before that.

"Why are you here, Chief Inspector?" asked Mrs Martin, with a strong emphasis on 'you'.

There was no point holding back. "I'm afraid we've found a body in the town centre; we believe it might be your son, Gary."

"Believe?" hissed Mr Martin.

"I can't say more than that until identification is confirmed. There are formal processes to follow and we'll keep you fully informed. We should know pretty soon, I'm sorry."

Mr Martin wasn't thrilled by Day's reply. "Well, you'd better piss off then and get on with the formal processes!"

"You're absolutely right, sir," replied Day. "We'll be away. I'll contact you immediately I know anything. I'm so sorry, this must be agony for you."

Mrs Martin gave Day a sad smile of apology but her husband just shook his head. The two police officers left without further discussion.

Day didn't want to talk either, he simply gave Dipa Sindhu the address of the second marine and sat back in the passenger seat to contemplate his next moves.

-

Day's DAY 2

Just after midnight Sindhu pulled up outside an end-terraced house close behind Brampton Primary School. The call ahead had ensured that Red and his girlfriend were up and prepared to be interviewed. The smell of quality coffee filled the pretty little sitting room into which the two police officers were received graciously.

Day introduced himself and his colleague before refusing an offer of coffee he hoped would be made again after the main part of the interview was over.

The young man held out his hand. "Hi, I'm Steve and this is Angie."

"Chief Inspector?" remarked Angie. "And to what do we owe your esteemed presence?" The question from Red's girlfriend came with a smile and no hint of sarcasm.

Day groaned inwardly. In the next five minutes he was going to cause this young couple no small amount of distress. "Mr Hamilton, you're a Royal Marine colleague of Corporal Gary Martin?"

"Shiner? Yes, great bloke – we've been mates since school. We joined up together. Okay, what's he been up to? Oh, and call me Red – everybody does."

"Thank you. I'm sorry to tell you that Gary was reported missing at about 5pm this afternoon. We're concerned for his safety." Day had decided to leave the major blow for later in the interview. "When did you last see him?"

"No, that can't be right," said Red, "I didn't leave him till five. It was outside Wetherspoons – Spa Lane – he said he was walking to the taxi office near the museum. It must have been five?" He turned to Angie with a puzzled look. "What time did I get here, love?"

She laughed. "It was 5.30 when you knocked on the door and it's about a half hour walk from that end of town. You staggered in and I made you a bucketful of coffee. You proposed to me at exactly six o'clock. I made a note of the time in my diary; it was very romantic – not!"

"Tell us about your arrival in Chesterfield right up to the time you last saw Gary." Day's serious tone caused Red and Angie to lose their smiles.

"12.37 train was on time – miracle! The three of us got off and Chalky was picked up immediately by his mother. He doesn't drink and me and Shiner decided years ago not to drink in his company– but as soon as he left, we needed a few beers. Dutch courage; we'd both decided to propose before we discussed our ideas with our girls. We had a couple in the Pig and Pump then a few more in Wetherspoons. That's it really."

"Who knew you coming to town today?"

Red looked at Angie with raised eyebrows. "Just family and a couple of friends," he said. She nodded.

"I'm going to need a precise list of everyone who was expecting your arrival," ordered Day.

"This is getting a bit serious, Mr Day! What's going on?" Red was moving from curiosity to annoyance.

Day now knew there was no point in messing around. "I'm sorry to have to tell you that we've found a body. We're not certain, but we believe it might be your friend Gary."

Angie squealed and put her head in her hands. She looked up through her fingers at her devastated fiancée, "They said this might happen – they warned us!"

Day was intrigued. "What might happen? Who warned you?"

"Military police," said Red very quietly. "At the palace when we got our medals. It was very low key, just the three of us, girlfriends and parents. It was supposed to be kept quiet. We killed a lot of bad guys in Afghanistan – Taliban. The security blokes said we'd be up for retaliation from extremists if word got around, especially if we were bragging. The press was told we'd been wounded but not about the CGCs." He looked sideways at PC Sindhu.

"I'm not a Muslim," she said very quietly, "but it wouldn't matter if I was – you were doing your job. All the Muslims I know think the Taliban are crackers."

Red nodded gratefully.

"Now, about that list. Who knew you were arriving today?" asked Day.

"Nobody outside the families, I reckon. Did you tell anyone, love?"

"Just my mum. I told her I thought you were going to propose. I was going to tell all the girls as well but I decided not to – in case you didn't and I'd look like a twa... fool!" Angie was in shock.

"Did you say 'yes' to the proposal?" asked Day. Anything to try to put a tiny bit of pleasantness back into a day he'd just ruined.

Angie smiled tearfully. "Yes, but only after the other big news. He's put in his notice to leave the Marines and we're going into business together – all six of us!" Then another level of truth dawned. "Oh shit, poor Gary... and Gina!"

Red moved closer to Angie and hugged her. "How certain are you it's Shiner?" he asked Day, grasping at straws.

"Don't get your hopes up, Red. I've seen the body and I've seen photos of Gary at his parents' and at Gina's house. It's him." Day knew he was overstretching the rules but he didn't want to leave this lovely young couple battling with agonies of uncertainty. "We're going to have to do a full, detailed interview early tomorrow... sorry, later today, I'm afraid. Where will you be?"

"We'll stick around here. Call when you want us. Would it help if we came to Beetwell Street?"

"It might, but I don't want you wandering the streets. We'll be in contact. What I do need is contact details for your buddy, Chalky is it? Could you give us that info?"

"No problem." Red tore a page from a notebook and quickly scrawled a name, address and mobile number. "That's his mum and dad's place."

"Thanks," said Day. "I'm not going to talk to Chalky tonight; I'll leave it until daylight. It would be really helpful if you didn't talk to him first?" The emphasis on 'didn't' left the couple in no doubt it was an instruction not a request. "We'll leave now, try and get some rest. I'm a little bit concerned about the possibility you might have been spotted as well. Just in case, I'm going to give this address and Chalky's to our patrols; they'll do regular drive-bys. Keep your doors locked. Any suspicions at all ring 999, okay?"

Angie gulped but Day recognised Red's very different expression. 'Let the bastards try!' it said.

The police officers both apologised again for being the bearers of such bad news and left.

As they climbed into Sindhu's car, Day said, "Station, please Dipa." He rang in and asked where the duty ARV Car was. Having been assured it wasn't at the other end of Derbyshire, he gave the operator Red's address first. As he began to read Chalky's details from the notepaper, he groaned.

"Problem, sir?" asked Sindhu as soon as he put the phone down.

"Could be. Marine humour. Chalky's real name is Tahir Abbas. I've had dealings with his father. Very active Muslim lawyer, got a practice on Saltergate. Picks up a lot of ethnic minority cases. Good at his job... like a dog with a bone. He's always been alright with me but he's generally not a massive fan of the police. This is looking very much like a terrorist attack so it's likely we'll be talking to a lot of Muslims amongst others. We'll find out tomorrow if the distinguished Mr Ahmed Abbas is going to be help or hindrance!"

Chapter Six

2am Briefing, Beetwell Street Police Station.

"Get a sandwich if you're brave enough but not too much coffee; some of the lucky ones are going to be sent home for a very short sleep!" began the DCI.

'Daysway' – an expression first coined by Pug Davies.

Thanks to the super-efficient efforts of his mentor, photos of the head, the victim (when alive) and the immediate area of discovery were already on display.

"As you can see," continued Day, "it's 99% certain that our head belongs to Marine Corporal Gary Martin, aka 'Shiner'. This means we have a very, very dirty case on our hands. I'd be telling you it was definitely a terrorist attack if there wasn't a tiny doubt in my mind - but the beheading does suggest revenge on Mr Martin for his recent heroics in Afghanistan. What does worry me is the speed. With this kind of attack, terror is the key. An organised group would have kidnapped him and put all sorts of appalling images on the internet before killing the poor bloke. Maximum publicity! This suggests a group of amateurs but, if that's the case, how did they know this lad and his two mates were arriving yesterday and hanging around town for a drink? A kidnap in broad daylight – it just doesn't add up.

Enough of guesswork, let's look at what we do know; Internet, Phil? Any video? Claims? Chatter?"

"Nothing, sir – apart from 'what's going off in town?' nonsense on Facebook, etc."

"CCTV? Anything yet?"

"Nothing helpful, sir. We'll get an avalanche when all the local shops open; there's certain to be something." Phil Johnstone was ever the optimist.

"Look at cars coming in and out of town between 5pm and 6pm then dusk and 9pm. It'll be a nightmare of a job but we might drop lucky."

"Pug?"

DS Davies knew what was expected of him. "We suspect the head must have been carried into the churchyard in a bag of some sort. We've emptied every litter bin in the area and we'll find it if it's there. Too many footprints to be easy but we're photographing everything just the same."

"Dumping the head so soon after the murder is a puzzle, too, sir?" suggested DC Rutherford.

"Absolutely. My guess is whoever was doing the delivery thought someone carrying a bag through town at twilight would cause less suspicion than at midnight or later? I'm pretty certain they didn't expect the head to be found until morning, though – and that gives us a… start." Day just managed to avoid saying 'head start'. "Dom, did you get anything useful from the bar staff at either pub?"

"Not really, sir. Both places had been pretty busy. Some recognised the description of 'Shiner' with him being so distinctive but no one could recall if he was with anyone."

"Any CCTV?"

"Both pubs have promised everything they've got will be on my desk by breakfast," he replied.

"Good work." Day felt the need to publicly acknowledge Dom O'Neil. The DC had created something of a storm by beginning a relationship with a young woman who had wasted a lot of police time in a previous investigation. The attractive and wealthy Melanie Price had been lucky to evade prosecution and was not on most senior officers' favourite persons list.

"Righto," continued Day, "we know time of death was between 5pm and say 8pm and Doc Smythe says he might be able to narrow that down a bit more but we don't know where our victim was killed and mutilated – and that's a priority. We need to find the rest of the body and his mobile; that's where the real evidence will be. The uniforms are already starting a fingertip search but we need everyone out looking at first light. So - jobs!"

Day turned to his whiteboard and began allocating tasks. The list was long and in great detail.

"Those of you not on the list can go home in a couple of minutes and get some sleep but, before you do, a couple of general points. Our third marine is the son of our friendly neighbourhood solicitor, Mr Abbas and those of you who've had dealings with him before know he's as sharp as a razor and you'll have to be 100% on the ball. The potential for a lot of anti-Muslim rhetoric is high so do nothing to feed it. Everything is confidential; any leaks and there will be blood dripping from my office ceiling – no pun intended!" That statement made the message crystal clear and raised a half-smile from those officers who had worked with DCI Day the longest.

"Right; if you've no immediate job – go and sleep; back here by 8am. If you're on the list, get to it or wait here for further instructions. I'll be going to see marine number three at the crack of dawn so I won't be here until maybe 10am. Anything I need to know, call me anytime. Off you go!"

-

Home matters…
Disagreements in the Day household were rare.
Derek, Jess and the kids were happy in their temporary accommodation and that was the problem; they had no security. Jimmy and Sally Hammond could be returning from Australia in as little as four months. Although they'd had an offer on their own house, they hadn't made any decisions about their future; Sophie's state of mind was their priority.
"I've seen a couple of properties further out of town, Jess. Shall we go and have a look next weekend?" asked Derek with no small amount of trepidation.
Jess' smile evaporated. Despite being one of the most laidback individuals on the planet this was not an issue she felt comfortable with. "I'm not sure I want to move further out of town," she replied. "I like it here."
"Oh, come on, love, this isn't our house. It was always going to be just temporary – another few months at most."
"I know that! I mean I like the street, the estate. It's got a nice feel to it and we've made so many friends. There's often

34

houses for sale round here so let's concentrate our search locally?" It wasn't really a question.

Derek nodded. "I'm not sure, I want a house that I can protect. I'm not prepared to risk another incident like July. I can't have my job putting you and the girls at risk – we really ought to move further away from the area I work in!" He managed to keep his voice level but Jess picked up the genuine anxiety.

"I'd say it's safer for us all in the middle of a tight-knit estate where everybody knows everybody. All the neighbours know who you are and what you do and, I reckon if I shouted for help, there'd be twenty blokes here in less than a minute!"

Derek smiled. He suspected that Jess' looks and personality created more interest in the surrounding male population than his job – but he wasn't insecure. That wasn't even a part of his wish to move.

Jess interrupted his thoughts. "I'll go and have a look at the houses you've found if you'll agree to look at any that come up on the estate. Agreed?"

"Agreed!" said Derek.

7.45am

Knowing the Abbas family had a very busy life, DCI Day decided an early phone call was worth risking.

A female voice answered immediately. "Hello."

"Doctor Abbas?" enquired Day.

"Indeed; who is this?" Pleasant enough, given the hour.

"It's DCI Day from Chesterfield Police, doctor. I wonder if you son Tahir is available, please?"

Suspicion was immediately evident. "No, he's not in. What's this about, Inspector? Did you say Detective Chief Inspector?"

"Yes ma'am, I did. I'm aware your son returned to Chesterfield yesterday; is he not staying with you? I have some rather sad news for him."

"Oh dear! He is staying here but he's gone out. He left a note to say he's gone for a drive – in my car! His mobile is on the kitchen worktop and he'd better be back soon because I've got to get to work in ten minutes or so. My husband's out, too. Could you give me some detail?"

"I'd rather not, Doctor Abbas, but I'm sure your son will share the information after I've had a chat with him. He's not in any trouble... with the police." That tiny hesitation brought a more formal tone into the doctor's voice.

"Give me your contact number, Inspector. I'll tell him to call you immediately he returns. Ah, I can hear a car on the drive... yes, it's him and my car's in one piece by the look of it. I'll put him on." Thirty seconds elapsed. "Here he is, goodbye."

Day heard one or two words exchanged about the unauthorised borrowing of the car before a couple of clicks told him the phone had been picked up.

"Hello, Inspector?"

"Hello, Mr Abbas, Tahir Abbas?"

"Yes."

"I need to talk to you urgently. May I come to your parents' house now?"

The silence indicated a level of surprise and doubt. "Yes, I suppose so. Do you know where we live?"

"I do. I'll be there in less than fifteen minutes. Please don't leave the house before I get there. Okay?"

"Err... fine!"

Exactly fifteen minutes later, DCI Day pulled up on the drive of the large house on Somersall Lane. The door was opened before he knocked. Tahir Abbas was a powerfully built young man whose handsome features were only spoiled by the myriad of tiny white scars across his forehead and cheeks.

Day introduced himself and was invited in.

"Sad news, my mother said, Mr Day. What is it?"

"Yes, I'm afraid so. Do you mind if we sit?"

36

"No, come on through." Tahir led the way into a beautifully decorated lounge. As the two men seated themselves, a key was heard turning in the front door.

In marched Mr Ahmed Abbas. "What exactly is happening here, Chief Inspector?" demanded the solicitor.

Day stood and offered his hand. "Hello, Mr Abbas, good to see you again. Sad news rather than anything threatening; I've come to inform your son of a bereavement and ask him a few background questions."

Tahir Abbas was obviously annoyed by his father's interruption but stayed silent. His father remained on the offensive. "Does your visit have anything to do with the constant monitoring of our road by police vehicles throughout the night?"

"I'm afraid it does and I'm sorry if you were disturbed. The police presence was a precaution – we have concerns about your son's safety!"

"Explain!"

"I apologise for my father's behaviour, Mr Day. Perhaps you would now tell me this dreadful news?" The tension between father and son almost made Day wince.

"We found a body in the town centre last night. Formal identification hasn't yet taken place but I'm sorry to have to tell you that I believe it to be your colleague, Gary Martin."

A thousand emotions flashed across the young marine's face. "Shiner? Not possible! Shiner's indestructible!"

Day studied the young man's reaction but the unmoving expression told father and son that this was no joke, no mistake. Even the normally irrepressible solicitor was shocked into silence.

A full minute elapsed before Day continued. "It's my understanding you got off the 12.37 train together with Mr Martin and your other colleague? You left in a black Mercedes almost immediately?"

Tahir nodded. "Yes, my mother. She brought me here and we had lunch more or less straight away... didn't we dad?" Suddenly, the young man seemed very vulnerable; Mr Abbas senior appeared to be shocked by the use of the familiar term. Then a torrent of questions came from out of the deep shock. "You're a detective – was it murder? Does Red know? How did he die? Where? Does Gina know?"

Day interrupted. "Yes, it was murder and I'll answer your other questions in good time but, right now, I need to do the asking! You didn't see or hear from Gary after you left him with Red at the station?"

"No, no need. We'd already agreed to meet this afternoon, 5pm. All six of us."

"The three of you and your girlfriends?"

"Yes, we'd come up with a business plan we wanted to put to our ladies!" Day noticed a tiny crack in Tahir's voice on the word 'ladies'.

Day's question and Tahir's response caused Mr Abbas senior to recover from his shocked silence. "Tahir has resigned from the marines, Chief Inspector – much to my relief!"

"Where were you between 5pm and 9pm yesterday, Tahir?" Day's sudden blunt question immediately changed the atmosphere in the room.

The solicitor stood up. "Are you suggesting my son is a suspect?" he demanded.

"You know the drill as well as I do, sir. At this stage in a murder enquiry, everyone's a suspect. I need to rule out your son asap!"

"No problem, father," said Tahir returning to the formal address. "At 4pm I drove up to the hospital to pick up my fiancée; she's a doctor. We spent a couple of hours with her parents before I drove her to her apartment and then I came back here around 8pm." Tahir looked anxiously towards his father for confirmation.

"That's right, Mr Day. After that, he was with us all night. But now I think it's time to get to the real point of your presence here; you obviously suspect this is a terrorist murder, don't you? Islam is always the target when a soldier dies!"

Day shook his head and looked Mr Abbas straight in the eye. "We've had this discussion before, sir and I'd hoped that, by now, you realise I follow the evidence. I accept that you believe some police officers jump to conclusions but that's not the way I operate!" To end that destructive conversation, Day turned to Tahir and fired off another question. "Are you able to give me an idea about your business plan? I don't need confidential details; it's only from the point of Mr Martin making potential enemies, perhaps?"

"There's no secret. We're hoping to set up an outward-bound centre. Shiner had found a property we could convert. A perfect fit – between us, we have… had all the skills to make it work…"

"And my son will be able to return to university to complete his medical training!" interrupted Mr Abbas senior with an interesting mixture of pride and annoyance.

Mr Abbas junior subtly raised his eyebrows towards Day to indicate that was probably not part of his plan at all. "Of course, without Shiner, this all means nothing."

Day nodded. "I'm sorry, this tragedy really is going to shake up so many lives, so many plans." Day hesitated as he felt a vibration from his mobile. "Just one more question, then I'll leave you in peace. Your project sounds expensive; how were you intending to pay for it?"

Tahir raised a weak laugh. "Ironic really! We've all got some savings and Shiner had had some positive responses from potential investors but our medals were the clincher. We saw in the press that an ex-soldier had recently sold his Conspicuous Gallantry Cross for £80,000 – and we had three of them between us!"

'So,' thought Day as he left, 'an extra motive to consider.'

He looked down at his mobile before he started his car. It was a text from Andy Grainger. "Call me immediate!" was all it said – not even a 'sir'. Day drove off the drive and parked his car fifty metres down the lane before returning the call. There was a flash of silver as Mr Abbas senior's car overtook him.

"Andy – what's up?"

"Another body, sir!" Just a statement but Day hated those words – more lives ruined.

"What? Where?"

"The footpath that runs behind Ravenside and in front of B&Q. But that's not the worst of it. Dipa Sindhu is at the scene, sir – she says the body's Steve Hamilton – 'Red', the marine you both interviewed last night!"

Day felt sick; he had been thinking 'what a lovely couple' when he had left their house only a few hours previously. Guilt almost overwhelmed him; he hadn't done enough to protect them. Just one ARV with too much to do. He hadn't sufficiently emphasised the danger they were in. He should have challenged the young man's brash self-confidence.

Alarmed by the silence, DS Grainger spoke. "Sir?"

"I'm on my way, send for the cavalry."

"Already done!"

But there was one job Day had to do first. He turned his car and headed back to the house. Tahir opened the door and was given the sternest possible warning to lock up and not go out. Protection would soon be on its way. No more mistakes.

With a rising certainty that he was investigating jihadi revenge attacks, Day set off to view yet another body.

9.00am

Getting from the road to the crime scene was not easy. The footpath was almost crowded and Day fended off questions and had his photo taken half-a-dozen times before he made it through.

It was a very sombre-faced PC Sindhu who lifted the tape for DCI Day. "It's definitely him, sir. 'Red' - the Marine we saw last night err… this morning."

"What on earth are you doing here?" asked Day. "You should be home in bed."

"Earlies, sir. Our expeditions last night were on my day off, if you remember?" Sindhu did manage to crack a millisecond smile. "Nice start to the shift."

"I'll try to make it up to you – sometime," said Day. "Who found the body?"

"We don't know yet. Mysterious phone call from someone apparently without a name! Oh, Doc Smythe's on his way." She looked at her watch, "Eta 20 minutes."

As Day strode towards the covered heap on the path, he stopped suddenly. "Who are those two?" Day pointed to the two strangers standing under the trees. Both men were in crumpled grey suits and looked tired. The first was a big unit, well over six feet and with the shoulders of a successful prize-fighter. The second man was bigger. They stopped talking to each other and turned to stare at Day. He ignored their gaze.

"They're Military Police, sir. Drove up overnight from the south coast after hearing about our beheading. Andy's… err… DS Grainger… err… Acting DS Grainger's told them they can't get involved until you give permission." Sindhu's uncharacteristic stammering told Day that his wife's theory about the two officers being more than friends was probably quite right.

"Good," said Day, although he had hoped for a longer break before the inevitable outsiders arrived. "Let's have a look at the body."

Andy Grainger was standing close guard, writing in his notebook as Day and Sindhu approached. "Morning, sir. Bloody awful, sir. He was…"

"Hold it, Andy. Let me have a look first and then I'll be happy to take your input."

Grainger nodded and pulled away the blanket. 'Red' was face down on the tarmac. Shorts, t-shirt and trainers left no doubt about his reason for being out so early. The attacker had made a hideously botched attempt to hack off the head. The spine was severed but flesh from the throat was holding the body in one piece, albeit at a very peculiar angle. The pool of blood gave a clear indication that the knife attack had taken place right here but that wasn't definitely the cause of death. The feathers of a crossbow bolt protruding from the middle of the victim's back told the rest of the story.

Day studied the scene for a full minute before he stood up and looked at Grainger. "Go ahead," he said.

"Seems fairly straightforward, boss. Victim running along, gets arrow in back, falls on face, might have crawled a couple of feet, stops. Attacker runs up, draws big knife of some kind and starts to hack at the neck not caring whether victim is dead or not at that stage. Amount of blood suggests he was still alive – just. Very callous – hideous really. Distraction, witness turns up – attacker panics and runs for it."

"Agreed. Any suggestions where the attacker came from? Was he following or lying in wait?" Day's questions were academic, he believed he already knew the answer.

"Lying in wait would be my guess. Victim ran past and got the bolt as soon as the attacker could step out into the open and lift the crossbow. Trouble is, that suggests pre-planning. How would he have known when and where? It doesn't make any sense."

Day rubbed the back of his head. "Got to be OCD. I reckon this young man was obsessive about training and used the same route whenever he was on leave. His watch tells me he was timing himself. I've no doubt his partner will be able to tell us." Day studied the gruesome scene for two more minutes in silence before pointing and continuing. "Andy, have SOCO take a close look at those clumps of bushes; I'll bet that's where the ambusher was lurking. Send uniforms to canvas the area around Red's girlfriend's house – as soon as she's been told. Someone must have been watching the house to report if Red set off. One of the neighbours might have spotted the scout. Also, house to house at the Park Road end of the path to see if our victim was followed and round these shops to see if security men or shelf-stackers saw or heard a disturbance – we might get lucky and find the person who interrupted the attacker and/or the person who phoned in; we need that individual!"

Day turned to PC Sindhu. "Ms Sindhu, introduce me to our military friends." He indicated to the waiting SOCOs that they should continue their grizzly tasks.

"I'm afraid I don't remember their names, sir. Sorry, I should have written them down; I'm just thinking of them as Mr B and Mr VB," she admitted sheepishly.

"Big and Very Big?" guessed Day correctly but Sindhu didn't smile.

"This is DCI Day, gentlemen, SIO on the Martin murder." Sindhu made a very polite one-way introduction, hoping the two MPs would introduce themselves. They did but both glared at the young PC, immediately antagonising Day.

"Sergeants Bryant and Vernon, Military Police Investigation Branch," said the slightly less huge MP. "Anything we can do to help?" His tone was friendly enough.

Day looked up into their faces as he shook hands with both men. "Welcome to Chesterfield, gentlemen. This second murder must have come as quite a shock?"

"It did. Our C.O. ordered us up here 21.00 last night, six hours of driving, two Big Macs and then this… poor bugger," said Vernon.

Day glanced back at the body. "Did you know him – or Gary Martin?" he asked.

"Only by reputation. Their CGCs caused quite a stir in the Marine Corps – a lot of people thought they were very, very lucky!"

"How so?"

"The group of local squaddies they were supposed to be training was wiped out – not a great advert for the British military."

Day nodded. "Still, nobody deserves this kind of treatment."

"Absolutely!" said both MPs with one voice.

"I'm going to call a briefing to allocate tasks at noon at our HQ. You're welcome to come along and meet some of our team; they're a great bunch – very bright."

"Oh good!" said both MPs, once again in perfect harmony. They were each thinking, 'I bet they are.' – and Day read that on their faces.

"You can have a look at the body now, if you wish. Do you have protective gear?" said Day, with exaggerated formality.

"In the car."

43

"Fetch it then, and don't get in the way of my SOCOs."

As Day walked back to his car, an unusual confusion was circulating inside his mind. Everything was pointing to terrorism but his brain kept saying 'no'.

Chapter Seven

Noon Briefing
The team filed in armed with drinks and sandwiches courtesy of Pug's organisational genius.

"Right folks," began Day, "a couple of introductions. Sergeants Vernon and Bryant of the Military Police are joining us for this briefing and, if these crimes turn out to be terror related, will be very useful additions to our team. Welcome gentlemen."

The two MPs nodded and smiled to the officers surrounding them but their eyes said, 'plods from the sticks'. Once again, Day wasn't impressed.

"Before we begin to sort out this very, very bad situation a quick word about something close to home. DS Sharp; nearly all of you know Mandy pretty well. Her sick leave isn't up for review for a couple of weeks but I've been told by someone I respect that she needs to be back at work pronto. We all know what a good investigator she is so I'm going to bring her back unofficially. I'll give her my office and she will work exclusively for me handling all evidence as it comes in. No one, I repeat, no one is to give her any task without going through me, first. Strictly speaking this is against regs, so I carry the can if anything goes wrong, okay?"

Daysway.

The room was full of smiles, Mandy Sharp was a good officer and something of a hero. Only three faces registered any sort of disapproval. The two MPs were still thinking something like, 'what a load of amateurs' and Andy Grainger was looking down at his new shoes.

Day intervened immediately. "It won't affect your status, Andy. I don't expect you'll ever see the dizzy heights of Detective Constable again."

That brought about some tension-breaking laughter which Day very quickly silenced. "Two brutal murders! Two dead heroes in our town! Given the status of these young men, I think it all too easy just to write them off as victims of terror

45

revenge attacks. I have to say, that looking at the early evidence, I am far from convinced that is the case." He shifted his gaze to the MPs, both of whom were trying hard to disguise contempt.

They were firmly ignored. "Murder one; Gary 'Shiner' Martin. From what we can gather, Mr Martin was seized in the town centre at approximately 5pm yesterday. He must have got into a vehicle. We know he'd had a fair amount of alcohol, but this man is a decorated Royal Marine and yet he was taken without fuss, what does that suggest?" Day began writing a list of tasks then turned to survey his team.

"Acquaintance?" offered Dom O'Neil.

"It's got to be more than that, sir. He was picked up by someone he knew well – family – friend?" added Andy Grainger.

"Or the third Marine?" interrupted MP Sergeant Vernon.

"That's something we definitely can't rule out; a priority for today." Day turned to his tech wizard. "Phil, nothing on social media about last night?"

"There are no helpful claims of responsibility, sir. Some stuff on Facebook, Twitter etc from kids who were in town when the body was discovered but they're all guesswork. Nothing from anyone who actually knew any facts. I've scanned all the media favoured by terrorists and there's nothing."

"And we all know terrorism thrives on publicity. Anything on CCTV – cars in and out around 5pm – or, even better, someone carrying the head into the churchyard?" Day knew that Phil Johnstone had been working non-stop since midnight.

"Just under five hundred vehicles went in and out of town on the relevant route between 4.45 and 5.30pm. I've got my team gathering addresses and looking for any links with our victim. CCTV files from shops near the Crooked Spire are starting to come in; nothing so far," replied Phil.

"Anything from Doc Smythe, yet? Time of death – we know it was between 5pm and 9pm but more specific would be useful?" Day asked of no one in particular.

"I talked to the Doc twenty minutes ago, sir. He's working on the head as we speak. Shouldn't be long before we get the preliminary."

"Thanks, Dom. Any sign of the rest of the body?" Day's question brought a shake of the head from the officer coordinating the search. "Trev, can you set up an info-line and put out an appeal for anyone in the town centre around twilight and just after to come forward? We might just drop lucky. Try local radio asap."

"No probs, boss. Soon as we've finished here." DI Trevor Allsop was ten years older than Day but also one of his greatest fans.

"Andy, did you get round to talking to the boys who found the head?"

"No sir. But I sent Kam and he did the interviews."

"Kam?" Day turned to face the young Polish DC.

"Sorry, boss, nothing new. The one who found head first was still traumatised. I'm hoping to go round to their houses again this evening when, hopeful, they'll be more relaxed; all parents have agreed I can."

"Thanks. Let's consider murder number two. Marine Steven Hamilton; aka 'Red'. Found dead this morning only a couple of hours after I'd interviewed him and told him not to go out – obviously not forcefully enough. 5am on that path between the shopping complexes – it surely would have been deserted." Day pointed to each of the photos on the screen in turn. "Have we tracked down who found the body, yet? I'm hoping it was the same person who interrupted the killers; it could be fear that stopped him giving a name?"

"Not yet," responded Phil. "For some reason, he was using a phone reported stolen a couple of days ago – very suspicious, sir! Could even be the murderer?"

Like all the police officers in the briefing room, Phil could see guilt etched into Day's expression. They knew this was going to be an investigation where no quarter was given.

"Ms Sindhu, please visit the owner of the stolen phone. Any info about where and when it was stolen might help," ordered Day.

"Sir."

"Shot in the back with a crossbow then killed with several knife blows to the back of the neck; poor devil didn't stand a chance!" Day continued. "Ideas?"

"Girlfriend said he followed a regular route, sir. Timed himself – very obsessive but going out this morning was a last-minute decision. He couldn't sleep, obviously because of what had happened to his mate. He left around 4.45am, still dark, sir. Most of his route was footpaths, sir so he couldn't have been followed in a car," offered the young DC who'd been one of the unlucky ones to break the news to Angela Lake.

"Thanks, Tara. Sorry I had to land you with that dirty job; How did she take it? Sorry, daft question."

DC Tara Rutherford replied, "Upset obviously, sir but then quite strange. Almost as if she was expecting the news. I suppose, if your partner spends a lot of time being shot at, you harden your heart to receiving that sort of blow? Not something I could deal with. Then she told me about him setting off against her will; bit of an argument – then she went terribly quiet. She didn't report him missing because she thought he'd gone for breakfast or was grieving on a bench somewhere. Lot of guilt. We left her in the hands of Family Liaison."

"Okay, I'm off to see her later today. So, what does Tara's info tell us?" Day scanned the room again.

"Inside information, sir. Killers – and I'm convinced there was more than one, possibly three or more – knew his regular route and knew him well enough to know about his obsession with running. Must have been someone watching the girlfriend's house to warn the actual killers to get into place. They were lucky it was so early in the morning; not many people about but, after the killing, they were disturbed before they could take his head." Acting DS Grainger was confident enough to give more details of his theory. Day added another instruction to the long list on the whiteboard.

"I think you're probably right, Andy. Everything is suggesting to me that these crimes are personal, not terror-related. I can't think of any reason behind terrorists trying to disguise murder as a local crime." Day looked pointedly at the two MPs, one of whom was involved in a conversation on his mobile. The sergeant clicked off his phone but looked Day in the eye and silently mouthed, 'Tahir Abbas' while shaking his head. Before Day had time to continue, there was a knock on the door and in came PC Rouse.

Day had never seen Rouse look so flustered, or in civvies. "Mr Rouse, problem?" he asked.

"There is for me, sir. I've dropped a right one!" Rouse held up an evidence bag containing a DVD in a plastic case.

"Explain!" said Day.

"Last night, sir. I got back to my car about midnight and this was on the roof. I had no idea what it was so I threw it on the back seat and, to be honest, forgot about it. I remembered it a couple of hours ago so I came in and the DVD was still where I left it." Rouse was speaking more quickly as he got more into his tangled tale. "I put it in an old laptop downstairs, sir – just in case it was a virus trap or something. It wasn't. It's just got one video clip on it, sir. I think you should look at it!" Rouse looked devastated. "Now, sir."

Day was pleased to note that Rouse was wearing gloves. "That been checked for prints?"

"Not yet, sir but I'm afraid I handled it without gloves last night."

"Can't be helped. You can set it running for us."

As the team focused on the TV, the door opened again and in walked two women. The first was DS Mandy Sharp, whose appearance caused a tiny ripple of applause. She looked well but those who knew her best noticed that the previous confident, almost arrogant glint in her eyes had gone. Following on was Detective Superintendent Jill Halfpenny. She nodded at Day. "Carry on, Derek."

Day nodded back, "Ma'am."

Halfpenny looked terrible; her face grey, eyes bloodshot and with hastily-combed hair. But Day knew that his boss was a true professional – she'd been in her office since 7am and had read or heard every interview about both murders.

49

Maybe one day she'd tell him how her date last night had ended?

The TV screen lit up. Just one tiny file.

"Play it please, Mr Rouse," ordered Day.

The one brief clip on the DVD was quite sufficient to horrify everyone in the briefing room. There was no sound but the images would be hard to forget.

Gary Martin was slumped on a chair, chin on chest, eyes apparently closed, hands obviously tied to the chair behind his back. Round his neck hung a crudely written sign.

SO DIE ALL THEM THAT
MURDER MUSLIM BROTHERS

Two other figures were also in shot. Both were dressed entirely in black. Gloves, ski masks and oversized sunglasses completed the disguises. One was behind the chair but the other was in front and holding a wicked-looking machete.

The nearer figure pointed to the sign with the big knife then waved the blade in the air.

There was some kind of signal, presumably from the cameraman, and the figure behind Shiner suddenly lunged forward and grabbed the Marine's ears. As he jerked the head back, the other man swung the knife at Shiner's throat. At the moment the blade hit, the film stopped. That was it.

Nobody moved; there was stunned silence.

Day was the first to recover. "Mr Rouse, start the clip again and pause it immediately." The lack of 'please' in the instruction told everyone in the room just how horrified the DCI was.

"First," he said, trying hard to recover his equilibrium, "what kind of place are they in?"

Those who had been looking away returned to the frozen image.

"Concrete sectional building!" Surprisingly, the first response came from DS Sharp. "Looks like vertical eight by two sections bolted together. It's fairly new – look, no trace of rust on the bolts."

By the time she'd finished her sentence most people in the room had turned to stare at her.

"Good to have you back, Mandy," said Day in a gentle tone that encouraged all present to relax a tiny amount.

Three of Sharp's closest friends gave her a round of silent applause. There was no sarcasm intended.

"Very clean, sir, spotless almost," offered Acting DS Grainger, keen not to be outdone. "Not going to be much evidence when we find the place."

"Don't you worry," interjected Lyn Cam, the senior SOCO present. "You lot find me the building and I'll find you some fucking evidence!" Her mood summed up the tension in the room.

"Thanks, Lyn, I know you will!" replied Day, turning a blind eye to the expletive. "Now, the two killers? Comments?"

"Both male, sir?" offered DC Rutherford.

"I agree, Tara."

"No skin on view. No eyes. If they're Middle Eastern Arab types, they're taking a lot of trouble to avoid showing it." DI Allsop's contribution brought mutters of agreement from most people in the room.

"You're right, Trev – no voices either – possibly for the same reason?"

Day picked up only loosely disguised snorts of contempt from the two Military Policemen.

"Something to say, gentlemen?" Day's tone suggested they shouldn't bother at this stage.

Sergeant Vernon didn't take the hint. "Not all Islamic terrorists are dark-skinned," he said. "Some of the most vicious bastards are white converts! Anyhow, I'd like to see the whole clip again."

"Agreed. Go through until we've got a clear view of the victim," said Day.

A few seconds of play brought the focus onto the man tied to the chair. "Stop there. Right, have a good look at Gary Martin, a young man who definitely did not deserve to die. Remember this image throughout the investigation; we will solve this… these murders. Comments?" Day glanced at some of the younger members of his team, hoping to give them confidence to contribute.

"I hate to suggest this, sir but are we certain he's still alive at this stage?" suggested PC Sindhu.

There was a flurry of whispers, which Day silenced by saying, "I share your doubts, Ms Sindhu," replied Day. "Come on – I want opinions."

"There's no flicker of emotion as his head's pulled back!"

"Not even a blink."

"Lips don't move; no sign of a scream."

"They stopped the film before we could see any blood; that would have given it away."

Comments rolled in thick and fast but it was DS Sharp who made the critical observation. "Can we freeze the very last moment, sir?" When it was shown, she was able to continue. In the split second between Gary's head being pulled back and the slash of the knife, it was there to see. "He was dead, sir. Garrotted – with some kind of wire. I wouldn't mind betting he'd been dead before they got him into the room and set up this sham execution!"

There were murmurs of agreement. By the time the team had suffered the agonies of watching the clip another dozen times, everyone in the briefing room was convinced that Gary 'Shiner' Martin had been dead before his 'execution'.

Day turned to the two MPs. "Well gentlemen, you've had more experience in this sort of thing than the rest of us put together. It's time for you to give us your advice." Day was determined that no one could claim he hadn't given the outsiders a fair hearing - however rude they'd been to him and his team.

Bryant began. "It's all very crude. The sham execution was meant to disguise the fact he was already dead – no question. Delivery of the video clip also very hit and miss. Everything suggests this is a group of local individuals trying to prove their worth to some established Muslim terror group and, for that reason, I'm fairly certain that this is terror-related!"

There were gasps around the room.

"Please continue," said Day.

"It's so bad, it's good!" added Bryant. "This is a group of amateurs; one of two possibilities. They're either recent

Muslim converts; not over-bright, probably radicalised in prison just using religion as an excuse for mindless violence. We've seen that a dozen times before."

"Or…" demanded Day.

"Or they're far-right; trying to create some sort of witch-hunt against Muslims!"

Day had to admit to himself that he hadn't considered the second scenario. "Which do you favour?" he asked.

"Eighty percent first one, twenty percent second," came the reply. "But, in our view, it's definitely one or the other!"

DCI Day was not used to being wrong but maybe this was time to admit it – but not before he sowed the seeds of doubt. "I just don't get this crude thing. My limited experience of terrorist propaganda is sophisticated use of the internet. What do you think, Phil?"

"That's usually my experience, too sir, but placing files on the internet and making them completely untraceable is a lot harder than most people think." The Tech expert seemed genuinely puzzled. "I have to take our MP colleagues seriously; this method of delivery suggests amateurs, copy cats or professionals trying to throw us off. Equally it could be ordinary murderers trying to shift the blame onto an easy target."

Vernon came back into the discussion quickly. "The deciding factor here is that they've got some very accurate inside information and I, for one, know exactly where it's coming from."

Now he had everyone's attention.

"We're going to interview Marine Abbas. We've been watching him for some time. Despite his apparent heroism in Afghanistan, investigators over there had suspicions there was a correlation between operations he was on and operations that went tits-up – including the one where he got his CGC. Nothing concrete, just too many incidents to be coincidences. I reckon he's in contact with this local bunch of scumbags or he might even be the leader. We'll get it out of him. There's a team of Anti-terrorist specialist officers on their way here now. They're good lads; we've worked with

53

then before. Some more of our lads will be arriving, too. I need you to instruct your local boys to give us all the intelligence you've got on local Muslim activists. We're going to kick some doors down!"

Day was just about to make a strong statement about jurisdiction when DSupt Halfpenny intervened in the meeting for the first time. "If there's any kicking doors down to be done, I'll decide who, where and when. I trust my team and you are here to advise and support – at least until I'm ordered otherwise by somebody who's got a lot more clout than you two!"

Sergeants Vernon and Bryant were not impressed. They scanned the faces in the room with expressions that said 'you'll all be taking orders from us before the day is out'.

Any escalation in the confrontation was interrupted by a PC who burst into the room without knocking. She spotted Day and shouted, "Sir, it's on the internet – the murder, sir – Instagram!"

"The story?" asked Day.

She pointed to the frozen image on the screen, "No sir, the film, sir – it's horrible, sir!"

Day pointed to the whiteboard. "Find it," he ordered.

She jogged to the keyboard and, within twenty seconds, the film clip they had just watched was there for all the world to see on a public post.

"Let it run," said Day, "I want to see it there's any more."
There wasn't.

"Posted by someone called Damien Tagg, sir. Give me a few seconds and I'll have his location," said Phil Johnstone. True to his word, after less than a minute clicking keys, Phil was able to give an address in Whittington Moor. "No record except a Caution for drunk and disorderly last year. No known terror links.

"Pug, organise me a raid, I'll give you an hour. Get the house under observation asap. Full works, cordon off the area and armed officers. Go!"

Whittington Moor had links with previous terrorist incidents – could this be a coincidence?

Chapter Eight

1.30pm

The two big men flashed their IDs to the police officers seated in the unmarked BMW outside the Abbas residence before marching to the front door and ringing the bell.

After the second ring, Tahir Abbas opened the door and studied the visitors. "Yes?" he asked superfluously. A Royal Marine could spot an MP in civilian dress a mile away.

"Mr Abbas. Tahir Abbas?" asked the big MP.

"Correct. Who are you?"

"I'm Sergeant Bryant and this is Sergeant Vernon, Military Police." Both officers held up their IDs. "We've come to interview you regarding the deaths of your two colleagues. May we come in?" It wasn't a request.

"Of course, but there's not a lot I can tell you," said Tahir, as he stood back and gestured them to enter. He'd only heard about the second murder a couple of hours previously and was still in shock.

Before they had left Beetwell Street Police Station, the two MPs had tossed a coin to decide who would play 'bad cop'. Vernon had won. "I'm sure you're going to be able to help us a great deal!" he said in his best threatening voice.

Despite his anxiety, Tahir almost laughed. "I'll do my best," he replied.

"I'll do my best, sergeant!" Vernon repeated.

Tahir nodded, "Sergeant." He indicated they should sit. Bryant did – Vernon didn't.

"It's obvious to us that the murders of your two Marine comrades are linked," said Bryant before using a dramatic pause.

Tahir resisted the temptation to say 'stating the bleeding obvious'.

"What's just as obvious," said Vernon, "is that a substantial amount of knowledge concerning the whereabouts of the two victims was given to the attackers." Another pause; this time with a hard stare. "You know, we've been really struggling," he continued in a sarcastic tone, "to think who might have

55

that sort of personal and local knowledge. Can you suggest anyone, Marine Abbas?"

"Let's cut the crap; you two think I'm involved in the murders of my friends. Are you insane, you're talking about my best friends? When I joined the Marines, I got quite a lot of racist stick, nothing hideous but enough to make me think I was in the wrong place. Shiner and Red sort of looked after me and it was their support and friendship that gave me time to build some status and get myself accepted in my own right. I owe them everything. Damn it, we were going into business together when we'd all served out our notice. That's screwed now!"

"Big deal," said Vernon. "Who did Corporal Martin know well enough to jump into a car with?"

"I know the time he was picked up and I have a solid alibi!"

"We'll check it," said Vernon with undisguised contempt. "Tell us about this magnificent partnership; what was going to be your contribution?"

"Medical – first aid stuff. I did two years at Med School before I joined the Marines and I aim to complete some training once I'm out. It's all a bit confidential at the moment, but I've been given a provisional offer to do Paramedic training at a uni. down south."

"Paramedic! You will do no such thing!" No one had noticed that Mr Abbas senior had entered the house. His arrival had been deliberately secretive. The police officers outside had told him that MPs were in his house and he was anxious to know how his son was being treated. The last thing he expected to hear was that his son had changed his mind about becoming a doctor.

Tahir flushed. "I'm sorry I didn't tell you, Father but I got to be so proficient at battlefield medicine, it seemed a much more appropriate use of my skills for the future."

"Huh! I'll deal with you later! Now, what are you two gentlemen going in my house?" Mr Abbas made the word 'gentlemen' sound like the worst insult ever.

"Just an informal interview to allow us some insight into your son's relationship with his two deceased colleagues," replied Bryant. "He's helping us with our enquiries."

Tahir couldn't believe that definition of the interview so far. "Actually father, they've come to accuse me of being involved in the murders in some way!"

"What? How dare you? In my own house!" hissed Mr Abbas. "Tahir, have you told them you have alibis for both crimes?"

"We didn't really get to that stage; we were still in a general 'you're a Paki so you must be involved if a soldier's murdered' sort of conversation."

Even after many years of defending ethnic minority suspects, it was painful for Mr Abbas to hear his son use that expression. "Does DCI Day know you're here?" he asked the MPs with deceptive calmness.

"He does."

As Mr Abbas began to dial his mobile, he gave a very clear message to the two MPs. "You will leave now. If you wish to talk to my son again in relation to these tragedies and his undoubted grief it will be at Chesterfield Police Station. Make an appointment!" Mr Abbas was now in full solicitor mode.

As the MPs walked sullenly back to their car Vernon said, "Guilty?"

"As hell," replied Bryant.

Their minds had been made up hours before.

-

By the time DCI Day was tracked down and brought to the phone, Mr Abbas was not in a pretty mood. "Chief Inspector," he stated, "is it true that you gave permission for two military policemen to make accusations against my son without thinking to go through the proper channels?"

Day wasn't too happy either; he was in the car park at Chesterfield FC, strapping on a stab vest and listening to reports from the officers surrounding the target house. "That's not good, Mr Abbas!" he said. "I regret that I'm not in a position to give or refuse those two gentlemen permission for anything – yet!" The emphasis on 'yet' told Mr Abbas that the MPs were going to get some hassle but did little to curb his annoyance. Day's next statement helped a little. "As far as I am concerned, sir there is no evidence that your son was involved in these crimes in any way."

"Good! I can tell you, both as his father and his solicitor, that he has irrefutable alibis for both crimes."

"That would assume that you and he knew the precise times of the crimes, sir. Is that the case?"

"Of course we don't know the exact times, Chief Inspector, but the information we have received gives us enough detail to know that Tahir's whereabouts can be confirmed... he was definitely elsewhere!"

"That's good, Mr Abbas but I need to talk to him about all sorts of issues. I've no intention of making accusations but I will need to check and confirm these alibis. With your permission, I'll come to your house at five or, if you'd rather, please bring him to the station at the same time."

Mr Abbas gave a one-word response. "House!"

A time was decided and the call ended with the tension unresolved.

-

AMBULANCE RESCUE

At the end of a long shift, Detective Constable Derek Day was driving to his home in Brimington. He was looking forward to a shower, a Chinese takeaway and a bit of excitement with his rather gorgeous wife, Jess. However, when a call came out from an ambulance crew in trouble on Rother Avenue, he was first to respond. "I'm less than two minutes from there, I'm on my way!"

As he swept around the corner the flashing blue lights of the ambulance lit up a complex scene. The rear doors were wide open and there was a small huddle of bodies on the pavement by its side. More concerning were the two groups of teenagers facing off on the opposite side of the road.

58

Day pulled to a halt behind the ambulance and stepped out of the unmarked car. The youths were too focused on yelling abuse to take much notice of his arrival so he was able to approach the figures lying half on the pavement and half under the ambulance.

Two paramedics were protecting two casualties. An Asian boy was bleeding badly from a stomach wound and the young woman paramedic had her fingers in the gash obviously trying to stem the blood flow. The older male paramedic was attempting to cover, with his body, a semi-conscious youth from the stones being thrown at the ambulance by both groups of teenagers.

Day took in the situation. "Stabbing?" he asked.

"Yeah!" said the female paramedic. "We think this one stabbed that one and then got a good smack on the head for his trouble. As soon as we'd assessed these two and told the others we were taking them away, all hell broke loose; they let fly with all sorts of crap! We need to get this one inside to the equipment or he's going to bleed to death – pretty damn soon."

"Right, I'll try and chase the others away," said Day, and he walked calmly around the front of the ambulance, held up his ID and shouted, "Police! We need to get your friends to hospital quickly! Go home now! Let the Paramedics do their jobs."

There was a moment's silence before a stone whizzed past Day's head and took a chunk out of the ambulance's jazz paintwork.

The detective had spotted the thrower in the middle of the group of Asian lads and decided to take drastic action.

He took a step in their direction then accelerated rapidly. Two of the larger boys stepped forward to block his path but he was having none of that. One was shouldered aside and the other received the palm of Day's hand hard in the face. Day swerved and grabbed a fistful of the thrower's sweatshirt and half pulled, half dragged him away to be cuffed to the ambulance. The whole manoeuvre took just ten seconds. Both groups of teenagers were startled into silence.

59

'Will that be the end of it?' thought Day.

No!

In the twisted logic of some young minds, the white lads clearly thought, 'White copper – he's on our side'. "Let's get 'em!" was the shout and they began a charge towards the Asian lads - who were still reeling from Day's assault.

Day had always been baffled by racism and the shouts of "Get the Pakis" increased his determination to put a quick stop to this nonsense. As the rush of teenagers got closer, he stepped into the road in front of them.

The voice of his mentor came loud and strong into his head – 'spot the leader – take him out – the others will back off!'.

One side step was all it took to get into the path of his chosen target. Day crouched. As the young man attempted to swerve around him, Day sprang forward and up pushing his shoulder into the teenager's groin. With Day's carefully calculated amount of force, the target did a slow-motion somersault over the detective's shoulder and landed flat on his back on the tarmac beyond. Ouch – badly winded, it was game over.

Once more, Day commanded both groups to go home. "If your friends don't get inside the ambulance in the next two minutes, they'll both die!"

Day would never know if it was the power of his words or the timely arrival of a response car that ended the fracas.

The white youth Day had flattened wasn't seriously hurt and he was dragged to his feet as soon as his buddies had disappeared. "ID?" demanded Day.

"Haven't got any," snarled the still shaken youth.

Before Day could respond, the youth was snatched away by one of the uniformed officers who'd just arrived.

"Oh look, it's little Steve Fletcher! You up to your usual tricks again?" The PC turned towards Day and said with mock politeness, "Would you like me to deal with this young gentleman for you, Detective Constable Day?"

Day replied in kind. "I would certainly appreciate that, Constable Hammond; feel free to do with him as you would wish!"

60

"I will do just that, Detective Constable Day!" The joke over, the boy was dragged to the response car and pushed inside.

The ambulance crew were by now inside their vehicle tending to both injured parties.

As Day uncuffed the stone-thrower he shouted up, "Everything okay, now?"

"Yeah, we think we've sorted them both temporarily – we'll be off in two minutes. Thanks, mate."

"I take it from your position under the vehicle, you didn't see what just happened?" asked Day.

"Not a thing, officer. Not a thing," they both replied.

That was a relief.

Day then turned to face the young man. On closer inspection, he was just a kid; no more than fifteen he guessed. "ID?"

Clearly terrified now the gang had dispersed, the boy replied, "None, sir."

"Name and address!"

The boy gave the information requested rather promptly. He lived in 'White City' only a two-minute drive away at this time of night.

"Get in the car, I'm taking you home!"

The boy's nervousness increased tenfold on the short journey. The door of the semi-detached house was opened immediately on Day's knock.

"Detective Constable Day, Chesterfield Police, sir," said Day to the middle-aged man who stood just inside the door. "Is this your son?"

The man studied Day's ID very carefully before replying, "He is, what's he done?"

"I'd like you to have a long talk to him about the dangers of throwing stones at police officers, sir."

There was a sudden movement and the boy's father was brushed aside. A brightly dressed arm shot out and the attached hand grabbed the boy's collar and dragged him inside.

61

The boy screamed - but not as loudly as his mother. "You throw stones at policemen! You bring police to our door! Get upstairs!" More slapping and shouting noises ensued – followed by more teenage screaming.

Day managed not to smile at the father, still standing in the doorway. "I was going to arrest him, sir but I gather from the reaction of your family that won't be necessary?"

"It will not be necessary, officer; he will be dealt with – severely! Thank you for your patience and for bringing him home."

Day considered briefly whether he should enter the house to protect the boy from his mother – but he didn't. He got back in his car and laughed all the way home.

Of course, at the time, young DC Day did not know that particular family was closely related to the esteemed local solicitor Mr Ahmed Abbas. As he climbed the promotion ladder, Day would meet Mr Abbas on several occasions and they would develop a rather grudging mutual respect.

Chapter Nine

2pm

The raid on Damien Tagg's house was a bit of a flop.

In just over an hour a mass of research had uncovered almost everything to know about the 24-year-old. Until recently, he'd been a welder but the company had gone bust and now he spent most of his time at his parent's house glued to a computer. From what Phil Johnstone could discover, the man was a habitual gamer and viewer of porn but there was no trace of anything terror-related until this morning's post on social media.

Tagg's parents were believed to be at work and current activity suggested he was, as usual, on the computer.

Pug's brilliant organisational skills left nothing to chance. The terraced house had been under intense scrutiny front and rear; no one had come out or gone in.

Fortunately, the two MPs had decided that interviewing the suspect they'd already convicted was more pressing and they had left the local 'plods' to it. They were now on their way but wouldn't be allowed to interfere. Even though they'd caused trouble it would take time to resolve, that suited DCI Day very well.

The detectives and armed back-up were kitted out and ready to breach the door when an urgent message interrupted their approach.

"Sir, it's Phil. I've just intercepted a social media communication between Tagg and one of his mates. The mate asked where he'd got, I quote, 'the brill clip' from and Tagg replied he'd found it on a DVD on a car roof when he was walking back from town last night."

Day didn't approve of swearing but he used a few choice words under his breath. The breakthrough had been whisked away. Worse still, two van loads of uniformed strangers appeared just outside the cordon. A ferocious array of equipment was quickly unloaded. An Inspector forced his way forward to talk to Day as he cast an experienced eye around the assault arrangements Day and Pug Davies had set

63

up. He was just about to start criticising when Day explained the situation had changed drastically in recent seconds.

Obviously just as disappointed as Day, but for different reasons, the Inspector bowed out gracefully. "It's all yours," he said.

Day was a great believer in the 'better safe than sorry' philosophy so all the armed officers except one were sent just out of sight. Day took position on one side of the door and the armed PC the other. Day knocked in what he hoped was a non-threatening way.

After five seconds or so the door was opened by a small, grey-haired, rather elegant lady. She calmly looked Day up and down and, apparently reassured by the large 'POLICE' printed on his stab vest turned her attention to the fully kitted-out PC. Day admitted later that he was, for a moment, lost for words. She studied the PC's automatic rifle then looked him straight in the eye.

"That's a big one," she said.

Day somehow managed not to laugh. "Detective Chief Inspector Day. Sorry to disturb you, madam, may I ask your name?"

"Elsie Tagg; you can call me Elsie if you like?" The information was provided with an angelic smile.

"Thank you, Elsie, we're looking for Damien Tagg. Is he in?"

"Oh, what's he done, now? Yes, he's upstairs on his computer." Before Day could ask a question or give an instruction, the lady turned and yelled, "Damien, get your arse down here!"

The young man had obviously been alerted by the knock on the door and appeared very rapidly. "What's up, Gran?" he asked before getting a full view of the two police officers. "Shit!" he said.

His Grandma gave him a very creditable thump on the arm and said, "Watch your language!"

"Damien Tagg? I'm DCI Day, Chesterfield Police. We need to come in – right now. May we?" It wasn't a question.

Within a few minutes, Day had all the disappointment confirmed. Tagg had indeed picked the DVD case off the roof of a parked car as he walked home from the town centre. Despite admitting to being a bit worse for wear he could remember the exact location and even the make of car. He'd put the case in his coat pocket and forgotten about it until a couple of hours previously. He was very cross with himself for putting it on Instagram – having just realised that one of the TV News channels might have paid him a fortune for it.

The DVD and case were seized and Tagg driven to the police station to make a statement and have his fingerprints taken. Bugger!

By the time Day and his team were back inside Beetwell Street HQ, it became clear that more recordings had been left lying around and at least one had made it to SKY News. The avalanche of reporters and anti-terrorist police was beginning.

3pm

Detective Superintendent Jill Halfpenny studied the street outside her office window. It was a bright Thursday afternoon in the best September for years but she was far from happy. She had a real headache compounded by an excessive number of phone calls from self-important people making demands. The report on the raid fiasco had soured her mood even further.

Beetwell Street was almost blocked by TV company vans - and a couple of uniforms were trying unsuccessfully to make sense of it all.

She ignored the knock on her office door in the hope that the caller would take the hint and bugger off.

He didn't. The door opened with indecent haste and there stood an imposing male in a dark blue suit that must have cost at least as much as Halfpenny's favourite Jimmy Choo's.

"Commander Perry, Anti-Terrorist Squad," the newcomer announced.

65

'Shit, the big knobs are arriving now,' thought Halfpenny.

"Good afternoon, sir – do have a seat," said Halfpenny. "Welcome to Chesterfield."

"Hmm, a trip I would rather not have made," he said.

"I share your sentiments exactly," replied Halfpenny ambiguously.

The Commander gave Halfpenny a suspicious look before continuing. "Am I right in thinking you've been giving my officers the run around, Detective Superintendent?" It took well-practised skill to make a senior officer's title sound like an insult.

"On the contrary, sir, we've been supplying them with every bit of intelligence we have on local terrorist sympathisers. I understand they've been sifting through it with great skill. I expect they'll be bringing people in for questioning any time now. We've offered interview rooms, so I fail to see what more we could supply, apart from some more local knowledge if required."

The Commander didn't look impressed. "Huh! This SIO of yours, Day isn't it? Any good?"

"Yes."

"He has a reputation for being an ass-kicker, I've heard?"

"When necessary."

"I could do with some serious ass-kickers in my unit. Is he ambitious enough for a move into the big-time?"

"He's ambitious – you should ask him," said Halfpenny.

'He's not ambitious – you haven't got a prayer,' thought Halfpenny.

"I might just do that – when I've seen for myself what he's made of. What bugs me is that he's still pursuing non-terrorist lines of enquiry."

"He's that sort, sir. He'll explore every avenue and rule them out one by one. Proverbial dog with a bone."

"Fair enough. I'm going to tell my lads and the MPs to concentrate their efforts on terror suspects and let your DCI Day fanny about on his own theories. Then we'll see how quickly he comes round to my way of thinking. Tell him to keep clear of my investigation in the meantime, will you?"

"Of course, sir," said Halfpenny.

'Not a chance,' thought Halfpenny.

3.30pm

After the disappointment of the unsuccessful 'raid' and confident that everything that could be done was being done, Day decided to put fifteen minutes aside to welcome DS Amanda Sharp back to 'informal' duty.

"Mandy, it's good to have you back – even if you're not actually here."

Sharp laughed, recognising an attempt to break the ice and make her feel welcome at the same time. She knew that, up until today, her boss had done everything in his power to keep her away from the station. "Good to be here, even though I'm still at home," she replied, extending the joke.

Day smiled and nodded. "You have to make me a promise – if it gets too much for you at any time, you tell me and disappear off home immediately."

"Promise."

"Looking after your mental health is my number one priority," he continued. "In reality, I'm just being selfish; during the last couple of years you've been my greatest asset."

Mandy Sharp started imagining the one thing Day could do that would boost her mental well-being through the ceiling – right now if he asked. On his desk. Some detail was involved in the fantasy and the silence perplexed Day.

"Mandy, you okay?"

Sharp jumped. "Yes sir," she said, "can we talk about the case, please? With all due respect, I've been talking about nothing but my mental health for two fu… months; some proper police work would do me the world of good." She was relieved she managed to stop herself swearing - almost.

"Point taken. What did you pick up during the briefing? I've always valued your first impressions."

"Confused, I'd say. Like you, my first analysis says not terror-related but that dodgy film clip has made me doubt myself. It was so crude, almost deliberately unconvincing. At one point, I agreed with the MPs. If we are dealing with terrorists, and it's a big 'if', they're definitely amateurs. And, as you know better than anyone that has pros and cons. Amateurs will make more mistakes and be easier to catch but, especially if they're first-timers, we've no intelligence-based starting point."

"My sentiments exactly. As usual we are in total agreement. The only reason I'm even considering going down the terrorist route is because I can't see any other logical motive - although I've just learned that their medals might be worth as much as eighty thousand each!"

Sharp whistled. "Eighty thousand! People have been murdered for a tiny fraction of that before now!"

"Which would make sense if any of the medals were missing. But both these lads, despite being professional killers, seem to have been really likeable characters. I haven't found any trace of a personal motive – yet!"

"I'll go through all the early interview notes to see if I can find anything for you," offered Sharp.

"Thank you. Incidentally, how are you getting on with the Super? She supported my decision to allow you back early but is she being okay with you?"

"Scarily friendly, to be honest. She was a bit frosty this morning - didn't seen too lively – but, as you know, she came to visit me several times while I was off and we had long chats about my future. She's talking about pushing me for DI; she says, when she retires next year, she wants to leave a woman senior detective in the department to keep you blokes in check."

Day was mortally offended for a full second before he realised he was being teased.

Sharp saw the flicker of doubt and reacted. "Oh, come on, sir – best thing about the Super is her confidence in you; her game is to protect your back against the powers that be – so you can go out and catch the bad guys. The new Chief Constable is a bit of a 'strictly by the book' fella. The Super described him as a 'Scottish Twit' – pretty mild for her."

Although he was shocked, Day knew he could be frank with this brave DS. "Yes, our Mr Carruthers seems to be more interested in keeping complaints down than getting arrests up. Don't quote me on that," he said in a rare flare of unprofessionalism.

"I won't," laughed Sharp. "Anyway, no promotion for me until I've proved myself back in the field. I won't know if I've still got what it takes until the bullets start flying! Two weeks to go – hopefully!"

That awful expression! Day had been on the wrong end of a gun barrel only once in his career and he knew that most British police officers would never have to face that terror – but it was always there in the back of the mind.

"That's a definite, Mandy. No active service for you until you're back officially. You're strictly office-bound. It'll be a weight off my mind knowing you're coordinating all the info that comes in."

"Thank you, sir. Consider it done!"

As she left his office, Day allowed himself a brief self-congratulatory 'phew' of relief - no inappropriate words from either side!

-

Mandy Sharp liked Jessica Day but envy was also involved. Mrs Day had a family; two lovely girls and a husband who adored her.

Mandy spent many guilty hours deliberating whether she loved her boss or merely desired a few intimate tumbles to assuage her lust. The more she thought about it, the more she believed that total possession was the only satisfactory outcome but that had dire consequences. Was it worth three broken hearts?

Another complication was her confession. While lying ill in hospital, Mandy had admitted to Jessica that she loved Derek but had continued with a reassurance that she would never try to take him away from his family. Did Jessica believe her and, more crucially, would she tell her husband?

In her darker moments, Mandy considered the depth of DCI Day's debt to her. Would he be susceptible to pressure or even a gentle kind of blackmail? 'You owe me' was not a great motivation for beginning a liaison but Mandy thought just one serious bout of sex with her would turn Derek into an enthusiast for more. But could she? No, she had to pretend it was just a phase; now she was just a good friend and a reliable and respected colleague. Bloody hell, that was going to be hard.

Derek Day liked and admired Mandy Sharp but it had come as a terrible shock when his wife had explained that the attractive young detective had a crush on him. This was totally outside his limited experience and, both as a manager and a man, he had no idea how to deal with the situation.

Not normally one to run away from confrontation, Derek decided to say nothing and hope Mandy's 'crush' would dissolve in time. He would be a friendly, professional boss – doing nothing at all to make her think he felt anything for her. Oh dear, oh dear, that was going to be hard.

4.30pm

Much to DCI Day's surprise, Tahir Abbas had called to change the appointment for his alibi interview. He wanted to meet at Chesterfield Police Station – without his father being present. Day knew that would cause problems later but was happy to grant the request; the interview could be much more formal.

DS Sharp was still in the station and had jumped at the chance to take part. She switched on the recording apparatus and made the required legal statements.

"Do you want your father to be present?" asked Day, just to be on the safe side.

"No," said Tahir Abbas.

Day made another offer. "How about a different solicitor?"

"Not necessary, Chief Inspector." Tahir seemed edgy but not desperately scared by what was about to happen.

70

"Two of your friends have been murdered and we've checked your alibis. Both are very suspect! Care to explain?" Sharp was back at her quiet, menacing best.

"If I must?"

"Yes, you must – this is a murder enquiry!" Sharp not so quiet this time.

"How much of my story has to get back to my family?" asked Tahir.

"None of it if you tell the whole truth. Unless, of course, they need to be interviewed to check any details you give us." Day was in a much more conciliatory frame of mind than his DS.

"Right. I told you that yesterday I borrowed mum's car to collect my fiancée from the Royal Hospital at the end of her shift. That bit's true. As you know, she's a doctor there. I picked her up at 4pm and drove her to her parents' house. I hadn't seen them for months so we sat for an hour and had a chat. After that, I drove Lianna to her flat down near the cinema; she shares it with a work colleague." Tahir began to squirm with a mixture of discomfort and anger.

Sharp had limited understanding of pre-marital arrangements in Muslim society so was only half expecting to receive details of a torrid sexual encounter as she looked sideways at Day.

It was not as the DS had anticipated. Not quite. But Tahir's account of his next few hours was graphic enough to convince both detectives he was telling the truth.

"I left her there, with her flatmate. We're engaged but we've never been lovers." Tahir rubbed sweat off his brow. "Almost since I met her, I've known she's gay. She told me when our families first arranged our marriage but we were both weak and agreed to play along. We couldn't ever marry and I couldn't find the courage to tell both sets of parents; the disgrace would have killed them! It's one of the reasons I quit medical school and went into the marines. That was just a delaying tactic but it almost broke my mother and father's hearts. They'll have to know now but, please Chief

71

Inspector, let me find my own time to break it to them and to Lianna's parents – that's really going to hurt."

"I'm not interested in your love life, Tahir but I am very interested in your alibi. Where did you go after you dropped Lianna at her flat? We know you didn't make it home until 9pm," asked Day in a sympathetic voice that quite surprised Sharp.

"My girlfriend's… the real one!" he said looking directly into the gap between the two detectives. "She's not Muslim, you see. Not a doctor either. She's a shop assistant. My parents will go mad and probably disown me!" The rising distress seemed genuine. "I was going to train as a paramedic but that was part of going into business with Shiner and Red. I've no idea what to do now."

"Her name and address, please?" asked Day. "Same alibi for the morning, I presume?"

"Yes, I hadn't seen her for nearly eight months – we had to catch up – on things." Despite his obvious embarrassment and anger, a tiny glint of a smile touched Tahir's eyes.

The required information was passed over and Sharp recorded it for an alibi check later.

"Even her name will offend my father when he finds out," groaned Tahir as Sharp typed.

"Lisa White? she said to herself. "Maybe!"

"Well," said Day, "if that checks out, you're off the hook for direct involvement in both murders but that won't protect you from a whole bunch of MPs and Anti-terrorist Police who're convinced you're at least a terrorist sympathiser and informant."

"I've always known that Muslims in the military are under constant suspicion; I've tried to prove my loyalty to this country over and over again while staying true to my religion. The saddest part now is that the only two people who knew for certain I'm one of the good guys are both dead. Only people who've faced death together can ever be truly certain of each other's loyalty – love almost!"

Day became acutely aware that DS Sharp had turned to look at him. He froze.

72

Sharp was thinking, 'Almost doesn't come into it'.

Day turned to face his colleague, desperate to think of something appropriate to say. "Yes," he said. He knew the loyalty between them was unconditional but was there more than that in Sharp's eyes? Confusion. He'd have to ask Jess; surely she'd be able to explain it?

The temporary silence of both detectives confused Tahir into thinking it was some kind of crafty ploy. He coughed. "So, what happens now?" he asked.

"We check your alibis. I don't suppose any third party can confirm when you were with Ms White?" replied Sharp.

"The old lady who lives in the bedsit below Lisa saw me around teatime; you should have seen the filthy look I got, so I'm positive she'll remember. This morning several people would have seen the Merc outside, if that helps?"

"Sounds okay, but we've still got to be certain you've not handed any information over to extremists – even unintentionally," said Day.

"I don't even know any fucking extremists!" hissed Tahir, Marine experiences overcoming his conservative upbringing. Sharp smiled inwardly at Day's discomfort – but then she went for the jugular. "Your dad does!"

Tahir put his head in his hands. After twenty seconds he looked up. A pleading glance at Day then a hard stare at Sharp. "He's a solicitor! You know damn well he specialises in representing ethnic minorities. Everybody in Chesterfield knows he's defended people accused of terrorist offences – that doesn't make him a terrorist. He can't stand racism and he can't stand injustice. He can be bloody difficult with me but I can't imagine any living person of any colour more boringly British than my father!"

"Right, Tahir," said Day in his most soothing voice," let's say I believe you're totally uninvolved in these crimes – just give me five minutes history of your relationship with Red and Shiner followed by another five minutes on your future plans together. Let's look there for motives."

The past was no help and the three comrades' future plans suggested little. The Conspicuous Gallantry Cross angle was worth considering. Were they really so valuable?

"Where do you keep your CGC, Tahir?"

"Since I found out how much it might sell for it's been locked up in my father's safe."

"I'll make a note, sir. We need to double-check the other two medals are where the relatives think they are!"

"Very sensible, Mandy. Now Tahir, let's go through this once more – just to be sure."

7pm

DCI Day and DC Rutherford were invited into the house by the Family Liaison Officer who had spent most of the day with the second murder victim's fiancée. The FLO was grateful for Day's instruction to take a short break.

"I'm so, so sorry about this, Miss Lake; I really should have done more to protect Steve. The car I'd ordered to keep an eye on you two and Mr Abbas was called away on an emergency. I know that's no excuse and I can't begin to imagine how you feel right now."

"Stop it, Inspector. You told us there were risks and it was Steve's decision to go out running. We had a row about it. In fact, the last words we exchanged were in anger and that just makes everything so much worse." Angie Lake was managing to talk coherently despite the intermittent sobs.

Day thought talking facts might help the discussion along. "I'm guessing Steve was pretty strong-willed and a creature of habit?"

Angie tried to smile. "Both – and, even worse, being a Marine, he was pretty convinced that, away from the battlefield, he was immortal. In fairness, he was more than a match for virtually anyone in a fair fight."

"I'm afraid the killers never had any intention of fighting fair. It was a cowardly attack and nobody would have stood a chance. I intend to get these people, Angie but one thing is puzzling me. I'm guessing someone was watching the house

74

just in case Steve set off for an early-morning run and you've already hinted he was pretty predictable. I don't believe he was followed; this was a planned ambush! But how could they anticipate his route?"

"I don't know how long they've been planning this and watching him but Steve always ran the same route – he used to time himself. He'd come back really fed up if he hadn't beaten his previous best." It was time to pause; the tears were flowing freely now.

Just as he had expected. Day was embarrassed to admit to himself that, in his twenties, he'd been victim to the same obsessive behaviour; he got up and went to the kitchen to bring a glass of fresh water. DC Rutherford moved closer to the other young woman.

That seemed to comfort Angie but, suddenly, she sat up and stopped crying. "Hang on," she said, "this was his first night home in ages. It must be eight months since he last ran that route so these bastards must have been making plans since before he became famous for getting that bloody medal!"

Day agreed. "And they must have tracked him several times before they confirmed he was so predictable. Unless... did any of your friends know about his running habits – it's just possible someone might have given up the information unintentionally?"

"I knew his route, of course. I tried to keep up with him a couple of times and I'm bloody fit but I couldn't get near him! He was so competitive he wouldn't slow down even for me."

"Anyone else?"

"Earlier this year Shiner went with him a couple of times when they were both on leave and they argued for days about who had the best average times - but that's no help! Oh, and Gina knew the route; she went round with me once when the lads were abroad. We put our times on Facebook, after we'd knocked a couple of minutes off. Needless to say, they didn't believe us."

The sad smile that flickered across Angie's face almost broke Day's heart. Someone was going to suffer for causing this misery.

"One last thing, Angie, do you know where Steve kept his medal?" asked Day.

"Yes, it's behind you in that cabinet. Is that what you think got him killed? I don't think it's ever been out of the box since the day he collected it. I brought the bloody thing home after the presentation at the palace." Her shoulders began to shake again and Day needed a distraction.

"Do me a favour, would you, check it's still there?

Angie nodded and left the room. She returned a minute later with a small key which she inserted into the lock of the top drawer. There was the sound of rummaging and things being dropped on the floor. Another drawer was opened. More searching. Suddenly, Angie slammed both drawers shut, returned to her seat and put her head in her hands.

"It's gone!" she said.

Chapter Ten
Day's DAY 3

Friday: 8am Briefing

Although Commander Perry was doing little to disguise his contempt of the locals' theory that the crimes were not terror related, he did deign to attend the briefing. There were now three MPs; a younger female officer had arrived and Day was pleased to see the two sergeants were appearing rather less arrogant. She was clearly the boss.

Day acknowledged the presence of the newcomers and began in what he hoped was a conciliatory tone. "I'm not ruling out terrorism in these two appalling crimes and I'm pleased to leave that angle of investigation to the experts." He nodded in the direction of the visitors. "I have, however, interviewed Tahir Abbas at length and I do not, at least currently, regard him as a suspect at any level." That comment earned him a dirty look from both MP sergeants. Their officer's expression didn't change. "Right, to business – still no sign of Mr Martin's body; Trev, widen the search area, will you?"

DI Allsop nodded.

"Have we tracked down the stolen mobile used to report the second murder?" Day asked, looking in Dipa Sindhu's direction.

She responded immediately. "I saw the girl who reported it stolen last night, sir. She knew to within ten minutes when it was lifted and she told me where she was during that period. I'll be checking CCTV as soon as we've finished here."

"Good, but this is priority. Phil, get your team on it right away."

Sindhu passed a paper to Phil Johnstone and he made a brief phone call.

"Post mortems?"

"Doc's completed both, sir," said DC O'Neil. "As we suspected, he's suggesting that Martin was already dead when the bas... they cut off his head. Hamilton died when his spine was severed. He would have died from the

77

crossbow bolt within a few minutes anyway. Doc's conclusions were supported by some bigwig up from my home town." He smirked at the MPs.

An angry silence filled the room.

There was an uncharacteristic crack in Day's voice as he continued. He'd already turned to write on the whiteboard so people couldn't see his expression. "DNA? Anything on either body?"

"None found yet, sir. Doc and his new best friend said they'll keep probing."

"Check the bolt, Dom – outlets and internet! House to house – make sure you include the shops backing on to the second murder site – check again if any security people were on duty – or shelf-stackers." Day was pleased to note that his team were being more professional in hiding their anger than he was.

"I know the beheading clip is all over the internet but how many DVDs have turned up now?"

"Six, sir," replied Phil. "Random locations, all apparently placed on Saturday evening; no pattern, no fingerprints or DNA, so nothing helpful, sorry."

"Can't be helped. Here's a new angle. Steve Hamilton's Conspicuous Gallantry Cross has gone missing. As you know, one sold at auction for eighty thousand pounds recently." Two detectives whistled at Day's announcement. "We have another potential motive but Gina Thomson still has Gary's. The medals are engraved so only an underground collector would buy one knowing it to be stolen. Tara, get on your computer – find out who are the shady medal traders and buyers."

The list of allocated jobs grew until Day was satisfied. "Back here later, folks," he said. "You'll get a call notifying you of just when - and if you find out anything call me immediately. Time for some detective work!" Several officers smiled as they left the room – it was always good to end positively – however angry you felt.

Daysway.

8.30am

After the briefing, Dom O'Neil stopped Day in the corridor. "Sir, do you remember Melanie Price? I'm dating her now."

Day tried hard to hide a frown but a little glimmer must have seeped through because O'Neil immediately went on the defensive. "Not to worry, sir – it's not that important."

"Spill it, Dom, it must have been important enough for you to raise it – come on, I trust your judgement!" Day was trying hard to re-establish a good working relationship with the DC.

"You sent me out to do a follow-up with the first victim's girlfriend's family…"

Day held up his laptop. "I did indeed," he interrupted. "Your report's on here, I'll be reading it in the next hour."

"There's something I didn't put in the report, sir but I thought you ought to know…"

As O'Neil hesitated, Day filled the silence. "Oh, the old detective's itch, Dom? Come to my office in ten – I'll be happy to give you a few minutes."

When O'Neil arrived ten minutes later, he gave Day the impression that he'd thought things through and was more confident about telling the boss about his so-called 'itch'.

"Well, it's two things joined together, sir. Dipa Sindhu told me how weird the brother was when you went to break the news. More interested in talking about his posh motorbike than being concerned about his sister and her boyfriend?"

"True, Dom. I felt the same."

"It was the name, sir – Will Thomson. I'd heard it before – recently. Mel was telling me about him the other night, she used to go out with him."

Day wasn't interested in pillow talk. "Where's this going, Dom?"

"Mel was saying what a lovely bloke he could be one minute and the next he'd go really weird. We know he's got that computer shop down Chatsworth Road and he's a proper IT genius, but did you know the bike he's got is worth over fifty

79

grand – and he's a member of an exclusive club called the Jean Vincent Thousands?"

Day had read something about that club in one of the local lifestyle magazines. Despite their name, the group didn't have large numbers of members. Less than twenty, he'd read. The 'thousand' referred to 1000cc bikes and the 'Jean' was about members scorning posh leathers and wearing a denim 'uniform'. The bikes were all Vincent collectors' items – you had to be very wealthy to become a member. On the positive side, they did quite a bit of charity work. The article in 'Reflections' magazine hinted they were 'good eggs all round'.

"And?" offered Day.

"And they get up to some very funny stuff, sir; that's why the relationship didn't last. She described some of their social functions… quite disturbing…funny attitudes to women."

Day was already rather interested in Will Thomson. "Thanks, Dom. I'd like to talk to Miss Price. See if you can arrange for her to come here – at lunchtime if at all possible. Thanks again, this might be relevant!"

-

DC Rutherford knocked on Day's office door. "Sir, I know you're up to the neck in it but Jimmy Hammond's downstairs and he's asking if you can spare him five minutes?"

The complications of the case vanished in an instant – to be replaced by domestic complications! Jimmy Hammond – what was he doing here? Six months in Australia, he'd said – just two months ago.

Day almost swore. Instead, he said calmly, "Ask him to come up, Tara, please." He turned to DI Allsop and said, "Sorry about this, give me five, please Trev."

A minute later, after a brief knock, in walked Day's landlord. To break his own tension, Day said without preamble, "Wow, Jimmy, that's an impressive tan!"

Jimmy laughed. "This is a winter tan, sir… Derek. Can you imagine what I'd look like after a good summer?" He laughed again.

As they shook hands, Jimmy became very aware that his presence was causing no small amount of anxiety. "I know you're very, very busy Derek so I'll make it quick. I'm back for two reasons. One, my brother Sam died." He continued before Day had time to interrupt with condolence. "You didn't know him, he lived down south. To be honest, we didn't see much of him either. It was quite sudden apparently. Anyway, I'm back for the funeral and to help settle his estate. The other reason affects you." He paused then took a deep breath. "Sally and me… we're staying in Australia. My son-in-law's in security and he's offered me a job but, much more important, getting Sally away from the grandkids would be bloody nigh impossible! So, it looks like we'll be able to arrange a long-term, if not permanent, stay. Reason I needed to see you – is it okay if I put the house up for sale? Sorry, I know I promised you six months."

Day's brain went into overdrive. First, a flash of near panic, followed by a whirring of cogs. If they were able to buy Jimmy's house, he would be able to make all the security alterations he wished. He'd be happy; the girls would be happy – and Jess would be over the moon!

Jimmy took Day's hesitation as disappointment and began a profusion of apologies.

"No, Jimmy, don't apologise. I'll tell you what I'll do – with your permission, of course. We've still got four months of our informal contract to run; so let us arrange the sale of the house for you. We'll get it valued, deal with the paperwork, show people round etc. If you're happy with what turns up, you can do all the signing from down under. If you send us a list of what you want sent over, we'll sort that, too."

Shock, then delight crossed Jimmy's face. "You'd do all that for us, sir?"

"Of course we would. You did us a massive favour when we were desperate. It would be a pleasure. Jess is a genius at that sort of thing; how quick a sale do you need?"

"Not hugely urgent. Before Christmas would help but it's not essential."

"Okay, Jimmy, we'll do our best for you – make sure you get a fair price! I'll get moving on it as soon the current situation is dealt with." Even though he was completely confident Jess would leap at the chance of buying, there was no point in raising everyone's hopes just yet.

"It's terrible, sir. Hideous crimes. I know you'll sort it though. I'm off to London in a couple of hours so I won't see you for a good while. I'm really grateful for your offer; goodbye... Derek." Day was pleased to see that Jimmy was positively oozing relief.

As Jimmy left the office, Day called after him. "Oh, Jimmy – there's one condition!"

The older man stopped. He turned. "What's that?" he asked.

"Australia's on our bucket list and we're hoping to go over in a few years – can we put Hammond House on our itinerary for, say, a couple of nights?"

"A month!" laughed Jimmy Hammond. Day could still hear him laughing right down to the end of the corridor.

Day laughed too, but only for a few seconds. One of the major problems in his life had possibly just been eradicated. Now to deal with the other. He got back to work.

Chapter Eleven

12.30pm

Melanie Price was obviously not at all relaxed as she was ushered into the company of DCI Day and DS Amanda Sharp; their previous encounters had been fraught to say the least.

Once again, Day was amazed by how attractive the young teacher was – almost on a par with his wife, Jess. "Thanks for coming in, Ms Price. Dom tells me you have some background information on Will Thomson? Anything you tell us will, of course, be in confidence. Now, Dom said you told him some of this motorcycle club's antics were – quote – 'disturbing'. How?"

"It depends what you already know about them, Inspector."

"Chief Inspector," said DS Sharp surprisingly quietly.

"That's fine, don't worry. The answer is virtually nothing, only what I've read in the Reflections magazine – which was quite complimentary. Start from the beginning, please." Day was all smiles.

"That's the image certainly - and they do lots of good work. Some of them ride for Blood Bikes, they raise quite a lot of cash for the Hospice and once a year they take busloads of poor children to the seaside. Delightfully old fashioned really. Will Thomson was recommended to me as a super computer expert; I wanted a top-of-the-range PC building and I gave him the job. Fourth or fifth time I went into his shop, he asked me out. At that time, I thought he was just a reasonably good-looking and very clever bloke so I said yes. Great – he took me to some very expensive restaurants and I started to feel relaxed in his company – but then he asked me 'do you like motorbikes'? You'll remember from our previous meetings that I'm a bit of a petrolhead so I said yes. So, he introduced me to his pride and joy, a Vincent Black Shadow. Admittedly, it was a magnificent piece of kit, seventy years old but in perfect condition. Worth a small fortune, he said."

Day was struggling to avoid looking at his watch but he didn't interrupt the monologue.

"Tell him about the Club, Mel!" said DC O'Neil.

"Once I'd told him I liked the bike, he couldn't do enough for me. 'I'm meeting the lads from the club at Matlock Bath on Sunday." he said. 'Fancy a trip out?' I agreed and, much to my surprise he turned up the day before with a parcel of clothes. Blue denim jeans and jacket; good quality, though - apart from a really naff club logo on the back of the jacket. He told me I had to wear it for our outing the day after. I thought that was being a bit cheeky but I agreed anyway. It was a good fit so I never gave it back; it's in my wardrobe at home. The following day, I met the Jean Vincent 1000s. There was a dozen of them, all with these antique bikes worth a fortune. Very smiley and pleasant with me and basking in the admiration received from the owners of modern bikes who were crowding round. A chauffeur-driven Bentley turned up and the Vincents all crowded round but it only stayed for ten minutes. Some facts, Chief Inspector: twelve blokes in their thirties and forties each accompanied by a young woman; all, and I mean all, the girls were very physically attractive individuals – sorry if that sounds immodest?"

There was a barely audible, 'pah' from DS Sharp.

"Carry on," said Day while raising his eyebrows at O'Neil.

Dom did a thumbs-up and nodded. "It's coming," he mouthed.

"They were obviously wealthy blokes, Vincent 1000 bikes in perfect condition are worth around fifty grand and upwards. Business owners and professional men, all of them. All white, Chief Inspector – no ethnic minority members. As the event wore on, some bad taste jokes started doing the rounds. I can laugh at a good joke but I'm not into sexist and racist stuff and I told them that. That got Will some nasty looks from his mates but I stood my ground. None of the other women objected."

"Good for you," said DS Sharp.

"When we getting ready to leave, I noticed a lot of discussion with occasional glances in my direction. I work with young children and I have a highly developed sense of hearing. I kept picking out the word 'eight'. We had a meal together that night and I asked him for the significance of the number. He coloured up immediately but eventually confessed it was my score out of ten on some sort of weird good-looking scale they use. He reassured me that eight was a good score – apparently, there were a couple of members' girlfriends who scored nine, but there was no one rated ten out of ten. I'm not interested in men who judge women solely on looks so that was it, I got up and left."

"Is that it, Ms Price?" asked Day, seriously disappointed. That had been a waste of time – apart from the little itch that had formed in the back of his brain. He lost concentration for a moment as he focused on a mental image of his wife – surely a perfect ten?

Seated next to him, Mandy Sharp was comparing her own 'out on the town' image with Miss Price and thinking positively about her own score. She knew it would be high, but didn't give a toss! Still, it was a pity the boss didn't notice.

"No, I had to go back to Will's shop to collect some kit and he persuaded me to give him another go. There was a charity 'do' in the offing and he said I'd enjoy it. I did – it was a great night out and the club raised a bucketful of cash for a couple of local charities. I talked to some of the other women during the auction and found out one or two things. The club is run by a chap called Simon Coy – he owns a big dental practice in Sheffield apparently but he's not the man behind it all. The real power – and the wealth, is the man who lives in Millthorpe Hall. His name is Paul something-or-other but they all call him 'Vince'. He's very secretive, almost a recluse; I've been told he was a city trader and made a fortune before the crash. He got out of London just in time, bought the old Manor house and apparently spent a fortune on it. That's one of the reasons the club doesn't have a website – it's as exclusive as it's possible to be. Now, this is where it gets interesting…"

'About time!' thought both the detectives seated across the table. Dom O'Neil was still looking on with starry eyes.

"What I'm going to tell you, Inspector, is not from personal experience but I'm pretty sure it's true. I've picked up too many overlapping little snippets for it to be made up." Day could see the young teacher was warming to her task – but was it going to be just gossip?

"Have you seen the film, Eyes Wide Shut, Inspector?"

"No, I don't think…"

"The *Chief* Inspector hasn't seen it but I have; continue!" interrupted Sharp. "I'll explain it to him later," she said. 'In considerable detail,' she added silently.

"Give me a clue," said Day.

"Intellectual porn," replied Sharp.

DCI Day's experience of porn was limited to say the least. He got all the excitement and joy he needed in bed with his wife. Of course, he'd seen the odd flash of nudity in mainstream movies but that never caused more than a flicker of interest. On the dark side, like most senior police officers, he'd seen naked people on the post mortem table – definitely not a turn-on.

Melanie Price was a little puzzled by the delay but, urged on by her partner, continued. "The Jean Vincents have parties twice a year. Big events at Millthorpe Hall. Members only – no girlfriends. Oh, and twenty or thirty top-class escorts! Basically, from what I've heard they're proper 'anything-goes' orgies. Big security, no phones but members pay a fortune to attend. I've been told it's like a fortress. Some of the girlfriends found out about them through pillow-talk; they didn't like being compared to professional ladies. Apparently, there's quite a turn-over of girlfriends in the Jean Vincents!"

Day still wasn't over enthusiastic with this storyline and couldn't see a link to the current investigation. Okay, next time a party was going on at the Manor house, he might send a few officers over to see if any crimes were being committed but there was nothing here of any immediate use. He was just about to dismiss his two guests when Dom O'Neil asked a peculiar question.

"Sir, who's the best-looking woman you've seen in the last couple of days? In the flesh that is."

Day was offended by the question. He was male and therefore registered exceptional female beauty but he certainly didn't mark out of ten or store the information.

Sharp was also offended. When she made an effort, she was equal to anyone around here except possibly Jessica bloody Day. "What's that got to do with the price of fish, Dom?"

"I don't think you've met her, Sarge but I know Mr Day has. These motorcycle nuts are in competition to have the best-looking girl – and – they have no respect whatsoever for them as human beings; they're possessions, arm candy - nothing more. Sir? Best looking woman you've seen recently?"

Even Melanie seemed desperate to hear his response.

Day forced the image of a naked Jessica from his brain and concentrated. It clicked. Dom was wrong, Day hadn't seen a beautiful woman in the flesh but she'd been in the same room as a beautiful photo. The beauty on the living face had been distorted by grief. "Gina Thomson," he said.

"How's about that for a motive, sir?" asked Dom, who looked like he'd just won the lottery.

Day still wasn't convinced and his face made that obvious. It was up to Melanie Price to seal the deal. "They talk about Gina a lot, Mr Day. I'd say the blokes in the club were obsessed with her and her brother knows it. I think that's why they tolerate Will despite him not being as well off as the rest."

This was tenuous in the extreme but DCI Day now knew he had a motorcycle gang to rule out of one murder. But what about number two?

"Oh, and Chief Inspector…" Melanie Price left the best to last. "The next Vincents' weird party at Millthorpe Hall – it's tomorrow night!"

87

Chapter Twelve

2pm

The procession from the Islamic Centre along Union Walk was silent and dignified. Thirty people of all ages and colours were carrying their placards by their sides. They turned right along Saltergate and joined another twenty or so like-minded individuals in the Town Hall car park.

The group listened intently to the man giving instructions about their route and behaviour. He used the word 'dignity' at least a dozen times.

At last he was satisfied all knew what was expected of them and the column moved off, two abreast into the town centre, placards now held high. So quiet was their advance that many shoppers didn't hear them coming and were surprised to see these brightly dressed, serious-looking people marching through the Market Square. Some read the placards in silence; some applauded. A few jeered and there were at least a couple of racist comments but the column continued undaunted down through the town towards Beetwell Street Police Station.

That morning, uniformed officers had ordered all the press and TV vans away from the street in front of the station into a cordoned-off area of a nearby car park. That didn't deter a dozen or more reporters from standing around the station steps.

As the fifty demonstrators lined up on the pavement opposite, all cameras turned on them. A TV crew arrived as if by magic. The placards were held high but the only sound came from reporters trying to encourage comments.

The man who had given the instructions earlier stepped forward and declared he would not make a statement until all the major TV stations were represented.

Several uniformed police officers appeared from the front doors of the station but made no attempt to intervene.

High above, Detective Superintendent Jill Halfpenny studied the street outside her office window. It was a bright Friday afternoon in what was still the best September for years but she was far from happy. Her hangover-fuelled headache was long gone but she was already getting flak from so many directions she really didn't need this additional distraction. At least they were behaving themselves. She began to read the placards left to right. 'Islam is the Religion of Peace'. 'We are not terrorists'. 'Black Lives Matter.'

She watched as a uniformed sergeant approached the man who was obviously the instigator and have a brief discussion. The sergeant retreated and spoke into his radio. A minute later she saw her second-in-command appear on the station steps, cross the street and shake the man's hand.

"Good afternoon, Mr Abbas," said DCI Day.

"Good afternoon, Mr Day," said Mr Abbas.

Microphones were thrust into the two men's faces.

"Comments, gentlemen?" was shouted.

"This is not the place, sir," said Day, "could we talk inside?"

"No Mr Day, we have a point to make and we shall make it… peacefully, if your officers don't intervene."

Day realised he was trapped and the only way forward was to let the solicitor have a moment of glory. "Go ahead, sir," he said. "Please make your point."

Mr Abbas turned to address the TV cameras. "I requested Detective Chief Inspector Day's presence because I know him to be a reasonable man." He paused for effect. "Yesterday and the day before there were two tragic crimes in our town. Two young men brutally murdered. These unfortunate men were serving soldiers and, in such cases, it is regrettably the norm in this country of ours for the blame to be placed on the shoulders of Muslims. In the past twenty-four hours, many young, innocent Muslim men have been dragged from their houses and interrogated at length – returning to their homes shattered by the experience." He turned back towards Day and raised his voice. "You, Mr Day have always assured me that Chesterfield detectives follow the evidence. Our young men have been put through torment without a shred of evidence against them!"

Day was completely blindsided and so he did what he always did when he was in a tight corner – he told the truth.

He looked into the closest camera and put on his most earnest face. "Mr Abbas is correct; these were two brutal murders and we will make every effort to find the killers! There are two lines of enquiry. One is assuming the crimes are terror-related, the other that these horrible events are theft related. My team is pursuing the latter theory. The terror angle is being investigated by national police agencies that are not under my command. If and when either angle is ruled out, we will all concentrate our resources on the most promising lines of enquiry. I will, of course, cooperate with any investigation into alleged police misconduct and, if required, apologise to any member of any community who is mistreated by officers working for me."

When blaming someone else – don't make it too obvious. Daysway.

"In the meantime, I understand your concerns and I also appreciate that your demonstration is peaceful but, I would point out, that it is causing an unlawful obstruction. Thank you for the message and I would now respectfully request that you disperse." To be factual, the demonstrators were on the pavement, it was the gathering storm of reporters that were blocking the road. But, looking into the eyes of the demonstrators, Day judged that he might just get away with the conciliatory approach - when another figure entered the spotlight.

Commander Perry was unimpressed by Day's method of dealing with this type of situation; small-town coppers needed an example of how to handle troublemakers. It wasn't as if he was aggressive – just very unsubtle to the point of rude. Sort of 'grandstanding' for the cameras.

The conversation became rather more heated despite Day's attempts to moderate. After five minutes he gave up and left them to it. Eventually, Mr Abbas did agree to disband his group and end the demonstration but he did make one final promise. "If this harassment of my community continues, we will be back this time tomorrow. Not fifty – but five hundred!"

Chapter Thirteen

4.30pm

DCI Day borrowed PC Sindhu to accompany him to a follow-up interview with Gary 'Shiner' Martin's girlfriend Gina Thomson. There were two reasons for this: Sindhu had enormous potential for detective work and, less altruistically, Day wanted to check out his suspicions of racism in the Thomson household. In fairness to Sindhu, he did warn her she was part of the test.

Thanks to Sindhu's assertive driving, they arrived right on time.

Day rarely thought about female beauty. Even after twelve years of marriage, he was still completely in awe of his wife. But this was different. It was the first time he'd seen Ms Thomson when she wasn't crying. Even with a negligible splash of makeup, this young woman was staggeringly beautiful. What made the effect more startling was that she either didn't know it or, more likely, really didn't care. Her expression oozed an innocent sweetness that was only slightly tempered by the sadness in her eyes. Day didn't do lust - but he was very good at compassion.

The two police officers were invited to sit and Gina offered tea. Both refused but the offer was repeated more forcefully. After the reluctant acceptance, Gina instructed, none too politely, her mother to go and organise the refreshments. The young woman clearly had things she wanted to say to the visitors without her mother's interference. Dipa Sindhu offered to help with the tea and was firmly rebuked as the mother stormed out - but that didn't stop the young PC following.

Gina began immediately. "My family all thought I could do a lot better than Gary. Over the years they've all very gently tried to put me off. Will must have brought a dozen of his mates around to chat me up. My mum wanted me to go into acting or modelling; can you believe it?"

Day could.

"I can't act to save my life and, who in their right mind, would want to be gawped at for a living. 'Be a model and you'll marry a millionaire' was my mum's favourite comment. All the time I just wanted to live with Gary. Him leaving the Marines and wanting to set up in business with me and the others was my dream come true." She stopped to think. "And… family members aren't the only ones who've tried to make me go off Gary; stranger attempts have been made."

"Care to elaborate?" asked Day.

"I once met a woman at a works leaving do in town. She wasn't with our group but she came up and stood next to me at the bar when I was getting a round in. She opened her purse right in front of me and inside I saw a picture of Gary. You can imagine how shocked I was. It took some time to get served and eventually I worked up the courage to say, 'Who's the lucky fella?'.

She explained his name was Gary and he was a Royal Marine. 'A real man', she said. Then she went into some detail about how he didn't get to Chesterfield very often but, when he did, he'd give her a 'right seeing to'. Her words, not mine, Chief Inspector. I told her my boyfriend was a Marine, too and made up a name on the spot; I just wanted to keep her talking. I should have been suspicious straight away because she just went on and on about Gary - but I'd had a few drinks and wasn't thinking too clearly. You know what it's like, Chief Inspector?"

Day didn't - but he encouraged her to retell the story for the benefit of Sindhu who had just returned with a tray of tea. There was no sign of Gina's mother.

"She knew a lot about my Gary. His taste in music, sports etcetera. She described some of the events they'd been to together. At the time I was devastated and I made excuses and went home early. Later on, I started to think and I looked up the dates of some of the events she said Gary had taken her to. On one he was definitely overseas and another he was with me. Whatever she was trying to achieve, that woman's research wasn't up to much."

"What did you do about it?" asked Day.

"First, I asked the girls I'd been with if they'd set it up as an elaborate bad-taste joke. They all denied it. Some of my friends also occasionally gave me a hard time for being with Gary. I mean he was no oil-painting but I did really, really love him!" The beautiful face began to crack.

"You never met the mystery woman again?"

"No. I even went back to the same bar several times but I never saw her again."

"Sounds like a set-up?" suggested Day.

"I reckon so but who on earth would go to so much trouble to do such a thing?"

"Someone who wanted to put a wedge between you and your boyfriend?" offered PC Sindhu.

"I can't think of another reason," added Day.

"Fair enough," said Gina, "but why? What's so important about us… about me?"

Day took that as a rhetorical question and decided it was time to explore a theory that had been wandering around his brain since the previous evening. "Have you ever had anything to do with the motorbike club that Will's involved with?"

"The Vincents? Yes. I've been to a couple of their events, why?"

"Good?"

"The charity events were really good; great fun - but there's no way I'd ever go to another club meet. Being a woman amongst all those rich show-offs was like being a piece of meat on a butcher's counter. I've had a couple of arguments with Will about it; I don't understand how he can put up with it!"

Day was fascinated by a simile that seemed to support Melanie Price's point of view. If both the murder victims had been women, he would have certainly pursued it. "What was his answer to that?" he asked.

"Business," he always said. "These are wealthy blokes and they bring him plenty of custom; apparently they made a huge difference when he set up by himself. He thinks he owes them a lot. Plus, of course, he's mad about his classic bike!"

Day nodded to create the illusion that that was the end of that line of questioning. It didn't work.

"Why are you so interested in the Jean Vincents, Chief Inspector?" A sudden dash of alarm caused her voice to rise. "Surely you don't suspect them? I mean, it says on the news that Gary and Red were attacked by terrorists. Why would a load of rich bike fanatics want to attack Marines?"

PC Sindhu and DCI Day exchanged glances. To them, it was beginning to make sense – but not to the lovely innocence of the woman opposite.

Then the two officers watched the penny drop.

Gina put her hand to her mouth. "No, it's not possible," she stammered. "It's ridiculous! Will would never allow it!" But there was no conviction in her tone.

Day had gone from sceptic to suspicious. He wanted to know if Will Thomson was involved, at some level, in two murders.

"I think I'd better have a chat with your brother: where is he likely to be this time on a Friday afternoon?" asked Day.

Gina's reply was so quiet, both police officers struggled to hear. "He's got some big project on – for the Vincents – he'll be in his workshop – behind the shop." The young woman's beauty disappeared in a tangle of denial and confusion. Tears flowed.

Day went into the hall and called for Mrs Thomson to come and sit with her daughter. The mother returned and, much to Day's surprise, nodded to PC Sindhu.

On the way back to the station Day asked the inevitable question. "What happened with Mrs T?"

"Intriguing! You were right about the racism thing but, in fairness, she does have a reason even it's totally illogical. We wondered if there was a Mr Thomson senior and there isn't. Poor devil was killed in a hit and run five years ago. When our lads finally caught up with the driver, he turned out to be Asian and, to make matters worse, a well-known drug dealer. He's just got out of the nick.   I remember

94

reading about it in the Derbyshire Times – it was just before I joined up."

"As you say – illogical," replied Day. "Very sad, though. Now you tell me, it does ring a bell although I wasn't directly involved; it might have been one of Trev Allsop's cases. How did you persuade the mother not to come back in?"

"I didn't. She was so upset retelling the story she finished making the tea and went to bed pretending to have a migraine. Maybe our chat was therapeutic?"

6pm

Dipa Sindhu dropped DCI Day off at Beetwell Street Police Station. As expected, DS Sharp was in his office.

"Still here, Mandy?" asked Day, stating the obvious.

"I'm enjoying myself and, to be frank, I've nowhere else to go at the moment."

"Okay then. Make yourself useful; find out everything you can about the 'Jean Vincent Thousands' motorcycle club and their mysterious leaders. Simon Coy's a dentist in Sheffield – and Paul something is the owner of Millthorpe Hall."

Five minutes later, Day was in DS Andy Grainger's car on his way to Will Thomson's Computer Shop on Chatsworth Road. They were discussing how to unsettle the computer genius.

Unlike in police TV dramas, where there's always somewhere to park right outside the required location, Chatsworth Road was busy and the two detectives had quite a walk from their parking space.

The sign on the door to 'The Computer Shop' stated 'CLOSED' but a bright light was visible through a door behind the counter. Grainger knocked gently at first – and then much more assertively as he realised he was being deliberately ignored. Day was just about to order his DS to see if there was a back entrance when Will Thomson appeared in the shop. The computer expert shook his head and pointed to the 'CLOSED' sign. Day pushed his face close to the glass panel in the door and held up his ID. It was obvious that Will Thomson recognised the face before the ID because he went from shocked, to frightened, to calm – all in the space of five seconds.

The door was opened very quickly. "Chief Inspector, so sorry. If I'd realised it was you, I'd have come straight away, of course!"

"Not a problem, Mr Thomson. Can you spare us ten minutes, please?"

"Certainly, do come in."

As they were ushered inside, Day introduced DS Grainger and noticed that Andy had been practising his 'scary look' – still not as effective as Mandy Sharp's, but getting there.

Will quickly made spaces amongst the chaos of his workshop for all three of them to sit. Day, who knew the basic functions of computers but had no idea how they worked, was genuinely awe-struck. "Wow, what a place!" he said.

Will Thomson was visibly relieved. Perhaps these two visitors were here just for background information?

Andy Grainger was studying the contents of a workbench. "What are you on with here?" he asked.

Now on safe ground, Will became more animated. "Oh, it's updated internals for a very complex security system for one of my wealthier clients. Rich bugger, actually, worth a fortune! This stuff will control all the locks, the cameras, gates, intercoms – even the lights and curtains. Entertainment too, of course. He's a bit of a recluse; means he doesn't ever have to meet or even see anyone he doesn't want to. Strange, but it's a good bit of business for me. He wants it installing and up and running tomorrow so I'm on an all-nighter."

"Tell me about your relationship with Gary Martin?" asked Day suddenly. The atmosphere in the workshop changed dramatically.

Desperately trying to disguise his discomfort, Will began, "Gary? Good bloke. I like him... liked him."

"Would you describe him as a friend?" asked DS Grainger.

96

"Of course. Yes, we sometimes go out for a pint together. Yes, we get on well, why do you ask?"

Day ignored the question. "How long have you known him?"

Will thought for a few moments. "Must be at least seven or eight years; since Gina first brought him to our house, why?"

"Background," said Grainger. "Would it be true to say your family thought Gina could do a lot better for herself?"

Will Thomson looked down at his feet then nodded. "It would be true, yes. Oh, we all liked Gary well enough but would you like it if your sister wanted to marry someone who made his living shooting and being shot at, Chief Inspector?"

Day didn't have a sister – but he had two daughters, so he could see the point. "Fair enough," he said. "How hard did you try to put her off?"

Thomson laughed. "Not very! Bad jokes and teasing, mainly. The more we tried, the more adamant she became about sticking with him."

"You introduced her to other men when Gary was away?" asked Grainger.

"Guilty!" admitted Will.

Day nodded to Grainger and the DS changed tack again. "This bike club, you're a member of – the Vincents is it?"

Thomson was clearly shocked at this line of questioning but decided to play for time. "Chief Inspector, I've forgotten to tell you something I really should have told you straight away - the other night when you came to the house to tell us about Gary." He stopped and waited for approval. Neither detective blinked. "I'd talked to Gary about his first day back on leave a couple of weeks ago." No reaction. Thomson continued, "He'd told me he was going to propose to Gina so I'd said 'great' – and offered to pick him up from the station." Not a flicker. "Gary said he was going to need a couple of beers after he got off the train so I offered to pick him up a bit later in the town centre. He agreed but I told him it'd have to be before four because I had a dental appointment at five." Now Day was interested but still didn't react.

"When he didn't call before four, I thought 'sod him' and went off to see the dentist. I feel bad. If I'd called him and persuaded him to stop drinking and see Gina earlier, he might still be alive!"

"Why didn't you?" asked Grainger.

Thomson shrugged. "He's a grown up, he can make his own decisions."

"Not any more!" said Day flatly.

"Sorry, wrong tense. This is awful, Chief Inspector. To feel partly responsible for a friend's murder, there's no worse feeling. And, to add insult to injury, I was late for the dentist and I got flashed by a speed camera on the way into Sheffield; I expect I'll be getting a ticket in the next couple of days." Will Thomson was saying all the right things in just the right tone but, with every passing syllable, DCI Day believed him less.

"Every cloud has a silver lining," said Day. "Perfect alibi – if you needed one."

Now Thomson did look alarmed. "Do I need an alibi?"

"No, of course not, this is just getting some background. Now, you were going to tell me about your motorbike club?"

"Do you mind telling me why?" asked Thomson.

"Background!" Day repeated. "They seem to be a secretive lot and I don't like secrets when I'm investigating murders."

Thomson took a few seconds to compose himself before he responded. "I'd say exclusive rather than secretive. There's plenty about them on the web…"

"But they don't have a website, why's that?" interrupted Grainger.

"I've offered to build a site many times but again, it's an exclusivity thing. We're not looking to recruit new members. Our secretary keeps a check on what's happening on the vintage Vincents market and, if he likes the look of a new owner, he'll be approached."

"He?" asked Day.

"Oh, there's no bar to ladies but the old Vincents are heavy bikes."

"So, the membership criterion is simply owning a classic bike?" asked Grainger.

"And a great deal of wealth?" added Day.

Thomson blushed, then laughed. "Embarrassing, but true! I'm afraid I'm the exception; I'm not exactly hard up but most of the other members are millionaires or even multi-millionaires. Keeping a seventy-year-old motorbike in perfect running order isn't cheap. They tolerate me because of my computer skills; I do a lot of sophisticated stuff for most members."

"Any other qualifications required – like colour of skin, for example?" Grainger asked the question that Day had devised in the car.

The reaction was predictable. Bluster. "Bloody hell, sergeant, no! Nothing like that. I admit we don't have any ethnic members but that's an economic thing not racist. How many black millionaires who like classic motorbikes do you know, sergeant?"

As planned, that put Will Thomson off guard – so Day could ask the question he was really interested in. "My understanding is that all the members are men with very attractive – no, startlingly attractive – female partners. Is that coincidence or a requirement?"

That struck a nerve; Thomson's eyes flashed from one detective to the other as though seeking a clue for the most acceptable response. "Rich men attract…"

Day didn't let him finish – he knew all he wanted to know… almost. As he stood up to leave, he asked for one more piece of information. The names of the other members.

"I only know a couple of complete names, Chief Inspector – at club meets we always use first names only."

"The Membership Secretary's name, then?" asked Day.

"Simon Coy, he can be…"

"Ah, Simon Coy, the dentist! I've heard of him. Is he your dentist, Mr Thomson?"

They didn't wait for an answer. Satisfied with the results of the interview, the two detectives stood and left. As Andy drove back to Beetwell Street, Day made a couple of phone calls. Appointments made for a very busy Saturday morning, the DCI went home, unaware that his plans would be shot to pieces.

Will Thomson waited for five minutes and then made a phone call. It took a distressingly long time to be picked up.
A quietly tentative male voice said, "Yes?"
The young man was now shaking so badly he had difficulty speaking. "It's Will; I think they're on to us…"
The line abruptly went dead.

Chapter Fourteen

Home matters…

As often happened, Jess and the girls had already eaten but there was a more than adequate plated-up meal waiting by the microwave. After the 'ping', he carried it on a tray through to the lounge where Jess, Alice and Sophie were watching something about endangered tigers on the TV. Jess immediately pressed 'record' and switched off the box.

"Not necessary!" said Derek. "I don't mind looking at the odd stripy thing."

Both girls laughed but Jess responded with fake seriousness, "It doesn't matter, they'll still be endangered tomorrow."

There followed the usual family discussion about who had done what with whom during the day. By the time Derek had finished eating and that line of conversation exhausted, both girls took his hint to go upstairs for a while.

"What's that about? It's Friday night, they always stay up on Fridays!" said Jess. "Are you okay, D? Had a bad day?"

"Mixed, as usual. Hideous crimes as you know and lots of outside interference but I think we've made some progress. I don't want the girls to go to bed yet, I just wanted us to have a ten-minute talk before we tell them something."

"Oh dear, that sounds ominous!"

"Probably not. Jimmy Hammond is back from Australia and…"

"Oh no, he wants us to move out!" Derek was shocked by Jess' expression as she interrupted.

He realised this was not a matter for levity. "No, quite the opposite. They're not coming back for a long time, if at all. They want to sell the house."

"Oh no!" she repeated. Then realisation. "Can we buy it? Can we afford it? Do you want it? When is this going to happen? What shall we do?"

He laughed. "Exactly which question would you like me to answer, first madam?" he replied in his best detective voice. But now Jess was all seriousness. "Do you want it?"

"You love it, the girls love it and I can make it safer – so, yes," he answered bluntly.

Jess smiled briefly. "Can we afford it?"

"You know that better than me. If we get our asking price for Brim, and it looks like we will, yes we can." The offer made on their Brimington house had been confirmed and the legal stuff was about to begin.

Jess collapsed back into the sofa with the biggest possible grin on her face. "So, what do we have to do?"

"Well, I told Jimmy that we'd make all the arrangements, get it valued, show people round etc."

"Wait, you didn't tell him we wanted it?" Jess was incredulous.

"No, I wasn't a hundred percent sure you'd go for it and, more important, if I'd said that he would have started offering all sorts of discounts. I didn't want that – they must have a fair price."

Jess shook her head. "You're a proper idiot, you know, but I do love you. No actually, you're right, they've been good to us, they deserve a fair price."

"Okay, so we're agreed. As soon as this case is sorted, I'll put the wheels in motion."

"Sod that!" exclaimed Jess. "I'll put the wheels in motion – tomorrow morning! Let's tell the girls!"

For the next two hours, the four of them toured the house deciding what they would change and where their own furniture would fit when it came out of storage.

They went to bed exhausted and happy – but Derek wasn't exhausted enough to refuse the well-earned reward Jess had in store for him.

PART TWO
Chapter Fifteen

After replacing the receiver, the man who took the call from Will Thomson didn't hesitate before tapping another number. It was picked up after the third ring.

"Go ahead caller." A simple statement.

"Mr Jones, I need you back up here, preferably tonight or at least first thing tomorrow. Your usual team and your usual fee. Plus, this time, there will be a substantial bonus."

"I'll make the calls; see you later."

A CRIME WAS PLANNED

Gary Martin was a little surprised to receive a call from Gina's brother. The two of them didn't speak that often when Gary was away on duty but Will obviously knew Gina very well, so Gary saw it as an opportunity to ask for advice. (His Marine friends tended to be over-expressive when giving advice about matters of the heart.)

"I'm going to propose when I come up next week – and I'm going to tell her how much progress I've made with our business idea. We're nearly there, mate. I'm crapping myself though; what if she says no to either – or both?"

"She won't mate, she's crazy about you. I saw how happy she was when you told her you'd put your resignation in. She told all her girlfriends you were going to propose. Don't ask me why – you're such an ugly bugger!"

Gary didn't laugh. "I know, that's the trouble. What a fucking contrast – beauty and the beast! But, come on, which should I do first?"

"Doesn't matter, mate. She'll say yes to both questions. Listen, when you come up next Wednesday, have a few beers on the train; Proper Dutch courage – not too much, mind!"

"Can't do that. The three of us will be travelling up together and you know Tahir doesn't drink. Me and Red have a pact – we don't drink in his company." Gary, in his nervous state, was looking for problems not solutions.

"That's easy enough, have a couple of beers in town when you get off the train and then ring me so I can pick you up and drop you off with Gina. Just give me twenty minutes notice and I'll be fine. I'll go back to work then you can call me again when you're ready to go to your folks' place. I'll come in with you then we can go for another beer to celebrate her saying 'yes' – twice!"

"Cheers, buddy – you're a good 'un!" Gary put his mobile down and raised a little smile. Maybe it was all going to be alright? It was good to talk.

Day's DAY 4
Saturday 6am

DCI Day was already up and getting dressed when the phone rang. It was DS Sharp. After she announced herself, Day interrupted, "What on earth are you doing up at this hour, Mandy – you're supposed to be taking it easy?"

"I've been at the station all night checking on stuff coming in but that's not important, things are kicking off here. The MPs have had a tip-off that Hamilton's medal is in the Abbas garage. At the same time a big file of damaging material has just arrived from Afghanistan. Your name is mud and the MPs are almost dancing with joy; gearing up for a mob-handed raid – there'll be shit flying everywhere!" Sharp was dangerously excited.

Ten seconds of whirling brain then Day knew exactly what was happening. "Too obvious! It's got to be a set-up! Tell the MPs before they get in bother. Those two sergeants have met Mr Abbas, he'll make their lives hell if they barge in. Don't let 'em do anything before I get there!"

"Huh! I already told that Sergeant Vernon exactly that and his response was far from polite. If I'd been feeling a hundred percent, I'd have smacked him!"

"Do everything you can to keep 'em there until I arrive; I'll be less than ten!" Now aware that his carefully planned-out day was ruined, Day accelerated the process of dressing.

Will Thomson would have liked to have changed his mind but things had gone too far. The silent couple seated just behind him in the Peugeot van gave off such sinister vibes he was having difficulty keeping his voice and body steady.

When the call came through, it was obvious than Gary was feeling pretty mellow. "Ready mate?" was all he said.

"Okay, Gary," Will replied, "layby opposite the Spire, five minutes." He hoped there was no obvious tremor in his voice.

As he put the mobile back on its mount, he felt a gentle tap on his shoulder. "Very good, William, your plan seems to be working," said Mr Jones.

And there was Gary Martin, nonchalantly leaning on one of the electric car-charging points, flight bag in hand. He moved smoothly enough as he approached the van and opened the door.

"Hi Gary, alright?" said Will as his passenger climbed in awkwardly, struggling to get the case comfortable on his knee.

"Great," Gary replied. "I think I've had precisely the required amount of Dutch courage! Hello, who's this?" he asked with only the slightest slur.

"Mr and Mrs Jones, very good customers of mine. They live in Old Whitt so I've offered them a lift home."

"Oh great. Good to meet you!" said Gary, trying and failing to turn sufficiently to offer a handshake.

"We understand congratulations are in order?" offered Mrs Jones as the van pulled out into the traffic.

"Too soon to…" began Gary.

"I'm just going to turn down here to get us pointing in the right direction," said Will. The van turned left at the lights into the complex of car parks and Will pretended to look for a quiet place to spin round.

"You were saying?" said Mr Jones as he looked intently around. No one was moving.

Gary didn't have chance to reply. A rope flashed down past his face and was pulled very tightly against his throat - thrusting his head back into the headrest. Mrs Jones pushed both of her knees into the back of Gary's seat and pulled with every ounce of her strength. Gary yelled almost silently as he struggled to get a grip on the rope but five pints of beer had taken the edge off his survival skills. It took slightly longer than Mrs Jones' record but she had obligingly used a thicker garotte than usual because she didn't want to make a mess in Will's borrowed van.

Now visibly shaking, Will drove out of the complex. Mr Jones had placed a baseball cap on Gary's distinctive head while Mrs Jones helpfully held his body upright. Seven minutes later the deceased Marine was transferred to the boot of the black Mercedes and Will was sent away to develop his alibi.

A further fifteen minutes later, Gary Martin's corpse was being tied onto a chair in a concrete storage unit behind a big house. Sometimes you just have to admire professionalism.

Chapter Sixteen

6.10am

As DCI Day shot down Newbold Road in the direction of the
police station, he caught a brief glimpse of a white van with
a small 'THE COMPUTER SHOP' logo travelling in the
opposite direction. He just had time to think, 'So, Will
Thomson has finished his rebuild and is on his way to
Millthorpe to set it all up for the big party tonight', before
his mobile rang.

"Mandy, sir. Couldn't stop them, they've set off!"

Day braked hard and did a u-turn in a builders' yard
entrance. "Contact the uniforms protecting the house and
order them to delay the raid as long as possible. Then contact
Jill Halfpenny and ask her to work her magic on Commander
Perry and see if he can put a stop to this nonsense!" He
didn't wait for a response but concentrated on driving. Not
for the first time, he wished Dipa Sindhu was in control of
the car.

CRIME TWO

Mr Jones was hidden in the shadows opposite Angie Lake's
terraced house. He'd been there two hours already and
watched the same police car drive by three times. This was a
nuisance; it was obvious the coppers had found the other
soldier's head much earlier than anticipated and were on
high alert, but Mr Jones had all the qualities required to
succeed in his chosen profession. High levels of patience and
adaptability complemented each other.

A light came on upstairs in the house. Even at that distance
he heard a brief explosion of angry words. He hoped it
wouldn't disturb any neighbours. A downstairs light came on
and went out again five seconds later. The front door opened
and out into the darkness stepped his target – in full running
gear.

So far, so good. No sign of the police car. Mr Jones took his
silenced Glock 17 out of its holster just in case Steve

Hamilton took a different, unexpected route. He didn't; the Marine looked around and up at the sky. He did a few stretches then clicked something on his wrist and set off at impressive speed. Mr Jones loved predictable people and now he knew his team could stick more closely to the brief they'd been given.

The gun was replaced and the phone came out. Mr Jones said one word, "Coming!" He waited until the upstairs light went off and counted to five hundred before crossing the road and working his magic on the door lock. Burgling an occupied house was always risky but he liked to practise his old skill set.

Game on.

By the time Mr Jones had completed his allotted task and then jogged his victim's route, the deed was done. The Marine was face down on the footpath with his head almost severed.

Jones' young accomplice was checking the area for any traces they might have left and Mrs Jones was stripping off her boiler suit and stuffing it in a bag. Both were immediately congratulated. "Good effort," he said. "The filth will be convinced we were interrupted and waste valuable time looking for whoever interrupted us. Some poor sod is going to have a very shitty start to his day!"

All three laughed silently. Having checked the area thoroughly they departed in different directions. Fifteen minutes later they regrouped at the black Mercedes. After a brief detour to the Abbas household on Somersall Lane, where Mr Jones skilfully avoided being seen by two police officers, he opened the side door of the garage and left a small gift. An hour later, Mr and Mrs Jones were dropped off at Derby Midland Station – where they caught the 7.03 train to St Pancras. By 10.30am, both were having breakfast in quite separate homes.

Robert Jones (still not his real name – professional nickname 'Archer') drove to a dodgy area on the outskirts of Nottingham and parked the Mercedes on a side street, leaving the keys in the ignition. Confident it contained no evidence and would be stolen and trashed within a couple of hours, he carried his overnight bag and crossbow around the corner to his girlfriend's SUV. They kissed and set off home.

-

Back in Chesterfield, the poor sod destined to have a shitty day was called Daniel Thorneycroft. Like so many young men who had experimented with recreational drugs, he had become an addict. Like so many addicts, he had become a thief.

His speciality was removing expensive phones from the unguarded back pockets of teenagers with more money than sense, but he'd had a lean couple of days so decided to have a wander round town in the early hours and look for opportunities. He'd removed an expensive leather jacket from the rear seat of an unlocked car and was confident he'd get fifty quid for it, so he was feeling quite chipper as he walked along the footpath in the direction of his flat in Hady. He saw the bundle in the half-light of the path up ahead but didn't realise it was a body until he was almost close enough to touch. He studied the corpse for a few seconds. That was just enough to disturb the kebab he'd eaten a few hours before.

He began to run even though he knew it would create suspicion in any observer. He was lucky; unseen, he made it home before he threw up.

Despite his many misdemeanours, Daniel had a conscience. An hour after the remains of his kebab had been consigned to the sewers, he used a stolen iPhone to report the location of the body. Immediately after the anonymous call, he removed the battery and the sim before placing the phone in a drawer. He planned to sell it on in a couple of weeks.

His description had been vague and, by the time the young PC had walked the length of the footpath to the correct spot, several people were on the scene. All had their phones in their hands; one was reporting finding the body but the others were busy taking photographs.

Images of murder victim two were on the internet before any detective had seen the body.

-

Day arrived at the chaos on Somersall Lane just in time to be of no use whatsoever. He took in the scene quickly.

Commander Perry, looking like the cat who'd just discovered a bucketful of fresh cream – and a kipper, was leaning against the bonnet of a response car. The two local officers seated inside the car looked totally bemused by the situation.

Four armed MPs were on the drive covering their colleagues who were well into the action. One turned and briefly pointed his gun at Day before Perry shouted, "Local police!"

The MP Captain was trying, unsuccessfully, to reason with a very irate and dressing gowned Mr Abbas senior. Sergeant Vernon had Mr Abbas junior already handcuffed, pinned against the garage roller door. There was no sign of Sergeant Bryant; presumably, he was already inside with a search team.

Abbas Senior saw Day arrive and called out, "Mr Day, stop this nonsense, at once!"

As he strode up the drive, Day received an instruction from Commander Perry. "DCI Day, here please, now!" Fortunately for the anti-terrorist officer, Day didn't hear him say, under his breath, "If you value your career!"

DCI Day had always struggled with obeying senior officers if he knew he was right and they were wrong but, in this case, he was only about ninety-five percent sure. "I'll be with you in a few moments, Mr Abbas. Please stay calm and I'll sort it all out!" He turned and walked back to Perry.

"Good man," said Perry, asserting his authority. "You think Marine Abbas is innocent – he isn't. We've finally received the report from our colleagues in Afghanistan. That young man was passing information about training methods and Afghan Army operations to Taliban agents. He's an extremist and, in my book, that makes him a very likely candidate for involvement in our two murders!"

110

At that moment, there was a yell from inside the garage and, seconds later, Bryant appeared holding a medal case in his gloved right hand. "Got it!" he shouted. "Hidden in a toolbox!"

Now Day was certain the young marine was being framed; in every Hollywood crime movie the stolen loot was always hidden in a toolbox.

Abbas junior looked shocked; Abbas senior looked horrified; everyone else in the scenario looked elated – except Day, who looked murderous.

"Still not convinced, Chief Inspector?" asked Perry.

"Less than ever, sir!" replied Day. "I can't comment on your info from Afghanistan, but this is the most blatant stitch-up I've ever witnessed."

"I can't help but admire your sense of self-belief," said Perry, "but it's time to admit you're wrong." He turned away and shouted to the MP officer. "Captain Church, I suggest you get your prisoner out of here right now!"

She left Abbas senior and marched over to Vernon and Abbas junior. Together, they half dragged the reluctant Marine to their car and pushed him inside. Ten seconds later all the MPs were back inside their vehicles and ready to leave.

The captain came over to Perry and gave a very stiff salute. "Thanks for your support, sir," she clipped.

Perry didn't return the salute. "You're welcome, Caroline. Be off with you now."

She was about to say something to Day but didn't get the chance. The DCI was on his way to sooth one extremely angry and influential solicitor.

"Could we go inside, please sir?" asked Day, now conscious that many neighbours were out on the street.

Mr Abbas opened the front door and indicated that Day should go first. Mrs Abbas, also in dressing gown, was waiting in the lounge. As they both sat on an oversize sofa, the solicitor appeared to regain some of his equilibrium. "This is a very, very bad situation, Chief Inspector!"

111

Day seated himself opposite. He hated making promises unless he was totally sure he could keep them and, on this occasion, there was no certainty. After what he had just witnessed, however, he felt he had to be positive. "I know, for a fact, that Tahir wasn't directly involved in either murder and I will prove it to the outside agencies. After speaking to your son at great length, my experience told me he wasn't involved in planning the crimes either but…"

"That report from Afghanistan has condemned him!" interrupted Mr Abbas. "What can it possibly say? I refuse to believe my son would ever give away information that would put his comrades in danger!"

"Just what I was going to say," added Day.

"Can you help him, Inspector?" pleaded Mrs Abbas.

"I intend to solve these crimes, Mrs Abbas and I believe that a thorough investigation will exonerate your son. In the short-term, however, he's a serving soldier in the hands of the military police and there's little I can do to protect him. Just to reassure you, I've no reason to believe he's in any immediate danger."

"Not good enough, Day! No more platitudes, I want this sorted – today!"

DCI Day realised he was getting nowhere with this conversation. "Not sure I can do that, but I'm going to send a team of my SOCOs to examine your garage before the military lot arrive. With a bit of luck, they might find traces of whoever planted that medal."

Nothing he said was going to impress Mr Abbas, so he expressed his sympathy, made excuses and left. On his way back to Beetwell Street he woke up Lyn Cam, his trusted Senior SOCO and persuaded her she should get to the Abbas house in double-quick time.

When he arrived at the station, he found Mandy Sharp looking exhausted and immediately ordered her home. She obliged, but not before she'd handed over two files. One was a print out of the report on Tahir Abbas' misdemeanours in Afghanistan and the other was the results of Sharp's research into the mysteries of Millthorpe Hall and the Jean Vincent bikers.

It only took Day five minutes to read most of the report on Tahir Abbas' actions in Afghanistan. The content appeared to be very circumstantial. Yes, the young Marine had been seen leaving the camp without authorisation and visiting some local houses. This wasn't unique, others had been involved with local women, but the two families Tahir had repeatedly visited didn't have any females in the likely age-group. At first, it had appeared to the watching MPs that Tahir's claim he was taking some kids a few treats had credibility but, what eventually damned him was the death of a young man from one of his frequently visited families in a recent gunfight with an Afghan Army patrol. It had become apparent the deceased had been a Taliban sympathiser for some time, possibly including the period when Tahir was visiting his home. Day concluded that evidence alone would be unlikely to gain a conviction in a civilian court but that, almost certainly, wasn't where Tahir Abbas was heading.

The information in the other report was comprehensive but told him very little. Mr Paul Wilbourn aka 'Vince' and the Jean Vincents were very, very good at telling outsiders only what they wanted them to know.

Chapter Seventeen
8am

In some ways, the briefing was disappointing for DCI Day but the outside agencies were not present so his team members were, at least, a little more relaxed.

He had resolved to get all the routine stuff out of the way before expanding on his theory that the Jean Vincent Bike Club might be involved in at least one of the murders. However, Dipa Sindhu and Andy Grainger were clearly anxious to impart some discovery they'd made overnight.

"Come on then, Andy, tell me you've got a breakthrough?"

"PC Sindhu will explain, sir. She did most of the hard work on this one," replied the DS.

The grins on both their faces confirmed Day's suspicions they were at, or near, the stage of being an item.

Dipa Sindhu was in civvies and Day knew she was putting in a lot of voluntary hours. "I looked at town centre CCTV at the times the iPhone was stolen – the one used to report Hamilton's death, sir. I spotted the victim straight away; usual thing, gaggle of teenagers - some using their phones and the rest with expensive kit sticking out of their back pockets asking to be stolen. Walking just behind and looking very furtive, I saw a young lad I'd had dealings with before. Petty thief and druggie, Daniel Thorneycroft. CCTV didn't catch him actually taking the phone but I'm ninety percent sure it was him; right place, right time."

"Good work, Dipa," said Day. "When did all this excellent detective work happen?" The stress on the word 'detective' reminded everyone that Sindhu had yet to make the leap from PC to DC.

"Overnight, sir – I was off duty, if that's what you're asking?" Sindhu wasn't sure if she was being complimented and criticised in the same sentence.

"Thank you, well done," offered Day, anxious to clear up the misunderstanding he realised he'd just caused.

"Thank DS Grainger, too, sir. We were at it all night!" Sindhu's remark brought howls of laughter from some members of the team - plus a couple of red faces.

Day, trying to return the meeting to business, continued. "What do we know about this Thorneycroft – is it likely he's a killer?"

"Very unlikely, I'd say, sir. He's a bit pathetic to be honest. I could flatten him with one hand behind my back; he wouldn't have stood a chance against someone like Hamilton," replied Sindhu.

"With a crossbow?" Day was uncompromising. "He have anything to do with motorbikes?"

"From what I know of him, he couldn't afford to run a pushbike, sir. He spends everything on drugs."

"Killer for hire?"

"No sir. I'd bet my life on that!"

"Okay, thanks. As soon as we've finished, the pair of you track him down and fetch him here. Don't take risks, I'm not betting your life on anything, take four armed officers with you. We can't assume he's not our killer, yet."

This was obviously not the breakthrough they'd all been hoping for but left an opening for Day to give out the news about what he'd witnessed a couple of hours previously. "Earlier this morning, the MPs arrested Tahir Abbas for Steve Hamilton's murder; they found the missing medal in his garage. That explains why we aren't enjoying their company today. They think it's all over – but it isn't, because I'm certain that Abbas didn't kill either victim!"

There was a silent uproar in the room. If DCI Day said 'certain', that's exactly what he meant. Everyone else was wrong.

"Don't get over excited," he added, noting the mood. "I'm not completely sure what did happen, or why but I'm thinking it's something to do with a group of rich blokes who ride vintage motorbikes, the Jean Vincents!"

DC O'Neil looked thrilled; he'd just earned a thousand brownie points for bringing Melanie Price's concerns to the DCI's attention.

Day continued, "The only link between this group of characters and our first murder is the family Thomson, who some of you have met. Gina Thomson was girlfriend, soon to be fiancée, of Gary Martin. Her brother is a lowly member of the Jean Vincents. Will Thomson does a lot of lucrative IT work for the other members. It could be said that his livelihood depends on them; if not his whole business, certainly the icing on the cake. Dom and his girlfriend put us on to this line of enquiry and DS Sharp has been researching them." Day paused while team members gave Dom a quiet round of applause.

"I've just had a few minutes to scan Mandy's report, but it's confirmed a lot of what I already knew from interviews. Exclusive club of owners of very expensive vintage motorbikes. All members wear identical denims, hence the misspelling of Gene. All white, all male, all rich. The club does some good charity work and some of its members occasionally ride for Blood Bikes." Day paused and nodded to DC Malysz, who also rode for that fine organisation. "But," he added, "and it's a big but, they get up to some very funny stuff indeed!"

At that moment the door opened and in came DS Sharp. She looked dreadful.

Day was horrified. "Mandy, what on earth are you doing here? Go home and get some rest. I've got everything I need in your report; I'm just going through it, now."

"I guessed as much," she replied, "but I've just found out a bit more. If you'd like me to continue the briefing, I will - and then I'll go home and sleep all fu… day." She'd stopped just in time.

Day reluctantly nodded and brought a chair to the front of the room. As the DS sat down, Day handed her file back to her. "Thanks, but I don't need it," she said.

She began to speak and her tone indicated a mood of exhausted loathing. "In 2007, a very successful, young City trader left his firm in London and bought the old hall in Millthorpe. Most of you know where that is. The building was apparently a bit of a wreck but he spent millions on

116

renovation. Paul Wilbourn is very, very rich. When he headed north, just before the financial crash, he was investigated by the Met. for all sorts of financial irregularities but nothing stuck. I've spoken to one of the senior officers who investigated him and been told that our Mr Wilbourn's wheeler-dealing was a major contributor to the 2008 disaster! In short, he's a complete bastard!"

Every eye in the room swung towards Day. They all knew his attitude to strong language.

Sharp continued, unfazed. "But he's a very clever and very secretive and very rich bastard. Almost a recluse now, he rarely goes out on club tours, although he's the registered owner of three vintage bikes worth hundreds of thousands. He does turn up at the big charity events but only makes brief appearances. His main interest seems to be the Jean Vincents club. He doesn't do the day to day running but all the members visit him from time to time. From what I can gather, they sort of pay him homage while their bikes are repaired. He's built a workshop in the grounds of the Hall and keeps a full-time expert mechanic on the premises. Also several security guards and servants. The club is actually organised by a smart cookie called Simon Coy. Some of you will be customers of his; he owns a chain of dental surgeries across South Yorkshire." She looked around but there were no nods.

"It's almost impossible to get a comprehensive list of club members. I think there are about fifteen of them from far and wide but I've only identified six so far, plus Thomson. All rich, white males. Apart from the dentist, I've got a couple of lawyers, three business owners and a consultant surgeon. Most of them seem to be in their thirties or forties – successful and arrogant is my guess. What I have picked up from several sources, all have an unhealthy obsession with attractive women; there's a sort of competition going on who's got the best-looking girlfriend." She hesitated. "So I'm going to go in undercover!"

There was a stunned silence because Mandy looked shocking. Nobody said a word! This was an attractive woman who was still recovering from a serious assault and hadn't slept for thirty-six hours. Day was just about to intervene when she broke the tension herself. Mandy pulled a strained expression and said, "Well not just yet, I might need a snooze and a dab of makeup, first."

The whole room erupted in laughter – through sheer relief. Mandy's spark was relighting.

Day was trying not to laugh and get some decorum back into the briefing but even he was struggling. Eventually, it was Mandy who brought the group to order.

"I haven't met her but I understand from those of you who have that the first murder victim's girlfriend is stunning."

DC Tara Rutherford agreed. "Yes, definitely."

"These men regard women as possessions, mere objects and, for that reason, I dislike them – a lot!" The tone of disdain immediately brought the briefing back to deadly seriousness. She continued, "As luck would have it, they're having a party at Millthorpe tonight. Very secret; men only – girlfriends sent away. We understand they bring in expensive prostitutes for the evening. For 'party', read 'orgy'. I for one, would very much like to attend and properly piss on their chips!" With that she stood up and headed for the door.

"Thanks, Mandy," called Day after her. "Get some sleep. Sorry, you can't go and spoil their chips but I'll do my best to do it for you!" Had the boss made a joke?

She nodded and left.

For ten more minutes the briefing continued at a pace. Day wrote furiously on his whiteboard as information came in and jobs were allocated. Other than Day's theory about the motorbike gang, there had been little progress and, in a rare moment of doubt, he hoped his suspicions would prove to be right.

Chapter Eighteen

Paul Wilbourn was above the law.

The fortune he'd made before his 30th birthday had given him a contempt for the normal conventions of adult life.

Cheating the financial markets in the City of London had become second nature. Unlike many others now serving long prison sentences, PW was very, very clever and, despite many investigations by various watchdogs and even the Fraud Squad, he had survived and prospered.

Money laundering for organised crime had also accelerated his accumulation of wealth and brought him into contact with people who would perform any service if the fee was right.

Unable to find a woman who met his exacting standards of beauty and compliance for an actual relationship, he regularly resorted to short liaisons with very expensive escorts.

The syphilis he'd contracted just before his 30th birthday had gone unrecognised and untreated for too long. His extended trip to Switzerland for discreet but straightforward treatment allowed him to break some of his links with the criminal fraternity but left his personality even more damaged.

Still sufficiently capable of realising his brain had lost its edge, he decided to leave The City and move to a place where he could indulge his fantasies unhindered.

Millthorpe Hall had been a partial wreck. The west wing was liveable but the centre and east needed extensive renovation. That didn't matter to a man with near limitless funds; the modifications he demanded ranged from exciting to eccentric - to bizarre.

The location was excellent, though. Isolated, and surrounded by almost two miles of sturdy high walls, Millthorpe Hall suited his needs admirably.

Spending more and more time alone, protected by a small team of extremely well-paid staff, Wilbourn's behaviour became obsessive in the extreme. He trawled the internet looking for an available woman beautiful enough to become his companion, but his demand for perfection doomed his search.

His life took a new turn as the result of a severe toothache. A private, and very expensive, dentist – a Mr Simon Coy, based in Sheffield - was his first choice. Wilbourn demanded personal service by the practice owner on a Sunday when no other clients were around and was prepared to pay for the privilege.

In discussions, during the period of time required for the anaesthetic to take hold, Coy introduced Wilbourn to the fascinating world of vintage motorcycles. Coy showed off photographs of his Vincent 1000 which he claimed was worth £70,000 - and his enthusiasm set Wilbourn's mind racing. The millionaire had never ridden a motorbike; indeed, he hadn't driven a car for more than five years, but he did recognise a thing of beauty, not to mention a good investment.

A new obsession! With Coy's advice and support, Wilbourn snapped up three vintage Vincents at auction within a year. Construction began of a state-of-the-art maintenance building with accommodation above to the rear of Millthorpe Hall. Coy recommended an elderly mechanic called Murphy who specialised in ancient motorcycles and, two weeks after the building's completion, the man moved in to a generous semi-retirement and became a permanent feature. Other Vincent owners were allowed to bring their bikes for service and those approved by Coy were introduced to Wilbourn.

Coy became the nearest thing to a friend Wilbourn would ever have. Their love of money, Vincent motorcycles and beautiful women, shared obsessions.

Careful manipulation of two would lead to access to the third. The 'Jean Vincent' Club was born.

9am

Day's call of the previous evening to Simon Coy had been difficult. The dentist told him he was far too busy this weekend to meet with mere detectives but offered a Monday appointment. Day said that wasn't good enough – it had to be Saturday morning. Under pressure, Coy agreed to visit the police station 'for ten minutes only' at 9am.

At 8.55am he had rung in to cancel, no excuse given. Although Day had never met the man, he already disliked him and determined to make his life unpleasant.

He would visit Millthorpe Hall and demand an entrance. He assumed Wilbourn would be there and guessed Coy might be, too. If Will Thomson was still there working on the IT system it would be three birds with one stone.

After a brief discussion with DI Allsop, Day sent for PC Sindhu. "Dipa, I've changed my mind. If you're okay with it, Tara can go with Andy to pick up Thorneycroft and you can come with me and DI Allsop. Before you agree, you need to know I'm playing the race card again. I want to test these two blokes with your presence. I know you're off duty and it's a pretty distasteful thing I'm asking so, if it offends you, feel free to say no."

Sindhu laughed. "Of course it offends me, sir but nowhere near as much as racists who treat women like these scum apparently do. Count me in and give me the nod if you want me to be properly obnoxious!"

The steady drive to Millthorpe took fifteen minutes. The Hall, invisible from the road, was surrounded by an ancient two-metre tall stone wall that had obviously been recently renovated to a very high standard. There was nothing ancient about the steel gates; impregnable was the first word that entered Day's mind. Six cameras and the sign on the gates made it clear how the owner felt about uninvited guests:

MILLTHORPE HALL
STRICTLY PRIVATE
NO ADMISSION WITHOUT APPOINTMENT

However, there was an intercom built into the wall – deliberately designed so uninvited guests would be forced to leave their vehicles for the benefit of the cameras. Day climbed out and pressed the button. The response was immediate and, much to his surprise, a rather posh voice said, "Good morning, how may I be of assistance?"

Day always made a point of being polite to people who were polite to him. "Good morning," he replied, "Chief Inspector Derek Day, Derbyshire Police – I'd like to see the owner, please."

"I'm so sorry, Chief Inspector, Mr Wilbourn does not see anyone without an appointment."

"Who am I speaking to?"

"My name is Henderson, sir. I am the butler, here. May I make you an appointment, sir; Mr Wilbourn has some slots in November?"

Being rude politely was a great way to put unwanted visitors off their stride but Day was an expert in dealing with such people. "Mr Henderson," he said, "how long is your drive?" It was a rhetorical question; Day had studied all the plans and images of the Hall's grounds he could find.

It did, however, catch the butler by surprise. "About half a mile, I would guess." No 'sir' this time.

"Good, then please make me an appointment to see Mr Wilbourn in exactly five minutes!"

Henderson recovered quickly. "May I ask what your visit is connection with?"

"No, you may not!"

"Then it's not possible, I'm afraid."

"Mr Henderson, which part of the word 'police' don't you understand?"

"The part where you didn't use the word 'warrant'!"

Cheeky. Had Day met his match?

Not really. "Mr Henderson, please tell Mr Wilbourn that, if I leave now, I will be returning this evening with a warrant and about twenty of my friends!"

"Just a moment, sir." The intercom clicked off.

Day turned and raised his eyebrows at his two colleagues still seated in the car. Both were grinning.

There was a loud click from the intercom and Henderson's polite tone returned. "I regret that Mr Wilbourn really is unavailable, sir, but one of his senior associates will meet you at the gate in a few moments." The intercom clicked off before Day had chance to respond.

Now, his limited sense of humour had evaporated. He jabbed the button again but was ignored.

His mental image of a large tow truck ripping the gates away from the wall disappeared with the approaching burble of a red E-type Jaguar. The personalised number plate told Day that the 'senior associate' was none other than Simon Coy, the man who had broken his appointment only a few minutes before.

The car stopped close enough to the gates to allow them to open but it still effectively blocked the drive. The car door opened and out stepped the bulky figure of the millionaire dentist. He smiled and, as he approached the gates, they opened exactly the right amount to allow him to walk through. In an act of blatant defiance, the gates closed behind him. The whole scene was being played out for the benefit of someone watching via the array of cameras.

Sindhu and Allsop climbed out of their car and joined Day. Coy approached the group and held out his hand in the direction of Day, pointedly ignoring the other two.

"Chief Inspector Day, what a stroke of luck! So sorry I had to miss our appointment but all's well that ends well, eh?" The man oozed charm.

Day looked him over. About forty-five, well-built and fit, good-looking and knows it, super-confident and very, very used to getting his own way. "Mr Coy! It is indeed a stroke of luck; I was hoping to meet you as well as Mr Wilbourn on this visit. Perhaps you would be able to facilitate that? I would hate to have to conduct interviews on the side of the road." Day hoped it was the right combination of threat and charm.

Coy smiled even more brightly. "Chief Inspector, I would be more than happy to talk to you for a couple of minutes by the side of this glorious thoroughfare but I'm afraid that an interview with Mr Wilbourn is impossible. I'm sorry to report that he has become a recluse, it's really taken over his whole personality." The contempt in his voice was well

123

disguised but Day picked it up and contemplated his response.

"Beautiful car," interrupted Sindhu, "is it a '63 model?"

Coy didn't turn to look at her. "You know your cars, young woman."

"Ms Sindhu is an accomplished rally driver," added Day.

"Is she really?" exclaimed Coy, as he glanced briefly at the PC with an almost imperceptible curling of the lip. He would never know how close he came to being punched at that moment. Three times.

"Right then, sir – shall we conduct this interview here, in the car or at the station. We'll be happy to give you a lift and bring you back after?" asked Day, subtly threatening.

It didn't work. Coy replied, "There will be no interview, Inspector. I am doing you the courtesy of talking to you for perhaps another minute. I am very busy today. Now, what exactly can I do for you?"

Day noted his 'demotion' and, for once, was relieved Mandy Sharp wasn't present. He realised he was on a loser with an arrogant man who had a precise understanding of his legal rights. "In that case, sir perhaps two favours? I would like a membership list of your motorcycle club and a further interview with Will Thomson, I guess he is still inside setting up the new security system?"

"The answer to both questions is 'no'." Coy turned and walked back towards the gates which silently opened just enough for him to pass through. As he climbed into his car, he said, "Ring my office on Monday, my secretary will make an appointment for you to see me sometime next week!"

Day had been treated with contempt many times before (all police officers know it's part of the job description) but this time he was deeply offended. Mr Simon Coy had made a dangerous enemy.

-

Daniel Thorneycroft, terrified by the sight of four armed officers outside his flat, had accompanied the two detectives to Beetwell Street without argument but, the moment he was placed in an interview room, he refused to comment and demanded a lawyer. A duty solicitor was eventually tracked down and DS Grainger and DC Rutherford began the questioning while Day watched on CCTV. The young addict was uncooperative for almost half-an-hour until Day lost patience and burst into the Interview Room.

"Enough of this nonsense," he shouted. "Charge him with murder!"

The solicitor responded with impressive alacrity. "On what grounds?"

"I'll find something before the day is out! Charge him!" Day, clearly fuming, swept out.

Thorneycroft immediately began to talk. He stated that he had not witnessed the second murder and had nothing useful to offer. He did, however, confess to eighteen offences of theft, including that of the leather jacket. He was passed on to uniformed officers who made sure the rest of his day was equally unpleasant.

Day's play acting had paid off but he was genuinely cross at the amount of wasted time.

-

Day's revenge on Mr Simon Coy and his cronies had begun almost immediately. Detectives O'Neil and Kamytz were sent to watch, from a discreet distance, the two roads that led to the gates of Millthorpe Hall. Their orders were to note exactly who went in - and arrest Will Thomson when he came out.

Within five minutes of O'Neil parking up, a blue BMW swept past and pulled through the gates as they were opening; it was clearly expected. Dom saw it was a young man driving but couldn't make out the shady figures in the back protected by tinted glass. He checked the registration and, discovering it belonged to a firm of solicitors in Wolverhampton, was taxed, insured and not reported stolen, he passed the information onto HQ.

-

Mr and Mrs Jones had been delayed in their preparations to head north once more and didn't manage to get a train until 6.30am. This was fine by 'the Archer' because it gave him an extra hour in bed before he had to get up and change the number plates on the blue BMW he had stolen the previous week. The car had been locked in a garage to keep it 'clean' but now it was perfect for yet another lucrative job. Cloning was just one of the young criminal's specialities.

At 9.14am Mr and Mrs Jones were met by their son at Sheffield Station - they never used the same station twice – and driven to Millthorpe Hall.

-

At 11.30am, there was another arrival at the Hall. A thirty-seater luxury coach, also clearly expected, drove in through the already open gates. Once again, the heavily tinted windows gave no clue to the passengers. There was no company name so Dom checked the registration and found that it belonged to a hire company in his home town, London. Everything was in order so the information was duly passed on to Beetwell Street.

12noon

After just three hours sleep, a slightly refreshed DS Amanda Sharp returned to the station and sneaked into a little-used office to continue her now personal vendetta against this group she believed to be racist abusers of women.

The first thing she saw was the registration of the BMW that had entered an hour or so previously. The PC tasked with tracking down the driver gave up after half an hour; it was a company car and it was Saturday. Sharp was more experienced and more tenacious. Eventually, she discovered the phone number of the Office Manager of the solicitor's firm. He told her that one of the staff had it for the weekend but was reluctant to pass on details. Sharp's persistence and the magic words 'murder enquiry' did the trick.

"At this stage, I won't give you his personal details but I'll call the member of staff concerned and ask him to ring you."

126

Sharp thought that would do for now, and set about discovering what the coach was doing at Millthorpe. She'd hardly started when her phone rang. It was the Office Manager again. With great delight, he informed her he'd spoken to his colleague and could confirm that the vehicle in question was parked on a drive in Sutton Coldfield.

An equally delighted Sharp thanked him and put the phone down to quickly call an internal number. "Boss, we're in luck. The Beamer reported entering Millthorpe Hall is a clone – we've got a reason to go in!"

"What on earth are you doing back here, Mandy?" protested Day but she could tell his heart wasn't in the protest.

"I've had some sleep and I've just given you a great big dollop of help!" she exclaimed.

"Point taken, but you really have to look after yourself. If you're not worried about your own wellbeing, think what'll happen to me if you go under from the strain of working unofficially!"

"Okay, but you've got your breakthrough. I'm just going to make a few calls about the coach, then I'll bugger off home again!"

-

DC Dom O'Neil later admitted he'd lost concentration when Will Thomson's Computer Shop van drove out of the Hall gates. It sped past him and he did a creditably fast three-point turn but the van was out of sight by the time he was heading in the right direction. He called in immediately and, within seconds, Day had made it a priority for Traffic to find and detain. O'Neil was ordered back to Millthorpe Hall.

People didn't clone cars unless crime was intended. Day now had a reason to demand entry to the Hall and, once inside, he was going to make a very large nuisance of himself.

He went to see DSupt Halfpenny to see if she would support the smashing down of the gates to Millthorpe Hall if he was, once more, refused entry. Halfpenny was dubious and decided to pass the request on to the Chief Constable's office. George Carruthers was tracked down on the golf course and angrily vetoed Day's suggestion. Fearing an enormous bill for restitution, he did however say he would support a reasonable number of officers scaling the walls. Plans were drawn up for a major raid at 2pm – but, unbeknown to Day, it would never happen. About five hundred people were going to get in his way.

Chapter Nineteen

Mr Abbas was still very angry about the arrest of his only son and, during the morning, he had made a large number of phone calls. It didn't matter that Tahir had been whisked away to a Military Police facility, Abbas' anger was focused on Beetwell Street Police Station.

At 1pm a crowd began to gather outside the station. Although the majority were Asian youths, there were women and children present. About a quarter were white sympathisers plus the inevitable handful of 'we hate the police, let's vandalise something, rent-a-crowd'. Once again, the banners made it clear that the feeling of the demonstration was 'police hate Muslims'. All available officers exited the station and formed up on the front steps. More were called back from patrol. In a calculated gamble, no riot gear was issued; the officers were trying hard to look non-threatening.

By 1.30pm, TV cameras and a plague of reporters had arrived in time to watch the arrival of Mr Abbas and many of his more elderly, respectable friends.

"This will be a peaceful demonstration," shouted Mr Abbas over his portable PA system. "But police persecution of law-abiding Muslims in Chesterfield must cease. My clearly innocent son, Tahir has been framed for a heinous crime by the military - and the police of Chesterfield have failed to protect him."

It looked to neutral observers that this was going to be a long speech but the solicitor was drowned out by the chanting of his own supporters. "Free Tahir Abbas, free Tahir Abbas!"

As well as interrupting Mr Abbas' flow, the loud noise disguised the approach of a far more sinister group. From the direction of the town centre came a bunch of forty or more young masked men carrying banners with a very different message. 'We are the White British' they proclaimed! The weapons they carried indicated that they had no intention of making their point peacefully.

The Superintendent in charge of the officers on the station steps quietly began to send his men and women back inside in small groups to change into something less comfortable. The first dozen suitably equipped officers were able to get between the two demonstrations just in time. For five minutes there was a stand-off, allowing a few more officers to strengthen their ranks. But it wasn't enough, as soon as they were confident the cameras were in place, the 'White British' charged.

The police line was just too thin. Many officers were flattened in a well organised attack and the first dozen racists broke through into the Muslim demonstration. The remainder of the officers on the station steps leapt into action even though they were ill-equipped to do so.

The twelve white supremacists who had broken through caused many injuries before they were overwhelmed by superior numbers of demonstrators and police and dragged towards the police station. That did nothing to pacify their thirty-odd comrades still held behind a now reinforced police barrier. Stones and bottles were thrown but the stalemate was not broken; it looked as though this situation was going to go on for some time.

Then, one of the White British looked behind. Five people were walking towards them. Two men and three women, all apparently unarmed – and one of the women was a bloody Asian – in a fucking police uniform! Then she had the cheek to yell –

"You lot are under arrest – get down on the floor!" DCI Day was surprised just how loud a voice PC Dipa Sindhu could project.

Of course, when the five of them had flung together a plan to break the deadlock, they knew if their timing was wrong, they were all going to get a good kicking - but DS Grainger (acting), DC Rutherford and DSupt Halfpenny had all, earlier in their careers, faced violent mobs and believed it was time to give their uniformed comrades some relief.

As expected, several of the thugs turned at Sindhu's shout and studied the newcomers behind them.

Even at a distance, Day could read their thoughts. "Come on – three women (pause for contempt) and just two blokes – and they don't look much – not big men! Who are they – the black bitch is a copper so they must be too – extra points for smashing detectives!"

Exactly as Day had planned, half the demonstrators peeled off from the pushing match with the police line and charged the five tempting victims behind them.

-

Dipa Sindhu was the only child of a couple who desperately wanted a boy. Despite their disappointment they resolved to give their daughter the very best start in life.

By the time she was eight, the little girl had, without any coercion from her parents, turned into a proper tomboy. She fought with her boy cousins and played with their Lego Technik. She read books about cars and trucks and loved Maths at school. Her mother and father didn't know whether to be shocked or thrilled.

They were horrified when they asked Dipa about her ninth birthday present and she replied, "May I have session driving a go-kart, please?"

After much debating between themselves, her parents gave in and took her to the local hire track. For the first fifteen minutes she was a disaster then something in her brain clicked and she was off. The proprietor spotted her natural talent and persuaded the parents to bring her again.

A deal was struck. "You work hard at school my girl and we will take you karting whenever you bring home a good report". Her Dad was struggling to deny his delight in his daughter's driving skill.

Dipa excelled at school. She was the only child of colour in her class but rarely received any hostility because she was friendly, bright, tall, pretty – and tough. Outside school was a different matter; at least once a month she would get into trouble for punching a boy who had been stupid enough to call her 'Paki'.

131

By the time she was sixteen she had passed ten GCSEs and was the best driver (including the owner) by far in the Chesterfield Karting Club. That was when she was spotted by Sheffield garage owner, Paul White. He ran a couple of rally cars and was rapidly coming to the point when he would be too inflexible and fat to get in and out of his favourite motor. He approached Dipa's parents and impressed them that his intentions were honourable. With strict chaperoning, he was allowed to take Dipa under his wing.

She passed her driving test on the day after her seventeenth birthday and came second in a local rally a fortnight later. There was considerable pressure on her to apply to join the big professional rally teams but Dipa had already made her mind up about her future career.

Three good A levels later, she joined Derbyshire Police. Her ambition was to become a traffic cop – but then she met a detective called Day.

-

The plan had been simple. Leave the station via the rear car park, turn right then right again up the narrow alley that would bring them onto Beetwell Street behind the White Britain demonstrators. Relieve the pressure on the line of officers separating the opposing factions by tempting some of the youths to chase after them back the way they had come. If only a few came, the detectives would turn and arrest them. If the attackers were too numerous, they would retreat into the safety of the station car park. Well, that's what four of them thought; DCI Day had a slightly different idea.

Day regularly walked up and down that alley and knew a particularly narrow part not covered by CCTV cameras. That was where he'd decided he'd sprain his ankle and let the thugs catch him. Day was feeling bitter about his humiliation at the hands of a posh racist that morning and thought letting off some steam with a few unposh racists this afternoon would be good for his soul. Oh, he'd let the first few through and just deal with the last half-dozen or so!

The five officers appeared to panic at the approach of a dozen or more demonstrators and fled back into the alley. This caused jubilation and near-hysteria amongst their pursuers.

The police ran past the Spread Eagle Pub to the precise point where Day had decided his ankle would become twisted. He stopped – shouting to his comrades to carry on back in the direction of the station. Although they were twenty metres away, they stopped, turned – and headed back. That was the moment Day realised, for the first time, just how much they thought of him – and how much he'd put them all in danger!

"No!" he yelled. "Go back – I can still run!" His ankle made an instant recovery and set off down the alley, carrying the rest of him with it. But it was too late; the most energetic thug caught up with Day.

Schoolboy error! The man grabbed Day's right shoulder with his left hand in an effort to spin the detective around. In one way, he succeeded – Day did spin round but, when an elbow smashed the thug's nose to pulp, he had just a split second to register he'd learned a hard lesson from a seasoned street-fighter.

As thug one collapsed towards the tarmac, thug two half tripped over him and, as his face went rapidly down, it met Day's knee rapidly coming up. Strike two.

The next thug received a massive blow to the solar plexus and went down with a very surprised expression on his face.

Thugs four and five hesitated just long enough for a screaming banshee to run past Day and flatten them both. The ginger-topped banshee yelled, in a raucous Scottish accent, "Yaahh bastaards!"

Day knew that DS Grainger had started out as a beat copper in Glasgow but, up till that point, hadn't seen him in hard action or heard such a strong accent.

Thug six got to Day and immediately wished he hadn't. His wild haymaker punch was blocked by Day's left and the right cross that followed instantly took the man into a world of stars.

Disappointingly, the thugs who had been lucky to be at the rear of the group decided their services would be more useful back on the street at the police line.

This gave Day a few moments to look how his female colleagues were doing. Very well, was the answer. DSupt Halfpenny had one man shoved up hard against the wall; he wasn't struggling – the extensive grazing on his face told the story. Halfpenny was complaining that the man had ripped her trousers during the scuffle. "Have you any idea what these cost, you twat?" she said with her usual decorum – as she winked at Day.

DC Rutherford also had a man in custody. His expression indicating his shock at discovering this delicate little opponent had recently achieved her black-belt at the local Karate club.

Dipa Sindhu had a man flat on his face with her knee in the middle of his back. He was screaming, "Get off me, you black bitch!" and flailing his arms in the traditional method of avoiding handcuffs. She managed to get one arm sorted but was struggling with the other until Day accidentally stamped on the free hand, breaking a couple of fingers. That felt good – Day really didn't get racism.

"Be careful, Derek!" shouted Halfpenny. "Watch where you're putting your feet, you careless bugger!"

There was a shout from the top of the alley and Day saw the remainder of the White British demonstrators running back towards the town centre pursued by the uniformed officers they had previously assaulted. A sergeant and five of her PCs peeled off and came into the alley, anxious to see what damage the thugs had done to the small band of detectives. She looked around at the carnage and, with a complete lack of sympathy, instructed her team, "Cuff 'em all – even the injured!" She took out her radio. "Ambulances to Spread Eagle alley, please. Three, if you can spare 'em."

Sergeant Smith shrugged her shoulders in the general direction of the detectives and their prisoners. DSupt

Halfpenny nodded in return and said, "Carry on, sergeant! – and well done for dealing with this group of miscreants. It's a terrible shame we were too late to intervene."

"Yes, ma'am," the sergeant replied, "always late, you detectives!"

Halfpenny was examining the rip in her trousers but still managed to laugh at the sergeant's response.

"Incidentally, ma'am, you might want to know that the Chief is on his way!" added the sergeant.

"Cue to leave!" ordered Halfpenny and the Infamous Five turned down the alley and headed back towards the police station car park entrance. With their rather dishevelled appearance, this was not the time to bump into the dour new Chief Constable.

As they walked, Halfpenny looked Day up and down suspiciously. "Your ankle seems to have made a speedy recovery, Derek?"

"Yes, ma'am," he replied.

"Stopping behind to fight wasn't part of our plan, Derek!"

"No ma'am."

"Are you sure it wasn't part of your plan?"

"Absolutely, ma'am."

Halfpenny knew he was lying and Day knew she knew he was lying – but he also knew he wouldn't be reprimanded in front of junior officers so he could relax for a little while at least. He'd get an earful soon enough.

-

At the front entrance, the demonstration in support of Tahir Abbas continued with very loud chanting. The press and TV crews, disappointed that the violence had ceased, lost interest and wandered off.

Fifteen minutes after returning to the station, a refreshed DCI Day went out to speak to Mr Abbas and the other senior members of his community. "We're struggling to find out exactly where they've taken Tahir and, to be frank, this isn't helping. I'm convinced I'm very close to the truth now and I reckon the MPs will have to admit they're wrong about his

135

involvement in the murder of his friends. Obviously, I can't make any comments about what's gone off overseas but, in my meetings with him, Tahir's convinced me he's a decent bloke. I'll do my best to get him released tomorrow, Monday at the latest."

It was no easy task but he managed to persuade the irate solicitor and two colleagues to encourage their supporters to disperse - before entering the building to meet with the Chief Constable.

Chapter Twenty

DCI Day, his frustration and anger abated, returned to his number one task, finding the killers of two apparently likeable young soldiers.

Phil Johnstone was waiting for him. "Sir, they've found Thomson's van unlocked in the car park at Sainsbury's in Matlock; no sign of the driver. They're checking CCTV and have promised to call as soon as they've got something for us."

The second thing he received was a handwritten page of A4 left by DS Sharp who, Day was pleased to note, was not in the station. The doodles around the outside of the sheet indicated that Mandy had been kept waiting on the phone for quite a while.

The coach that had arrived at Millthorpe Hall earlier in the day had been hired by a man named Raymond Briggs. Although the hire company claimed he was a regular and reliable customer, that name had obviously made Sharp suspicious and she had gone into her typical 'dog with bone' mode.

What the notes didn't indicate was the run of luck Mandy had hit when calling colleagues in London. The first detective she spoke to recognised the name of her target and passed her on to 'Vice'. Eventually, a detective sergeant named Don Moseley was brought to the phone. Mandy had met Mr Moseley on a course when they were both studying for their sergeants' exams. It had been to his great good fortune that he possessed a passing resemblance to (then) DI Derek Day. Moseley remembered those two nights with enormous pleasure and, despite being married in the interim, would have given his right arm for a repeat performance. He couldn't do enough.

Raymond Briggs, his real name as far as Moseley knew, was a low-level player in the capital's vice industry. Bouncer, minder, driver for a high-end escort agency. "Top of the range girls; mostly eastern European but all educated and attractive and very well paid for their services. Willing, we

137

believe, but the agency has the inevitable link to organised crime so you can never be sure." Moseley's conversation then drifted into nostalgia and a string of hints about a visit to London and a repeat performance in a decent hotel when he was on 'night duty'.

Sharp hung up. He didn't look that much like Day.

The two words 'organised crime', written in Sharp's copperplate hand and underlined, immediately caught Day's attention.

The third set of information was from the two DCs watching Millthorpe Hall. Thirteen riders on twelve vintage motorbikes had arrived and been allowed in. Registration numbers had been collected and processed; all were legally owned. Day now had a list of the all-male 'Jean Vincent' members in front of him.

It all pointed to an event rather like the 'Eyes Wide Shut' that Melanie Price had described. He really must watch that film.

There was sufficient dodgy stuff going on at Millthorpe Hall to justify a raid. He decided that the middle of an intriguing party would be a very good time to visit and began to make plans and phone calls – a lot of phone calls.

-

Millthorpe Hall

Saturday had been a busy day at the big house. Butler Henderson and his team of five staff were preparing buffet snacks in several locations. Beer, wine and champagne were distributed to easy-access convenient points around the building. Little-used bedrooms were tidied and cleaned. The old servants' quarters were prepared as dressing rooms for a large group of attractive young ladies.

Henderson knew what would be happening that night and, although he didn't approve, it was his very well-paid responsibility to see that everything went well. At 5pm he would send the rest of the staff to the Casa Hotel where they would enjoy a slap-up meal and a night's accommodation, courtesy of their generous employer. Henderson would then go to the Central Hub from where he could control all aspects of the security system, the CCTV and the movements of the hard-faced gentlemen who would be accompanying the young ladies up from London.

Will Thomson had been very nervous when he arrived at Millthorpe Hall earlier that morning. He'd expected to be greeted by Simon Coy, but the JV's Organiser hadn't yet arrived. To his horror, Henderson had welcomed him warmly and escorted him to see the big boss. Thomson had only met Wilbourn a couple of times before - and then at a distance, for a few seconds.

In Wilbourn's study, Thomson was offered coffee and placed in a large chair facing a gargantuan desk. The great man entered and offered his hand, an almost unheard-of honour. Will stood and shook the hand.

"Good morning, William," said Wilbourn, warmly. "Thank you for coming so early. It is, as you know, very important that the uprated security system master control is up and running before this evening's celebration. I do hope you will be able to stay for the function, William?"

"Of course, PW," replied Will, his mind racing. He'd expected a very different reception.

"I can see you're anxious, William. Don't be; I have the resources to protect all our assets and you, William are a very important asset. Steps have already been taken to distance our group of comrades from the sordid actions of the recent past. I can guarantee you will have no more trouble from the police."

Will struggled to contain his relief and gratitude. "Thank you so much, PW," he blurted. "The new system will be ready for testing by lunchtime and, of course, I will be staying for our celebration." What an invitation! Thomson knew he'd struggle to pay the party fee other JV Members were paying – but his services were valued.

"Good man! Get to it, then. Henderson has been instructed to provide you with any support you require." More smiles as Wilbourn waved him away.

A much happier Will Thomson got to work.

Mr and Mrs Jones arrived with Junior just before 10am. As previously instructed, they parked the BMW in the maintenance building, nodded to the mechanic, and went upstairs to the living accommodation, where more than adequate refreshments awaited.

The systematic preparation of the Hall was temporarily interrupted by the 11.30am arrival of the coach from London. The driver dismounted, followed by four tough-looking security men with tell-tale bulges in their jackets. After checking with Henderson that everything was in order, the other passengers were allowed to alight. Twenty-five young women, all tall, slim and attractive as specified. Most looked tired from their journey so were not yet ready for inspection. The butler gave them a brief tour of the main rooms then led them to their quarters for rest and refreshment. They were ordered to report, appropriately dressed and made up, to the Great Hall at 6pm where Mr Wilbourn would select those sufficiently stunning to grace his party. It would be an important decision as far as the young ladies were concerned; Wilbourn's approval would earn each of them an advance payment of £2,500 – for which they would be expected to do almost anything – and more, if they wanted to double their money with tips.

JV Members arrived throughout the afternoon. Three took their bikes to the maintenance building and requested minor adjustments.

Will Thomson was struggling to meet his deadline. The installation of the uprated electronic 'heart' of the security system was straightforward, as was most of the trialling of equipment but some of the original kit was almost obsolete and therefore incompatible. But Will was a genius and he worked as though his life depended on it. (It didn't – his life depended on something else entirely.) By 5pm, he was able to send a message to PW that everything was fitted, tested and working most satisfactorily. By 6pm, he had given Henderson some serious training on the modifications. The butler called his boss and confirmed the installation was satisfactory.

140

The exhausted computer expert walked outside to put his remaining equipment back in his van, only to discover the vehicle was not where he left it. In the exact same parking space were three people he had met before. The bottom dropped out of Will Thomson's life.

Elsewhere in the building, PW was looking at a screen as one of the guards filmed the line of London beauties. As he had expected, none scored ten on his scale of perfection. He rejected two women and they were sent back to their accommodation with a £500 'thanks-for-coming-now-keep-quiet' gift. Twenty-three obliging women would be more than enough to satisfy the Jean Vincents.

PW did not intend to participate in the wider party, he planned to have a private celebration with the only genuine 'ten' he'd ever met face to face. She'd be here soon.

-

"Now William, you've heard the expression – 'listen carefully, your life may depend on it'?" asked Mrs Jones. "Well, in this case, that is quite literally true. You've seen my family at work so you know we're good at what we do – agreed?"

"Agreed," he whispered.

"Agreed, Mrs Jones," she hissed.

"Agreed, Mrs Jones," he repeated.

"Good. Now there are several scenarios that might play out this evening and I want you to be prepared for all of them. Yes?"

"Yes, Mrs Jones."

"Good boy. Now, I'm going to invite your rather beautiful sister to join us here. If she refuses to come that would be quite bad for you - probably resulting in some painful maiming." She took secateurs out of her handbag and put them on the table in front of him. "Understood?"

He winced. "Understood, Mrs Jones."

"Good. Now, a much better outcome for you would be if Gina does attend and complies with my instructions and Mr Wilbourn's fantasies. In that case, you will be given a large

141

amount of money and put on an aeroplane to a country with no extradition treaty. Much better, yes?"

"Much better, Mrs Jones," replied Will, with a first trace of optimism. He was a clever man – but not clever enough to grasp that could never happen.

"So, you should do everything in your power to persuade her to take that course, agreed?"

"Agreed, Mrs Jones."

"Excellent! But there is another possible scenario, William. What if your sister does agree to come here but tells the police of the situation and invites them to come too? If that becomes the case, I have two options. Number one – I will garrotte you and bury you in a very deep hole that has already been prepared in the dark, dark woods…"

There was a snort of laughter from Jones Junior but it was cut short by a withering glance from his 'mother'.

She watched the little remaining colour drain from Will's face before throwing him a tenuous lifeline. "Number two: I will allow you to be arrested for the murder of Gary Martin. This is conditional on you agreeing not to say anything for thirty-six hours. After that a solicitor will visit you and tell you exactly what to say. You will confess to the crime but claim it was to protect your sister from an evil bully. You will go to prison but Mr Wilbourn's wealth will guarantee that you are protected inside. He will purchase your business – and your Vincent – and promise they are returned to you, in good order, when you emerge. Do you understand that you must convince Gina to cooperate in this?"

Will did understand but was too terrified to respond immediately. Prison was a lifeline. He would agree to anything to get out of this room alive. He looked directly into Mrs Jones' beaming smile for the first time in several minutes. How could this ordinary-looking middle-aged woman be having this one-sided conversation in the same matter-of-fact way a normal person would discuss Aldi or Tesco for the big shop?

"Do you understand, William?"

142

"Now, if you break any of these conditions, I should point out that my son, Robert..." The man who was not her son – or called Robert, gave a cheery wave. "...will kill your mother and, eventually your sister – when Mr Wilbourn has finished with her. Is this all acceptable to you, William?"

This time it didn't take Will long to reply. "Yes, Mrs Jones," he stammered.

"Good. So, let's hope Gina is sensible and does what's required of her. Keep your fingers crossed, William." She picked up the secateurs. "While you still have them."

-

Phil Johnstone, Day's tech expert, parked his unmarked van in Barlow Community Centre car park. He opened the rear doors and extracted his favourite drone. He rechecked the batteries, the cameras and the control surfaces before taking it on a short practice flight above the playing fields. The images on his laptop were clear and sharp. He called his boss to say he was ready.

Dom O'Neil pressed a few keys on the Briefing Room keyboard and the same images appeared on the large display. "All good here, Phil. Off you go – and keep it high!" ordered Day.

The drone set off on its two-mile journey to Millthorpe Hall.

Chapter Twenty-One

It was a pleasantly-spoken woman with just a touch of Essex. "Could that be Gina Thomson?"

"Speaking. Who's calling, please?" responded Gina, expecting to hear she'd been in an accident that wasn't her fault.

"Hello, Gina, my name is Jones, Mrs Jones; I'm a friend of your brother's."

"Hi. Where is he? Has he finished that big job at Millthorpe yet?" Gina was reassured by the measured tone of the caller.

"He has indeed, Gina and a brilliant job it is, too. I'm admiring his work as we speak; we're all very pleased. So pleased, in fact, we're going to give him a special reward. That's why I'm ringing, he said he'd like to have you here to see him receive it – could you get up to the Hall in, say, the next hour or so?"

"Thank you so much, Mrs Jones but I'm sure Will has told you I've recently suffered a bereavement – I'm not going out at all – at the moment."

Mrs Jones detected the first tiny note of doubt in Gina's voice. "Yes, Will did explain, my dear, but he said he thought it would bring you out of yourself."

Suspicion mounted. Will knew that his sister wasn't a big fan of the Jean Vincents – and now he was inviting her to their HQ – that just didn't make sense. "I'm so sorry, Mrs Jones," she said, trying hard to keep her voice level, "please thank Will for the suggestion and I do appreciate your invitation but I really don't want to leave the house at present."

There was a pause and then Mrs Jones replied in the calmest possible way, "So sorry to press the invitation, Miss Thomson but Will has asked that I insist on his behalf."

Now Gina was irritated. "Can I speak to Will, please?"

"Sorry, no. I'm afraid he's still making final adjustments to the system he's installed – that's why he asked me to call."

"I need to speak to my brother!" snapped Gina.

Mrs Jones' mood didn't change. "I will allow you to speak to your brother as soon as you confirm you will visit the Hall this evening, Miss Thomson." There was a subtle threat included in the statement.

Gina took a sip of water to calm her nerves. "Mrs Jones, please tell me what'd going on here?"

"Okay, my dear, if you insist. It is essential to you brother's wellbeing that you visit Millthorpe Hall very, very soon." The threat no longer subtle.

"Why?"

"I'm afraid William has caused our leader some inconvenience and I believe only a direct appeal for clemency from his nearest and dearest will guarantee his safety,"

Now Gina was frightened. "Clemency! What the hell do you mean?"

"You need to plead for his life, Miss Thomson!"

"You're threatening to murder him, you bitch! I'll have the police there in ten minutes!" Gina yelled.

"That would be too late, I'm afraid. He'd be dead long before they got here – and they'd never get in quickly enough. By the time they got inside, there wouldn't be a shred of evidence to find. A call to the police would be Will's death warrant." So calm, so factual.

Once again, Gina took a sip of water; her mind in turmoil.

Mrs Jones was persistent. "Are you coming to visit us, my dear?"

"You'll kill him if I don't?"

"Oh no, Miss Thomson, you've missed the point. We'll kill him if you call the police but, if you merely fail to attend, I'll begin to cut off his fingers with my new secateurs. I think I'll start with the little finger of his left hand."

There was a burst of noise in the background followed by a muffled scream. "Gina, she means it!" Definitely Will's voice.

"Naughty boy, William," said Mrs Jones in a tone that could have reversed global warming.

And Gina realised she wasn't just talking to a hostage-taker, she was talking to a certified psychopath. "I'll come," she said, quickly.

"Thank you so much, Miss Thomson. Now, it's important you look your best. A little light make-up and a revealing black dress, perhaps? Our leader would like that, so I'll give you ninety minutes to get here."

The time on Gina's phone was 6.15pm. "Okay, I'll be there before 7.30. Please don't hurt him!"

"Of course not – if you're on time!" The very polite psychopath disconnected.

Gina wasted her first five minutes considering her options So, all the 'leader' of the Jean Vincents wanted was for her to turn up looking good and beg for her brother's life? She could do that. Although she'd never regarded her exceptional good-looks as an important part of her everyday life, she'd always known she could exert power over inadequate men. She would not call the police.

Fifteen minutes tops to drive to Millthorpe. She wasn't exactly sure where the Hall was but two minutes on her iPhone sorted that out. Leaving a margin for the unexpected, she had forty-five minutes to make herself look stunning.

But, ten minutes later, staring at the tearful face in her dressing-table mirror, Gina realised she was being foolish. There was no fair-play scenario when dealing with psychopaths; Will's only chance of coming out of this horrendous situation was if she told the police. Not just anyone, though. That DCI who'd visited her twice, he seemed a calm, level-headed sort of man – he'd know what to do.

-

Briefing Room No2 was packed. Day was writing on the whiteboard while intently studying the video display with one eye. The clarity was amazing. As the drone skimmed over fields and woods it got higher and higher but the cameras remained in focus. There was the formidable wall surrounding the Hall and immediately after, a distant view of

146

the big house itself. The H-shaped stone mansion looked elegant as the evening sunshine reflected from masses of glass. The gently curving gravel drive came into view. It was too long for any kind of surprise; the occupants of the house would have time to hide evidence before Day's team could break in.

The array of aerials and discs on the roof of the east wing hinted at the location of the security centre and possibly the servants' quarters.

To the east of the main house was an elongated barn-like structure made of the same stone and with a slate roof. As the angle of viewing altered it could be seen that the front of the building was completely open. The grey coach that had been observed entering earlier in the day was parked alongside.

Several cars and motorbikes were visible within. Simon Coy's E-type was there but no sign of the cloned BMW that was intended to be the police's main excuse for gate-crashing tonight's party – hopefully without crashing the gates.

Fifty metres behind the east wing was a much newer two-storey building. The closed 'up and over' doors suggested garages of some sort. Curtains on the upper floor and an external steel staircase pointed towards accommodation. Just behind this building was a single storey storage unit of some kind – constructed, by the look of it, of 8 x 2 concrete sections. For one mischievous moment, Day thought that another reason to enter would be an obvious breach of planning regulations.

"Phil, see if you can get close enough to the side windows of that garage – I really need sight of that BMW," ordered Day.

As the drone tilted and swooped closer to the ground, the pictures abruptly vanished. The images on the screen were replaced by an Arctic blizzard.

"What's going on, Phil? Where are my pictures?" exclaimed Day.

"Bugger!" hissed the technician. "They're jamming everything – the cameras and my controls! I reckon they've crashed the drone – sorry, sir!"

Day didn't swear, but half the people in the room did. An expensive piece of kit like that could only be disabled by something at least equally sophisticated.

The BMW had been seen entering the Hall by a police officer but no one had seen it leave. Legal justification to enter the Hall grounds – just! But a reason for doing thousands of pounds worth of damage to gates that belonged to a secretive millionaire with lawyer friends; very risky!

The team had already discussed every possible motive for raiding Millthorpe Hall. They had suspicions about drugs being consumed, underage non-consensual sex, perhaps even organised 'crossing lines' crime – but absolutely no solid evidence to persuade senior officers to give the go-ahead.

Then, the whole investigation took a dramatic turn. The door opened and in came the head of a breathless PC. "Phone call for you, sir!"

"Take a message, Mr Taylor!" replied Day.

Constable Taylor persisted. "Sir, it's the first victim's fiancée, Gina Thomson. She seems very distressed and actually said it was a matter of life and death!"

No hesitation now. "Put her through!"

Within two minutes, Day had formulated a completely different plan and was explaining it to his colleagues. It was time to get moving and they left the station with high hopes.

-

Day recognised the butler's 'hello' immediately. "Good evening, Mr Henderson, DCI Day here. Would it be convenient to speak to the owner?"

"I'm afraid not, sir. We have a major social event here at the Hall this evening and Mr Wilbourn is totally absorbed in its organisation." All good manners returned.

"Fair enough," Day replied, "but I wonder if you would be willing to open the gates to my traffic officers so they can

148

have a look round for a stolen BMW we believe to be on the premises?"

Henderson made a RADA-quality shock/horror sound. "A stolen car? Here? Quite impossible! Mr Wilbourn's friends are all upright citizens; wealthy – and with important connections." A clear warning to keep away.

"I'm afraid I'll have to argue, Mr Henderson. One of my officers saw the car enter at 10.14am and no one has seen it leave," offered Day.

"I have no recollection of seeing a blue BMW today, sir. Perhaps your officer is mistaken? Although we do have a rear access route in the north-east corner of the estate; I can't remember when it was last used but I suppose someone with less than honest intentions might be tempted to try it?"

A rear access! Day was horrified – nothing was shown on the ancients plans he'd acquired or on rather more up-to-date Google maps. He put the phone on silent and ordered DC Rutherford, "There's a rear access, north-east corner – send a team to find it!"

Tara made the call.

"Let's put that disagreement aside for the moment, Mr Henderson. My other reason for wishing to enter is – I believe Mr William Thomson is present. I desperately need to interview him regarding a very serious crime." Day tried to match the butler's slimy politeness even though he now knew the man was lying.

"Ah, there I can help you. Mr Thomson was indeed here for several hours earlier today working on electronic installations but he left at, let me check, ah, exactly 2.20pm. Surely your alert officer observed him passing through our gates?" Henderson was now being openly sarcastic but it didn't bother Day one bit. Keeping the butler occupied had been part of the plan.

Day, DS Grainger, DC Rutherford and four very serious armed officers were seated with their backs to the boundary wall of Millthorpe Hall in a spot where Phil Johnstone had spotted a gap in CCTV coverage that made secret entry a slim but real possibility.

149

He double checked his watch and indicated the six officers should scale the wall, before continuing his conversation with the butler. "Okay, I'll leave it at that for now but I'll have to insist you make me an appointment to see Mr Wilbourn very soon."

"Please phone tomorrow, sir – when I will be able to access Mr Wilbourn's diary. I'll try to fit you in."

"Just one thing before you go. Do you have CCTV coverage of your mysterious rear entrance?" Day hoped Henderson would recognise the returned sarcasm.

"Oh, yes, sir!"

"Then you will know if the blue BMW left that way earlier today!" Check.

"I regret, sir, that that part of our surveillance system is rather old. The camera is working but does not record." All bases covered.

"Goodbye, Mr Henderson."

"Goodbye, Mr Day."

The DCI crossed his fingers then crossed the wall in pursuit of his team.

-

A mile away, Gina Thomson's borrowed Fiesta pulled up outside the Hall gates. Day had wanted to put one of his officers in the driving seat but his recent experience with DS Sharp's substitution plus the impressive array of CCTV cameras persuaded him to accept Gina's offer of taking the risk. She was angry and looking for revenge but was in the state of single-minded determination that had dominated her adult life.

She stepped out of the car and did a nervous twirl to show off the 'little black number' that could hide no secrets. She walked the two steps to the intercom button and pressed it.

"Yes?"

"Gina Thomson, I'm expected."

"Ah yes, so you are, Miss Thomson – and right on time," said Henderson.

"Listen," said Gina, staring at the closest camera, "you can tell your leader that I am willing to do anything, and I stress anything, to secure the release of my brother – but I have to know he's alive and unharmed."

Paul Wilbourn, seated immediately behind Henderson in the security hub, almost ejaculated in his pants at the image and accompanying offer.

"In fact, I must see him!" Gina continued.

"You're in no place to make demands, young lady!" hissed Henderson.

"True, but I'm not risking my life coming in there if my brother's already been murdered. I will only enter if you allow me to see Will before I see anyone else – or I'm off – that's it!"

"One moment, please," and the intercom clicked off.

'So far, so good,' thought Day as he listened in to the wire very well hidden on Gina's body. He concentrated on making no noise as he followed the armed officers through the squeeze of trees towards the Hall.

Henderson switched back on. "We have an agreement, Miss Thomson. Please enter. A quarter mile up the drive you will see a Landrover. It contains two of our security staff. One of them will get into your car and take you to see William."

"Thank you," she said with a tremor – and promptly dropped her car keys. She kneeled to show another camera a flash of cleavage as she retrieved the keys.

The gates opened but the car wouldn't start. She tried it again and again. The engine turned but it just wouldn't fire. Eventually, she stepped out and returned to the intercom.

Before she even had time to speak, a strange voice came on the line. "Don't cry, Gina – you'll spoil your makeup."

"I'm so sorry," she stuttered, "it started playing up yesterday but I thought it would be alright!"

"Stay there," commanded the voice, "my security team will collect you."

"Please don't hurt Will!"

"Your cooperation guarantees his safety; wait by your car."

151

Far from crying, Gina was trying hard not to smile. It had been her own idea to use her mother's old car – which was playing up and badly needed servicing. DCI Day needed information and time – and Gina was providing both. They couldn't launch a hostage rescue until they knew exactly where he was.

-

Still under cover of the trees, the police team stopped by the side of the long open-fronted barn.

They could see the three main sections of the Hall were being used differently. The west wing was mainly in darkness but with a couple of brightly lit, unshuttered rooms. The east wing was in almost total darkness apart from one heavily curtained room which gave off a flickering blue glow – clearly the security hub. The main action of the evening's proceedings was obviously in the central part of the house. The windows of the 'bar' of the H around the main entrance were shuttered but, with many tiny slices of light filtering through imperfect joints, they gave the impression of a fully illuminated interior.

The officers could hear classical music playing and Day was just able to identify Carmina Burana.

A black-clad man was walking a sentry's route back and forth across the front of the Hall and they waited until he was as far away as possible over by the west wing.

Suddenly, a bright light shone out as a completely naked woman burst through a small door and ran down the steps. She bounced onto the gravel, pursued by an equally naked man with obvious intentions. He caught her and swooped her up. She screamed - then laughed and kissed him on the cheek. All the way back to the house she wiggled her feet and giggled loudly. Someone was expecting a big tip!

Relative peace descended and Day gave an order. "Right Andy, do your stuff!"

DS Grainger set off along the edge of the wood in the direction of the main drive. When he was about a hundred metres from the rest of the police team, he found an ideal

152

spot for creating mischief with the half gallon of petrol he was carrying. He would light his fire as soon as Day indicated he knew where the hostage was located. A useful distraction plus an undeniable invitation for more arrivals.

-

Earlier in the evening, DSupt Halfpenny had phoned an old friend. Matthew Butterfield was Station Chief at Chesterfield Fire Station.

"Hi Matt," she said. "This'll sound like a daft question – but have you got a rather large appliance handy," she paused, realising the unintentional innuendo. "Sorry, a fire engine sufficiently expendable to smash down some iron gates?"

Butterfield laughed. He had dated Jill Halfpenny many years previously and remembered that intriguing combination of clever and crazy. "What are you up to, Jill?"

"It's not a joke, Matt; I've got a tricky hostage situation and I need a method of opening the gates that will look normal – sort of!"

Now he could tell she was being deadly serious. "Will there be a fire?"

"There'd better be – or one of my officers is going to get a kick up the arse!"

"In that case, I've got an elderly turntable unit with about a year's service left in it. Will that do?"

"Is it big?"

"Very!"

"Good. Look, is it okay if we worry about the insurance crap after we rescue our hostage?" she asked.

S.O. Butterfield knew he was risking his pension but he agreed anyway.

"Thanks, I'll send round one of my lads to collect it."

"You've got an experienced HGV driver, then?"

"No idea! I'll drive it myself if I have to!"

The image of Jill Halfpenny driving a twenty-ton vehicle into a set of iron gates horrified him. "No, hang on – I'll see if any of my lot will volunteer."

Half-an-hour later the turntable fire appliance was rumbling towards Millthorpe. In the cab, firefighter Deb Pierrepoint was accompanied by five police officers – all well strapped in and wearing firefighter helmets for disguise – and protection. Pierrepoint had volunteered immediately. "I know the truck and I've always wanted to smash down some gates!" she had declared. Now, her grin through gritted teeth said it all.

-

By the time the Landrover arrived to pick up Gina, she had totally flattened the battery so she used the slight slope on the pull-in to the entrance to roll the car a little further away from the gates. She made sure there was enough room for whatever large vehicle Day had commandeered to get a good run at its target.

The two Serbian brothers who'd climbed out of the Landrover had travelled to Derbyshire in the company of twenty-odd very attractive professional ladies but they'd never seen anything quite so perfect as a close-up of pure innocence in Gina Thomson.

"So sorry, gentlemen," she simpered to increase the magic, "it just won't start. Are you here to take me to see Will?"

In the few moments before the shock wore off, the younger brother would have driven her all the way to Paris, if she'd asked.

"Get in!" said the older brother.

Gina made a drama of locking the car, gave it a kick (no mean feat in five-inch heels) and waited for the younger man to open the rear door of the Landrover for her. As he rushed round to oblige, Gina caught a glimpse of the automatic pistol in a shoulder holster.

"Oh dear," she exclaimed, "you're not going to shoot me with that are you?" Clever Gina.

Within one minute, the dozens of officers surrounding Millthorpe Hall and the twenty more in the convoy behind Pierrepoint's fire engine, knew they were up against armed

154

opposition. Day's guess had been right and the tension went up a notch.

-

Day heard one of the guards jump out of the Landrover halfway up the drive. Afterwards, there was no more speaking, only the rumbling of the diesel engine. Even that background noise abruptly stopped as the headlights appeared round the closest bend. The wire had gone dead! The Landrover turned right in front of the Hall, drove around the east wing and parked close to the steel steps on the side of the garage. Slightly better.

The driver stepped out and opened the rear door for Gina. Day was relieved to see she was being treated with some respect; Wilbourn obviously wanted her unblemished. She was given some instructions and the driver pointed to the steps.

Gina climbed and knocked three times on the door at the top. It was opened by an older woman, who said something the detectives couldn't hear, and ushered her inside. But, just before the door was closed, they all clearly heard Gina shout, "Oh, Will darling, you're okay!"

Confirmation was good – but Day was furious – he had instructed Gina not to enter any enclosed space whatever happened!

The door shut – and all hell broke loose!

Chapter Twenty-Two

Mr Paul Wilbourn was disappointed and excited at the same time. Disappointed because he'd realised Gina had gone to the police so it wouldn't be convenient for him to enjoy carnal knowledge of her tonight – but he'd already waited more than a year for 'the perfect ten'; another couple of weeks wouldn't hurt. Excited because Will Thomson's modifications to the security system had enabled him to wreck a drone and override the wire. Better still, the night-vision cameras he'd had installed two years ago now worked beautifully.

Seated in the security hub in the east wing, Wilbourn and Henderson were watching twenty-two TV monitors. Half the screens were recording very explicit sexual activity in and around the Great Hall but, much more relevant were the security images.

They had watched flickering green images of the seven figures struggle through the dense undergrowth since they had crossed the wall - so that had confirmed that Gina had notified the police. Her brother would die for that – but not tonight. Why had the intruders gone straight towards the area where Will Thomson was held? Luck or an inspired guess? Either way, Wilbourn knew it would be dangerous to underestimate that particular detective.

They watched the Landrover arrive and Gina go up the steps. "Henderson, put some light on the subject," instructed Wilbourn.

The entire gravelled area surrounding the Hall was lit up brighter than the average Derbyshire summer's day.

"Henderson, dial 999 and report that we have intruders on the premises."

"Sir."

There was a flash of flame at the edge of the woods close to the drive.

"Henderson, call 999 and inform them that my favourite bird hide is ablaze."

"Sir."

"Henderson, inform our guests and guards that Emergency Plan 'S' is to be put into operation immediately."

A discreet alarm sounded throughout the building.

"Henderson, I am adjourning to the Safe Room – you know what that means, when the police seek to gain entry, don't you?"

"Indeed, sir."

"Henderson, instruct the girl Mareeta to go to the safe room before you lock down." If he couldn't have his chosen 'Ten' this evening, a 'Nine' would have to do.

As he turned to leave, he added, "Oh, and Henderson, don't forget to open the main gates!"

"Indeed no, sir."

Internal security barriers fell into place sealing off the Great Hall and the other rooms of the central bar from the outside and east and west wings.

-

Firefighter Pierrepoint was cross. She had calculated that, at 15mph in first gear, the weight of her vehicle would smash open the gates without terminal damage to either but, as the gates came into sight, they silently opened. The first part of the expected excitement that evening was cancelled but there was still a chance of more. She accelerated up the drive towards the brightly lit house until she drew level with a fire on the edge of the woods to the right. She pulled over and the rest of the convoy shot past.

"Everybody out" yelled Sergeant Smith and the five police officers rushed off to find out what was happening.

Pierrepoint was left alone with the wrong fire appliance and a blazing wooden building that looked as though it might spread an inferno to the surrounding trees. But firefighters are adaptable – she ran as close to the hide as she should get and, having decided no one was trapped inside, returned and connected a hose. A young guy dressed in black appeared from out of the shadows and asked, in broken English, if he could help. Together, they completed the four-man job in a

157

couple of minutes and put the fire out just as S.O. Butterfield arrived in his SUV. The foreigner disappeared.

Butterfield looked at the smouldering ruins of the hide, shook his head, walked around the front of the turntable ladder truck and examined it closely. Appearing satisfied, he returned to his colleague's side, pointed to one corner of the hide and said, "Bit more water there, Deb," before walking back to his car. As he climbed in, he said, "Clear up, find somewhere to turn round without getting in the way of the police operation and get back as soon as you can. Oh, and well done."

As she continued to damp down the ruin, she smiled to herself and whispered, "Twat!"

-

When the lights came on, Day knew he'd been completely outmanoeuvred. Time to make the best of a bad job!

The driver of the Landrover shot off into the woods like a scared rabbit. Day sent two officers after him. "We believe he's armed – take your time!" he ordered.

Day led the other three officers up the steps to the garage accommodation. Standing to the side of the door, he tapped lightly and said "Armed police, open up!"

The woman, Day guessed was in her forties, opened the door, smiled, noticed the armed police officers, put up her hands and shouted in falsetto, "It's a fair cop, but society is to blame!" – and burst out laughing.

Day was rarely lost for words but this was one occasion.

The woman broke the silence. Her face turned serious and she said, "Oh, you are real policemen? Is there a problem, officer?"

"There is, madam, may we come in?" responded Day at last.

"Of course. Welcome to my Dad's home."

The four officers were ushered into a scene of domestic bliss. In the centre of the large open-plan room, three people were seated around a dining table. Will and Gina Thomson and a middle-aged man all looked surprised at the new admissions. A younger man was lolling in an armchair to the

158

left and over to the right a much older man was standing in the kitchen area obviously waiting for the kettle to boil.

"Detective Chief Inspector Day," said Day as much to give himself thinking time as an introduction. Behind him, the three other officers held up their IDs.

The woman who'd let them in held out her hand. "Mrs Jones – but you can call me Angela." She turned towards the kitchen. "Dad, I think they really are real policemen – and woman. It's not another of Mr Wilbourn's jokes!"

"Doubt it," said the old guy.

Gina intervened. "They definitely are real police officers; I've met DCI Day on several occasions."

Day was not amused. "Introduce yourselves," he ordered.

"Allow me," said Mrs Jones. "This is my husband, Charles. Over there on the chair is my son, Robert, looking as though he owns the place. Making us all tea is my father, Mr Wilbourn's famous mechanic, Mr Murphy. My father's friend, William, I think you already know?" For someone being covered by two sub-machine guns, she was remarkably matter-of-fact.

This was turning increasingly surreal. "So, tell me what's happening here," said Day.

"Annual reunion," Mrs Jones continued. "We live in London; my son lives in a dreary little town called Darlington and my father lives and works halfway between. So, we meet up here at least once a year, simple."

"Darlington's not dreary, ma! I like it." (A Robert Jones did live in Darlington – but not this one.)

Still trying to get his head around the situation, Day asked, "When did you arrive, Mrs Jones?"

"Last night – and we're leaving tomorrow."

Day eyed the single bed in the corner of the room. "Where are you staying?"

Mrs Jones almost preened. "In the big house, of course. Mr Wilbourn loves my father and he's very generous to his children."

"And grandchildren," added Robert.

"Did you come by car?" asked Day.

159

"No, train and taxi from Chesterfield Station; £25 - ridiculous!" Mrs Jones seemed genuinely outraged.

But Day had had enough of this play acting. He looked directly at Will Thomson, who gave a good impersonation of someone who'd just emerged from a hostage situation and been told to 'look normal'. "William Thomson, I'm arresting you…"

He never finished. Gina Thomson leapt up, took two strides towards Day and slapped him across the face. Hard! "That wasn't part of the deal!" she yelled.

DC Rutherford shot forward but Day put out his arm to restrain the young detective.

"I'll ignore that," said Day, trying to stop his eyes running. He turned to the nearest officer. "You get that all on your bodycam?"

Armed police officers on duty tend to be very serious, but this one was struggling not to grin. "Yes, sir."

"Right, take Mr Thomson outside and complete the formalities. Take him to Beetwell Street and don't let him talk to anyone out there."

"Sir."

As the officer led a more-than-enthusiastic Will Thomson outside, three more uniforms arrived. Day's earpiece crackled; the officers outside were now ready to enter the main hall. He turned to DC Rutherford. "Tara, take statements and check the IDs of these four. Check the room for weapons while the backup is still here. Do not let any of them out of this room until you're satisfied they are who they say they are!"

Mrs Jones started to object but Day was having none of it. "Sit down and shut up! Right Tara, you're in charge, I need to get outside and see what's happening out there." As he began to turn to leave, he pointed a finger at Gina Thomson. "You," he yelled, "outside, now!" It was the angriest any of the officers had ever seen him.

-

Tahir Abbas was having a hard time; he'd been questioned for ten hours and still had no idea where he was. Looking back, he knew he had been guilty of some errors of judgement and very tiny thefts but nothing that warranted this kind of treatment.

Like most of his tough comrades in the Marines, he had a soft spot for kids who were caught up in war. When his patrol had been sent to clean up after an IED explosion, he found an injured child and gave him some fairly extensive first aid. The boy didn't live far away and Tahir was given permission to deliver him to his family. Tahir had been appalled by their living conditions. Although they had almost nothing left after the years of upheaval, their gratitude was enormous - and he melted.

They were a decent, devoutly Muslim family consumed with poverty, sickness and injury. For the next few months, Tahir would leave camp (without permission) and take them a little food, medicine and dressings. He taught them a little English and they gave him a grounding in Dari. In short, they became friends. At that time, he had no idea that one of the teenage sons was planning to run away to join the Taliban.

The revelation came when the MPs placed three photographs in front of him. The first showed Tahir smiling and talking to a young man outside a wrecked building. The second was of the same young man wielding an AK47 alongside three similarly armed older men. The young man also appeared in the third photograph – he was lying in a pool of blood and was clearly very, very dead.

"Is that you in the first photo?" asked Captain Church.

"It is!" admitted Tahir.

"Explain!"

"Look, I've already told you. I was helping out his family. I'm a medic – some of them were sick. I had no idea he was a terrorist."

To change tack, they put in front of him a series of large crowd photos taken at the previous day's Muslim demo in Chesterfield. "Your alibis for the two murders we're investigating are a bit thin but, for the moment, I'll give you the benefit of the doubt. So, you weren't present at either killing, but you were involved. Point out the people you were working with to plan the deaths of Martin and Hamilton."

Tahir shrugged his shoulders. "I keep telling you, Gary and Steve were by best mates. I would have given my life to save theirs. How can I make you believe me?"

"Try again."

Tahir couldn't be bothered to express his feelings yet again so he picked up one of the photos. "I know a dozen or more of the people on this – we go to the same mosque. Some are friends of my father's – they visit our house. None of them are terrorists, I'd stake my life on it!"

"You seem keen to give your life away; considering becoming a suicide bomber, are you?"

Tahir exploded. "Don't be so fucking ridiculous, I've got far too much to live for!"

"Explain that! Fighting for your perverted cause rather than your country? How about some truth, Mr Abbas?"

Tahir placed his head in his hands – again.

-

As Day hustled the young woman down the steps he hissed, "What's going on, Gina?"

She replied, more loudly than was necessary, "I'm not talking to you! I want a lawyer!"

Day was rapidly losing control of the situation. He recognised the nearest uniform and called over. "Mr Dawson, please put this woman in your car and don't let her out of your sight." Dawson obliged and Day jogged around the east wing to the front of the Hall.

What a show! Seven police cars and two vans were parked on the still brightly lit gravel frontage. There were more police officers neatly spaced out surrounding the building than Day had ever seen on a single operation before. Jill Halfpenny had certainly been pulling some strings.

DI Trev Allsop called over. "Ready when you are, sir!"

"Hang on a minute!" he replied. Day could see the Hall's security doors and screens were all in place. It was time for damage limitation. He phoned.

"Who's calling, please?"

"Good evening, Mr Henderson, it's DCI Day. Will you let us in, please?"

"Thank you for coming so promptly, Mr Day. And so many of you! Did you catch our intruders?"

"Yes," he lied. "Now we'd like to come inside and, before you ask, yes – we do have a warrant."

"Of course, I'll open the doors in a few moments – I'm still trying to get to grips with this new security system." More time wasting.

Just as Day was beginning to get very, very irritated, the security screens silently vanished and the main door opened.

A large man in a black suit appeared in the doorway, made an exaggerated bow and waved the police inside.

Day turned to his second-in-command. "Give me a minute's start, Trev, then bring a dozen in." Day always valued his first impression of any situation or crime scene. As he walked past the suit, he couldn't resist saying, "Butler Henderson, I presume?"

Henderson bowed again. "Indeed sir. And you are the famous Chief Inspector Day – I've seen your photograph in the Derbyshire Times."

The butler was huge; he looked more like a retired prize-fighter than a faithful manservant; eighteen years as a paratrooper can give a person that appearance. "Lead the way, please, Mr Henderson."

They were in a small, square, heavily panelled reception room with rather grand carved double doors in front of them. Henderson pressed a carefully disguised button on the wall and the doors hissed open, revealing a surprising scene.

Day wasn't expecting to see an orgy; they'd had lots of time to tidy that up – but he didn't expect a lecture theatre! There was Simon Coy, standing at a podium, addressing a group of about forty people. The large screen behind him indicated that the talk was about the history of the HRD Vincent

163

Motorcycle Company. Unusual in such a context, the women slightly outnumbered the men. Never had Day seen an audience so well-dressed or completely enthralled; not one turned to look at the source of the intrusion.

But Coy did. He turned sharply back to his listeners, "Thank you for your attention, ladies and gentlemen. I think this might be a good time to take a break. Coffee will be served in the Great Hall. Back in twenty minutes, please."

As the audience began to ease from their seats, Day commanded, "No, stay where you are! The police are here and you will all be interviewed…"

"No, we will not!" interrupted a man of about forty as he stood and marched assertively in Day's direction.

If he expected the DCI to flinch, he was to be disappointed. Day looked him up and down with a glare that stopped him in his tracks. "Name?" he demanded.

The newcomer was equally unintimidated. "Henry Boston – QC!" He almost spat out the initials.

"Mr Boston, my name's Derek Day – DCI," retaliated Day. "Are you a member of the organisation known as the Jean Vincents?"

"I am – and proud to be so!"

"Good, I'm so pleased for you; now, go and sit down!"

It looked as though an awkward stand-off was about to begin but rescue came from an unexpected source. Henderson glided up and placed a gentle hand on the QC's elbow. "My dear Mr Boston, let me take you to your seat and bring you a brandy."

Much to Day's surprise, Boston acquiesced immediately. Day followed the two men back to the seating area and, before Henderson could slope off to bring refreshments, he was firmly instructed to point out Mr Wilbourn.

Henderson looked genuinely surprised. "Oh, didn't you know, sir? Mr Wilbourn is not on the premises. In fact, he's away for a couple of days."

The absolute sincerity in the butler's eyes immediately told Day it was a lie. "You do realise I've got a couple of dozen officers waiting to search this place? If he's here, we'll find him; let's make this easy."

"Easy or not, sir – Mr Wilbourn left earlier today."

"Explain! You know I've had this place under observation all day."

"Indeed, sir – and so did Mr Wilbourn; that's why he borrowed Mr Thomson's van." Henderson's explanation was almost credible – putting Day in a tricky position.

Paul Wilbourn was lying in his safe room. The bed was comfortable and the rather beautiful woman working on top of him was mildly satisfying his needs as he studied two monitors. The one on his left was showing a looped silent recording of Gina Thomson's performance at the gates a short while before. The monitor on his right was showing a live feed with sound of the interrupted lecture down below. Centre screen was that detective, DCI Derek Day. The insignificant little shit had become rather annoying during the course of the day and it had become PW's pleasure to make trouble for him. Phone calls to influential contacts had been made and now PW was awaiting the results. He couldn't wait to see the detective's face when his mobile rang. Paul Wilbourn now had two obsessions – lust for a beautiful woman and hatred for Derek Day.

The stalemate in the hall was broken by the entry of DI Allsop and a dozen officers, all eager to get the search under way. Everyone in the lecture audience turned their attention to Simon Coy – who gave an almost imperceptible signal. The young women began to move. Some stood and wandered apparently aimlessly; others started to sob. The men reached for their phones and began to stab buttons frantically. Soon, it was bedlam.

"Nobody leaves this room without my permission!" ordered Day.

Trev Allsop put officers on each of the six doors, leaving only a tiny number to search the great house. "Weapons and drugs!" he announced, "Find me some!"

Henderson interrupted. "There are many guns in the house, sir. Mr Wilbourn has one of the finest collections of World

165

War Two weapons in the country. All of them deactivated, of course." More time to be wasted!

"Got some reports from the outside search team, boss," said Allsop.

Day issued more orders and told him to go ahead.

"We've rounded up four foreign blokes who claim to be security – none of them were armed."

"Tell the lads to put markers where they were found. At first light we'll search for the guns they've obviously thrown away." Not helpful thought Day. "Found the BMW?"

"Not yet, sir."

"Blast, what else?"

"Fire's out and SOCO's got inside that section storeroom; they had to snap off a very expensive lock."

"Good," replied Day. "Anyone got video of the naked woman being chased by the bloke across the front?"

"Yes, in surprisingly good quality!" Allsop just managed not to smile.

The noise level in the room was increasing. Despite threats of arrest, most people were refusing to give their names and addresses to officers. The QC was shouting instructions about how to be uncooperative and several people had managed to leave the room via a door that didn't look like a door! The chaos was very well organised.

Things went from bad to worse when Day realised that Henderson was missing. What he didn't know was that the only two people who knew how to get inside the saferoom – were already inside it!

Then Day's mobile rang. It was a very agitated DSupt Halfpenny. "Found anything yet, Derek? Stolen cars, drugs, guns, underage sex, trafficking?"

"Nothing concrete, ma'am."

He heard her say 'shit' under her breath before she added, "The Thomson twins?"

"Will should be in the custody suite by now and Gina's safe in a car outside – but she's playing silly beggars and I don't understand why now that her brother's safe."

"Bugger. Any evidence from the building you think was used for the execution scene?"

"SOCO only just gone in, ma'am."

"Pity, that would have been your lifeline. Get back here immediately. Tell Allsop to scale down and pull everyone out as discreetly as possible."

"Why?"

"Chief Constable is on the warpath! He's conveniently forgotten he authorised the raid and now he's looking for a scapegoat – or goats – and you and me are looking promising!"

Halfpenny was only a year away from her pension and Day couldn't let her take the heat for his mistake. "My idea, my fault, ma'am. I believed a young woman who'd lied to me before. I'll be back in thirty."

"Make it twenty – Carruthers is getting himself worked up into a frenzy. His phone keeps ringing and, apparently every call's making him worse."

-

After checking that Will Thomson was in a cell downstairs and his sister was safe at home – with a message to expect a visit at 8am, Day reported to the Chief.

"You saw the paperwork, sir – I had sufficient…" Was exactly the wrong thing to say.

"Yes, you bloody did! You had sufficient intelligence to bring down an avalanche of complaints on my head – on a bloody Saturday night – at a bloody golf club dinner!"

"Sorry about…"

"Sorry's no bloody good, Day. Have you pulled all your team out of Millthorpe or am I going to get more hassle?" The Chief Constable's face matched the scattered remains of his red hair.

"The Hall was cleared of police before we had chance to properly interview suspects so only one arrest was made," Day replied bitterly. "I've just left SOCO examining the sectional storage unit at the rear of the main building, sir.

167

The interior appears to be identical to the murder scene on the video so I thought it justified to…"

"Pull them out – tonight! Find some solid suspicions and you can try again later. Listen, Day – I know my predecessor held you in high esteem but I've been reading your file. God knows how you got to DCI rank with your maverick tendencies and a nasty, violent streak! Thank heavens you didn't punch anyone at that lecture tonight; that would really have given me a good excuse to put the kybosh on your career!"

"That 'lecture' was a sham, sir – put on for our benefit. It was an orgy – one of my team got a video of a naked man chasing a naked girl across the car…"

"Age? Coercion? Consensual? Not our business, Day! I've had calls from lawyers, councillors, even that bloody local author who's made a mint out of film rights for his stupid bloody stories!"

Day had recognised George Stuart at the Hall and knew he was a pretentious so and so.

"I presume it was your idea to burn down some kind of outbuilding? I'll be taking steps to see that you pay damages – out of your own pocket. The Chief Constable suddenly looked very tired and his demeanour softened. "Go home and get some sleep – you've got a busy day tomorrow. I'll be providing you with a list of people to call – to apologise."

As Day left the office, he almost tripped over DSupt Halfpenny; she'd clearly been trying to hear what was happening.

"Bad, was it?" she asked.

"Very."

"If you gave him a good smacking, I'd be obliged to give you a slight telling off – but I doubt others would be so lenient!"

Day was horrified at the suggestion but quickly realised that his immediate boss was trying to cheer him up.

"Those buggers at the Hall pissed on us, Derek – and I don't like getting wet. We are going to pay them back for that insult, aren't we Derek?"

A subtle vote of confidence. He felt a little better. "We are, ma'am." A statement of fact.

An hour later, in the comfort of a king-size bed, Jess also aided his recovery. Afterwards, she told him about her conversations with various estate agents. Two would be visiting to do valuations on Monday but she'd omitted to tell them it would be a closed sale and there'd be no commission. Her bubbling excitement was infectious and it enabled Day to clear his mind sufficiently to achieve four hours sleep.

Chapter Twenty-Three
Day's DAY 5

Sunday

At 7.45am, DCI Day picked up DS Mandy Sharp from her apartment. If anyone could find out what game Gina Thomson was playing, it would be Mandy. On the way to Old Whittington, they received a report from the team watching the main gate of Millthorpe Hall. People had begun to leave the 'lecture' at 4am, some in taxis - others in chauffeur-driven limousines. None on motorcycles. The coach, presumably London-bound, had departed at 7am; the suspension suggesting, to the watchers, it was fully laden.

The birds had flown. Even if Day obtained more evidence, it was unlikely he'd be able to satisfy his desire for justice.

8am

Acting DS Grainger was standing by the police car that had been parked outside the Thomson's house all night. A third person was needed at the interview; this was a precaution – Day didn't want to spend too much time alone with his number one admirer.

They were admitted on the first ring. Gina Thomson didn't look her best. She seated herself on the couch next to her mother. No refreshments were offered.

DS Sharp began. "Mr Day tells me you were brilliant last night, Gina. You had them eating out of your hand at first and it was, of course, down to you that we were able to rescue Will. But – could you tell me what went wrong after you entered that room above the garage?"

Gina had obviously rehearsed her reply and it was delivered flatly, without any trace of emotion. "The people in that room knew the police were outside all along. They explained that Will was in more danger from you than them. That proved to be correct as he was immediately arrested. My family's best interests will be served by non-cooperation with the police." Her mother nodded.

"Gina," continued Sharp, "all three of us have seen this situation before. It's obvious to us you've been threatened with God knows what, but we can protect you. It ⌐ make a statement about the phone call you received and u. subsequent visit, we'll have armed police watching over you until those bas… villains are locked up and no further threat."

Gina's damp eyes flicked across the faces of the three detectives, lingering longest on DCI Day. "I have no further comment," she said.

"Please, Gina. These are very dangerous people; we need to put them away." Day was almost resorting to begging.

"Gina! You told Mr Day that a Mrs Jones had threatened to maim your brother. You can't rescind that kind of comment! You need to put that in a written statement today!" Sharp being rather more sharp.

Gina ignored Sharp and looked at her watch. "I had great difficulty contacting my solicitor in the middle of the night, Mr Day, but he should be here any minute. He has advised me to make no comment." The first part was a lie; the solicitor had contacted her.

"I'm sorry you feel that way, Miss Thomson. I can see you're distressed so we'll leave it for now. We will, however, need to continue this conversation later today – at the police station," said Day as gently as he could contrive.

"Maybe so, Chief Inspector, but it will still be 'no comment'."

She watched the detectives walk down the drive. Day stopped to have a word with the two officers in the marked police car but then the three climbed into a Mondeo and drove away.

Gina shivered as she remembered the two mysterious thuds, exactly one minute apart, during the night. She had opened her bedroom window and looked towards the police car on the road outside. She could see the driver and he was clearly wide awake. She could also see the two crossbow bolts embedded in the window frame close to her left hand. The police couldn't protect her.

-

urn journey to the capital, twenty-three young

.e satisfied with the previous night's work. A

re £6,000 richer and the other participants in the

festiv.   , all had at least £4,000 to show for their night's work. The two considered not attractive enough were not so cheerful – the £500 fee was less than they would have expected to make from their normal duties.

Three of the four security men were annoyed, having failed to recover their pistols after they were ordered to throw them away before the police got too close. Still, they had no doubt new models would eventually be provided at Wilbourn's expense.

Also on the coach as it left the Hall were the three members of the Jones 'family'. Robert had hidden the blue BMW so well it just couldn't be retrieved. They weren't heading home. Mr Wilbourn had requested they stay local just in case their services were required so they were dropped off opposite the Old House pub in Newbold. In the car park was Robert's girlfriend in yet another of his cloned cars. She took Mr and Mrs Jones to separate hotels, where they registered under different names, before driving to the Casa Hotel for a few days of being spoilt.

9am

Day had never seen his team look so dejected. They were tired, yes – but that was nothing new. What made it worse was the certain knowledge they'd been out manoeuvered and hoodwinked by some rich, devious bastards – and their popular leader was in the shit.

On his arrival at Beetwell Street, Day had been presented with the list of contacts the Chief Constable had promised him. He decided to leave the apologies until later; he wasn't going to give up yet.

"Tara, did you get anything out of Will Thomson this morning?"

172

"No sir," said DC Rutherford, "just a string of very determined 'no comments'."

Someone had put very serious frighteners on the Thomsons. "What did you make of the Jones family last night?"

"As you know, sir, the interviews were cut short – but they all seemed very credible. I checked some of the background details they gave me and, at first glance, they appeared genuine. Having said that, I think Mrs Jones is probably the smartest, most cunning person I've ever interviewed."

Day was about to proffer his thanks when the door opened and in came Lyn Cam. The Senior SOCO looked shattered – she'd clearly been up all night. "Sorry I'm late," she said.

"No problem, Lyn. Got anything for us?" asked Day with genuine sympathy.

"I think so. No forensics – it ended up in a bit of a rush. I'm pretty sure that the storage unit had been steam cleaned in the last forty-eight hours – but I have got these." She marched over to the table and placed two lines of photographs on the surface. All were of the inside of a sectional concrete building. The top line was made up of stills taken from the 'execution' video; the bottom, of much better quality, were obviously taken by her team the previous evening.

She began to point. "There are no obvious distinguishing marks on the concrete panels but, if you look carefully at the specks of rust on the bolts in pictures five and six, I believe the patterns there suggest that this part of the building was the background in the video."

Everyone who'd managed to get close enough to see the photos was gobsmacked into silence until DI Allsop blurted out, "Bloody hell, Lyn – that's tenuous!"

"I agree," said Day, "but it's also brilliant! Well done you!"

Several officers took turns with magnifying glasses to check the similarities in the rust patterns. All agreed they were probably the same.

Probably. But everyone in the room now knew that Day had fallen foul of the new Chief Constable's wrath just hours before; was this evidence solid enough to justify another raid that would undoubtedly put their DCI's career at stake?

Day's self-confidence was at a low ebb. "This is good stuff," he declared, "but we need more – what else is there? Andy?"

"I've studied the recording of the naked woman in the car park several times, sir. It's not brilliant quality, but there's nothing to suggest she's underage – and she seemed to quite enjoy being captured."

Dejected as they were, the report still amused several of the officers present. Even Dipa Sindhu seemed to see the funny side – but that just added to her boyfriend's embarrassment.

Mandy Sharp wasn't amused. She turned to Day and said, "What exactly did Gina Thomson say to you on the phone when she first rang in – it must have been pretty explicit for you to alter the whole format of the raid?"

Day wasn't the only person who noticed the absence of respect but he responded pleasantly enough. "She gave me full details of the threats against her brother and offered to cooperate in the raid but, as you all know, if she denies it, it's her word against mine. The CPS won't be interested in taking it forward on that basis."

Phil Johnstone tried to break the tension. "How about I have a go at enhancing Lyn's photos?" he offered. "Enlarged and enhanced might just give you enough to go back to the Super and the Chief?"

"Worth a try, Phil. Go for it," said Day. "Now look, nothing's going to happen in the next couple of hours so I want some serious detective work. Andy, get your section, with Tara, to delve into the Jones family tree – I want to know who they really are. Mandy, we've now got a fairly detailed membership list of this bizarre motorbike club – find me some dirt on any or all of them. The rest of you, find out about the guys who hired that coach and their escort agency; we've heard there might be links to organised crime so find them. Dom, you've got the most contacts in the capital so pull in any favours. Incidentally, I don't care how many London detectives you get out of bed on a Sunday morning!"

174

Dom O'Neil groaned; he'd hoped for an early escape. Today, there was somewhere else he'd much rather be.

Further instructions followed and the weary detectives got down to some pretty tedious – and normal – work.

Reports from the officers watching Millthorpe Hall came in throughout the morning. More taxis had arrived and a few more vintage motorcycles had departed but nothing of any use to an increasingly impatient DCI Day.

The research being processed by the detectives wasn't producing anything useful either. Further information about the coach company and the escort agency came sporadically. The coach firm was apparently legitimate but was believed to have a few dodgy clients. The escort business was a large and successful concern. As far as the Met Vice Squad was aware, the ladies were all sub-contractors, over eighteen, willing and making very good money. Their offices were raided once a year just to maintain the status quo and it was suspected that a few senior officers occasionally got 'freebies' but the organisation didn't present enough concern to warrant too much police time. It was fairly common knowledge that the agency was paying a considerable amount of protection money to one of the Soho Serbian gangs but, for obvious reasons, no complaints had ever been made to the police.

One of Dom O'Neil's former London colleagues had risen to Detective Sergeant in the squad monitoring Serbian gangs and, despite it being Sunday, was willing to chat at length with the former drinking partner who'd gone north. After the business discussion ended, O'Neil and Lomax exchanged details of their recent conquests and O'Neil couldn't help boasting about the rich beauty he was currently dating. DS Lomax told some of the blokes in the office about Dom's good fortune with a lottery-winning bird called Melanie. 'He always was a lucky bastard' was the consensus. Scant details of the 'Eyes Wide Shut' party in Chesterfield were also passed on and they all had a good laugh about it. Except one – who thought it would be in his best interests to tell his Serbian contact about the enquiry from Chesterfield.

175

Several phone calls followed – the final one in the series being to Mr Paul Wilbourn's private number in Millthorpe Hall.

When the mobile vibrated, Wilbourn was lying naked on his four-poster bed admiring the hundred plus photographs of Gina Thomson surrounding him. That most had been taken without her knowledge only added to the excitement he felt; next Saturday she would be in this bed with him.

"PW, I heard you had some complications with your party last night?" said the voice with the thinnest hint of foreign accent.

"Nothing we can't handle, my friend. I put a lid on it all by leaning on the powers-that-be. I'll see that those of your staff who were inconvenienced will be fully recompensed."

"Of course you will," he responded ambiguously, "but I think you will find the lid is not put back on quite firmly enough. Many detectives from your town seem to be having intriguing conversations with many detectives from my city. One of them was an inquisitive and boastful Detective Constable – who apparently has a very attractive lottery winner for a girlfriend. Good for him but potentially bad for us, don't you think? It is important that your complications do not rebound on the peace and quiet of my life here, PW!"

"Definitely! Please keep me informed of the progress of any enquiries at your end and I will ensure they dry up very rapidly. Nothing will get out of hand; I have the Family Jones available to clean up after any serious problems." Wilbourn was not intimidated by the caller but knew his long-term wellbeing depended on keeping on his good side.

"Mr and Mrs Jones and son? I hope you are paying them well, PW – they're not a team even I would choose to make unhappy."

"Definitely! I appreciate the heads up. I will be in touch should anything potentially harmful to your interests occur." Wilbourn disconnected and called Henderson.

"Henderson, have the staff arrived?"

"Indeed sir – the clean-up is well underway," replied the butler.

176

"Did they enjoy their night off?"

"They did, sir. All asked me to pass on their gratitude."

"Excellent! Now, a memory test for you. I believe one of our members once had a relationship with a number eight who'd won the lottery; does that ring any bells?" asked Wilbourn.

"Not immediately, sir," Henderson replied, "but the troublesome Will Thomson did have a girlfriend whose parents had won the lottery a few years ago – could that help?"

"Ah-ah, I think you're right – well done! Apparently, the young lady in question is now dating a member of the team of local detectives who've become our very own private nuisances. I'm guessing she's the originator of DCI Day's interest in our club. Are we likely to have any details on her – name would be a good start?"

"Unlikely, sir. If she's the one I'm thinking of, she didn't last long. Would you like me to ask around the other members?"

"No, not necessary. I'm seeing Richardson in a short while before he goes on his way to visit Thomson in the cells. He can ask about the girl before he gives young William his instructions about exactly what, and what not, to tell the police." Wilbourn laughed to himself – he considered himself a much better detective than the genuine articles. Why work hard when you can get solicitors to do it for you? Richardson seemed to have sorted Gina out very effectively, now he could work the same magic on her brother.

12noon

Day's frustration increased throughout Sunday morning. He'd just heard that the MPs had formally charged Tahir Abbas with two murders and, to make matters worse, Will Thomson's solicitor had arrived late and was demanding at least thirty minutes with his client before formal interviews could begin.

Information filtering through from London didn't bring any breakthroughs. Mr Jones was a successful, self-employed painter and decorator and his wife was indeed a well-

177

respected piano teacher. Their son, Robert did live near Darlington and was an architect. All very uninteresting for the detectives – if only it had been the correct three people.

The enhanced photos had been returned but were only ten percent clearer. It was enough to confirm to Day that his SOCOs had been right but Halfpenny advised him it would not convince the Chief Constable without additional evidence.

Day was seated in his office considering whether it was time to send his team home to spend at least a fraction of Sunday with their families, when the phone rang.

"Call for you, sir – a Mr Henderson."

The last thing Day expected. "Put him through, please." Day looked at his watch. "Good afternoon, Mr Henderson."

"Good afternoon to you, sir, I do hope you are well?"

Day analysed the tone in search of sarcasm but could find none. The butler seemed to being polite. "What can I do for you, Mr Henderson?"

"Mr Wilbourn sends his apologies, sir. He has just returned to the Hall and learned of the events of last evening. He's sorry he missed you and wishes to make amends. He has called an Extraordinary General Meeting of the Jean Vincents 1000 Motorcycle Club this very evening, sir. Almost all members will be present and Mr Wilbourn is to instruct them to cooperate fully with the police. Admittedly, we are puzzled by your interest in our little club but do want to resolve any concerns you may have." Day still couldn't detect any irony. Henderson continued. "The meeting will begin at 8pm and there will be a short session of business unrelated to your enquiry so, if you feel able to attend at, say 9pm all members, including Mr Wilbourn will be available to talk to you or your officers – bring as many as you like."

To buy thinking time, Day made a frivolous comment. "Sunday night at 9pm? That'd make me really popular with my team!"

"Indeed, sir," responded the butler, "but I'm afraid you may not get another opportunity for many weeks. Mr Wilbourn will shortly be leaving to look after some of his business interests abroad."

"Fair enough, I'll bring a small group. Thank Mr Wilbourn for his kindness; see you later."

'What are those devils up to?' thought Day as he rang around to form an interview group.

-

At the same time as Henderson was talking to DCI Day, Mr Wilbourn was speaking on a very secure line to Mrs Jones.

"The young lady in question is called Melanie Price and she lives alone in Walton, which is not far from your current location," said Wilbourn. He gave her the address and continued, "At 9pm this evening she will be the victim of a burglary that will end in tragedy when she discovers the intruders. Does that sound feasible?"

"Of course, provided she will be there?"

"My information is that the woman in question is a dedicated school ma'am who works all day Sunday getting things ready for the kiddies on Monday," said Wilbourn, confirming his contempt for all public-sector workers. "There are two important factors. Nothing must link this terrible crime to the killings of the two marines so it is essential that you do not use your weapons of choice…"

"Okay, no garrotte and no crossbow – it sounds like a task for my 'husband'", interrupted Mrs Jones.

"Your decision, my dear. Now, the second factor: Miss Price thinks a lot about herself for a mere eight and has caused me considerable inconvenience and, for that reason, it is important that she suffers a great deal before meeting her maker. Is that acceptable?"

Mrs Jones had heard about the 'marks out 10' system before and, as a woman, heartily disapproved – but business was business. "Of course. To a client as dear as you, it will be done at no extra charge. Anyway, I think Mr Jones might enjoy that. I'll send Robert, too – double the pleasure, double the pain!"

179

"Very good," replied Wilbourn. "9pm precisely – that is important."

"You'll transfer the fee as per our normal systems?"

"Certainly, Mrs Jones. Have a nice day."

Wilbourn cut the call and immediately made another. "Simon, my friend, did you enjoy the party last night?"

It took some time for the call to be answered. Simon Coy sounded very drowsy but managed to put some enthusiasm into his tone. "I did, PW – it was great fun, thank you."

"I'm so sorry I missed your lecture – I bet it was fascinating!"

They both laughed. "It's always good to have something like that in reserve – just in case!" said the dentist. They laughed again.

"But I heard you got back to the proper business of the night as soon as the police had vacated the premises?" It was a rhetorical question; all had been recorded and Wilbourn had watched the juiciest bits on his monitors.

"Oh, indeed we did, PW, indeed we did!"

"Excellent! Now, I wish you to gather the members together this very night. I want as many as possible here at 8pm prompt. I know this is inconvenient but I have a plan to end the police's fascination with our club. Please impress on members that it will be in their best interests to attend - whatever they have to cancel, come tomorrow they will be very grateful they were here, believe me."

Chapter Twenty-Four

Mr Abbas was not good at sitting around doing nothing. When he had learned his son had been charged by the Military Police, his anger and confusion were close to overwhelming.

Tahir had an alibi! He was with his fiancée – a respected young doctor at Chesterfield Royal Hospital – why did they not believe her? She must not have been forceful enough when interviewed; she obviously needed coaching by a seasoned solicitor. Mr Abbas resolved to pay her a visit.

Lianna's very pretty and very white flatmate opened the door.

"Good evening, miss," said Mr Abbas, "I am to be Lianna's father-in-law and I would very much like to speak with her. I know she's not at work so I take it she is in?"

"How do you do, Mr Abbas. Yes, she is in, but she's in the bath." The woman held out her hand and, after too many moments of delay, Mr Abbas shook it. "I'm Katrina, please step inside and I'll tell her you're here. I'm so, so sorry about what's happened to Tahir – we all know he's innocent, of course."

"Thank you, that's why I'm here." He was too polite to add 'then why didn't you tell the bloody police that?'.

Katrina returned after a few seconds and invited Mr Abbas into the lounge. "Please have a seat, Lianna will be with you in five minutes."

There was little conversation. Mr Abbas was perplexed by the vibrant clash of cultures in the tiny room's décor and silently analysed every detail. He was forced to admit that the combination of IKEA simplicity and Asian flare worked wonderfully.

Lianna's entrance shocked Mr Abbas to the core, the image was not one of a demur young Muslim woman. She was wearing a white full-length dressing-gown and a matching towel on her hair. Her expression was an intriguing combination of anger and determination.

Mr Abbas stood and nodded a greeting. "Good evening, Lianna. I hope you are well? I've come about Tahir's…"

"Alibi?" she interrupted.

"Indeed," he replied. "I'm far from convinced that your support for his alibi was delivered strongly enough. Is your flatmate able to corroborate?"

"Please sit down, Mr Abbas, I have something to tell you."

Full of consternation, the solicitor went back to his chair.

"I gave the military police exact times when I was with Tahir. Katrina was present and also confirmed his alibi. However, the times Tahir gave to you were not the same ones he gave to the authorities."

"What!"

"Let me finish, please. Tahir did collect me from work and he did visit my parents but he did not remain here after dropping me off."

Mr Abbas stood up. "What are you saying?"

"After dropping me back home, Tahir went off to see his girlfriend!"

"What! He's seeing someone behind your back – I'll kill him!"

"No, no, no! This is going to be hard for you, sir but I beg you to be sympathetic. Tahir's other relationship has my blessing; we are not in love; we have never been in love." She continued despite Mr Abbas' attempt at interruption. "He is my friend, my loving brother - and I know he could not be involved in these dreadful crimes, but I cannot lie for him. Like you, he is loyal to his family, his religion and his country. I know this is difficult for you, sir but I cannot marry your son. I promise I will tell my parents soon but please, please let them hear it from me!" Tears rolled down both cheeks.

Mr Abbas was about to enter into the usual 'love will develop when you are married' litany when the obvious distress she was feeling silenced him. He left without another word.

It wasn't until he was halfway down the stairs, that the other thought occurred to him.

By 12.45pm, the solicitor, Richardson, had declared his client ready for interview. Day had made good use of the time, organising a small group of detectives to join him on his 'night out'. Andy Grainger, Tara Rutherford and Kamil Malysz all volunteered immediately and there was one late addition, Dom O'Neil.

Day didn't want DS Sharp out late at night so he invited her to the interview with Will Thomson instead. She was always an asset in tricky interviews; equally adept at being 'good cop' or 'bad cop'. Today, however, there were no decisions made about strategies because Day thought they were going to be facing a brick wall.

He was right. As soon has Sharp had completed the formalities, the solicitor interrupted. "Mr Thomson is anxious to cooperate. He is, however, still in a state of distress and shock following his arrest. Mr Thomson wishes me to tell you that he will be willing to make a full and complete statement about his involvement in the two crimes – tomorrow!"

Sharp was quick off the mark. "Mr Thomson, is this statement likely to contain a confession?"

Thomson looked at her and gave an almost imperceptible nod.

"Would you confirm that aloud, for the record?"

Thomson turned and looked at his solicitor then turned back to Sharp. "No comment," he said.

Ten more minutes of 'no comments' convinced Day the detectives might as well go home and enjoy a few hours with their families. All were sent home to rest with orders to be back at Beetwell Street for a briefing at 8pm prompt.

-

Dom O'Neil had no intention of going home to rest. This Sunday had been in his diary quite a while and working was not part of the plan. His girlfriend had booked a track day at Donnington Park and, despite Wilbourn's low opinion of

183

her, would be thrashing her highly tuned Mini around the circuit for most of the afternoon. Although he was no petrolhead, O'Neil knew he was onto a good thing and wanted to spend as much time as possible with a woman he suspected he was in danger of falling in love with.

An hour later he was on trackside watching the battered Mini hurtle round at terrifying speed. 'For God's sake, Mel, don't kill yourself,' he thought, but he knew she was highly skilled; he'd been in the passenger seat for a brief rally practice – and that was quite enough.

She joined him on the grass a little while later and was so pumped up with adrenalin, O'Neil thought she was going to jump on him and demand sex there and then. She wasn't – Melanie had other plans. "I'll be finished here before five. We'll go to my place, have a shower, then an hour's adventure, then another shower, then you can bugger off to see your lord and master while I get ready for school tomorrow."

And that was quite alright with him.

-

The afternoon at Chesterfield Police Station was rather quieter. A half-expected further demonstration by the Muslim community hadn't materialised and even the Sunday-lunchtime drunks seemed to be behaving themselves. The only bizarre incident of the day was in Holme Park where a teenage boy had been assaulted and his dog carried off. Very peculiar – it was a mongrel rescue dog – not one of the £1,000 plus pooches usually snatched in an increasingly common crime. Uniforms were investigating.

-

Robert Jones had picked his 'father' up in a stolen car at 4.30pm as arranged and they had driven to Walton to have a preliminary survey of their target's home.

Mr Jones was not happy. Within his very limited circle of assassin friends, he was well known for meticulous planning; impromptu murders were just not his thing.

184

A detached house is always preferable. One car on the drive - no sign of habitation caused some concern but neither man was easily flappable and their information was that Sunday evening was about preparation for the next day. Robert parked further down the road in a spot where they would see any returning vehicles.

Just after six, a dirty Mini, followed closely by a black VW Golf, passed the Jones' car travelling in the right direction. Mr Jones took the dog for a walk. He'd cursed Robert for choosing such a bad-tempered bloody thing and had already decided to break its neck when they no longer needed an excuse for walking up and down the street. They'd guessed right; the old Mini was parked next to its brand-new equivalent on the drive and the Golf was parked half on the pavement just behind them. Mr Jones continued his walk around the block then joined his 'son' in the stolen car. He made two more short walks to confirm the Golf was still there so plans could be made to dispatch two for the price of one. Not strictly true – he would charge extra if he had to kill a policeman.

By 7.45pm it was pretty dark and both men thought it appropriate to have supper. A flask of hot coffee was opened and pre-packed sandwiches shared. Mr Jones gave the dog a sliver of ham and broke its neck. There was a flash of headlights across the steamed-up windscreen and the black VW Golf sped past. Miss Melanie was now home alone – but every cloud has a silver lining.

Dom O'Neil had been a police officer for fourteen years and a detective for six. He wasn't the sharpest officer in Day's team but everything is relative. Why was a car, heavy with condensation parked on an affluent housing estate after dark? He made out the vague shapes of two figures in the front seats – he would have been less suspicious if they'd been in the rear. With only ten minutes to get back to the station, he didn't have time to investigate but he did remember the registration. He had two minutes to spare when he entered the building – just enough time to pass the car's number onto a friend on the desk. Traffic would be informed and take a look – eventually.

Mr Jones was good at shadows. After checking his automatic had a full complement of shells, he looked at his watch and stepped out into the night. It was 8.15pm. "Thirty minutes," was all he said.

While taking the now-deceased dog for a walk, he had planned his approach very carefully. Within three minutes, he was seated on the patio behind Melanie Price's house listening to the Billy Joel album she was playing. The occupant wasn't nervous enough to fully close the blinds and Jones was able to ascertain she didn't appear to be expecting more company; she was making a drink and some kind of healthy snack for one in the kitchen. Although her hair was still shower-wet and she was wearing no make-up, even in a bright pink onesie, she still looked more than the mere eight he'd been expecting to see. His anticipation increased. Shifting to gain a view into the through-lounge, he could see piles of notebooks on the dining table. 'The kids won't be getting their nine out of tens tomorrow', he thought. He crept a little further away from the house and texted a detailed set of instructions to his partner in crime.

-

8pm

The five detectives gathered in Day's office precisely on time.

"Thanks for coming back, folks," said the DCI. "I hope you've all had a few hours rest and are ready for what I think will be a very confusing series of interviews." He hesitated, noticing O'Neil's broad grin at the mention of the word 'rest'. "I really have no idea what to expect so I need you take detailed notes – tape if they'll allow it but remember they're volunteering so we can't insist. I'm ninety-five percent certain that the leadership of the Jean Vincents is involved in at least one of our murders. The other dozen or so members, I can't say, so I'll be relying heavily on your intuition this evening. If any of the ordinary members start to dish any dirt on Wilbourn or Coy, encourage it for all you're worth – divide and conquer is the methodology!"

Day paused for comments or questions. There were none.

"Now, we're sort of walking into the lion's den. I've been told there are lot of firearms on the premises and assured they're all deactivated but we're not taking chances. We'll be followed into the grounds by a firearms team but they'll stay outside unless we need them." He checked the group for anxiety, but his colleagues seemed to have total confidence in him. Day wished he deserved it.

"You've all got timelines of the crimes we're investigating. I want to know where all the Jean Vincents were at the critical times. Also, I'm keen to know more about Butler Henderson – he does a good impersonation of a smooth-talking manservant but I want to know about his background so, if you can entice that sort of info, do so. For some reason I really don't understand, the search warrant is no longer valid and we haven't been invited to search the house or grounds, but if anyone offers to take you on a tour feel free to go only if you're confident you won't be out of sight of colleagues. Anyone mentions anything about the Jones family, listen hard between the lines – I'm not convinced they are who they claim. Tara, for one, found them very creepy, agreed?"

"Yes sir," said Rutherford. "Very, very creepy but clever with it!"

"Any questions?" asked Day as he handed out notes. "Read these in the car."

There were a few technical issues that were quickly resolved before Day looked at his watch and said, "8.30 – right, let's go and meet our support team before we head out."

Chapter Twenty-Five

Mandy Sharp was bored, lonely and cross. There was nothing on TV and her boss had flatly refused her request to be included in the interview team for Millthorpe Hall.

She tried phoning a few friends but all were busy enjoying life with their partners and families. Her only escape was a trip to Beetwell Street Police Station – perhaps she'd catch DCI Day before he left and persuade him to let her join in the fun.

She was too late; the detectives' offices were pretty deserted. On her way down the stairs into the car park she was overtaken by PC Dawson.

"Hey Dawson, what's happening in the dull old world, tonight?" she asked with all the friendliness she could muster.

Dawson was surprised to see her but responded positively. "Hi, I'm heading up to Walton, sergeant. We were notified about a suspicious car an hour or so ago and I was hoping Traffic would take a look but both lots are tied up. The same car was reported stolen about five minutes ago when the owner returned home from a shift at the hospital so I'm going to take a look myself – see if it's still there."

"Oh good, I'll come with you!" said Sharp, sensing a break in her monotonous evening.

"Sorry sergeant, but Mr Day would kill me – you're not on full duty yet!"

It was a very short argument. It ended when Sharp climbed into the passenger seat of Dawson's response car. In truth, the young PC wasn't too unhappy, he'd fancied the detective since he first laid eyes on her three years before. Okay, she was six or seven years older and way out of his league but a bit of attractive company on a Sunday evening can't do any harm, can it?

-

At 8.55pm Melanie Price's doorbell rang. She pulled aside the blinds on the front window to get a good look at whoever was outside. A young man – he looked innocent enough.

She went to the door, checked the strong chain was in place and opened up a small gap. "Yes?" she said.

"Miss Price? Melanie?" asked the man with a beaming smile.

"That's me."

"Hi, I'm DC Jones. I'm a colleague of Dom's. There's been some suspicious activity in the area and he's asked me to check up on you."

She laughed. "Oh, that's very good of him – and you, too – but I'm fine, no problems here."

There was a dull thud behind her. She turned sharply but could see nothing out of place.

"I'd better have a look," offered Jones.

"Fine, please do," said Melanie and she unhooked the chain.

-

A little way down the street, the two police officers had arrived at the suspicious vehicle. No condensation now – the car was empty. Dawson put on his gloves and tried the driver's door – locked. He shone his powerful torch into the interior. Well, not quite empty. On the rear seat was a dog, clearly dead – its head facing the wrong way.

"Bastards!" said Dawson under his breath.

DS Sharp ignored him; she was standing, hands on hips, obviously trying to get her bearings.

"Hang on," she said, "Dom O'Neil's girlfriend lives round here somewhere. I visited her in the Summer. Melanie Price?"

"That must be right," replied the PC. "It was Dom who reported the suspicious reg when he was on his way back to the station."

"Price has been helping Mr Day find out about those bloody Vincents…"

"You don't think...?" interrupted Dawson.

"I bloody do! Which fucking house is it?" And they both set off at a run.

-

Melanie had no idea how long she'd been unconscious until the blurred clock on the front of her hi-fi told her it had only been a couple of minutes. She took stock. She was horizontal on her own sofa. There was some kind of tape across her mouth and a cable tie around her wrists in front of her. The onesie was partially unzipped so she knew one or both of the men seated opposite had had a crafty look inside.

The blow to the back of her head must have acted as a temporary sedative because she felt no pain. Hysteria tried to descend but failed to take hold – she had to think this through. These guys obviously knew she had plenty of money. They were robbers, pure and simple. They probably just wanted her gold card and the PIN number. She tried to sit up but didn't have the right leverage so she just pointed to her mouth with both hands.

The older man laughed and said, "I'll remove the tape, Miss Price, provided you promise not to make a fuss. Nod if you agree."

She nodded and the tape was removed. She didn't make a fuss, she pointed to the unit under the hi-fi. "My handbag's in there. All my cards are in it and I'll give you all the PINs if you'll just promise to leave without hurting me."

The older man raised his eyebrows. "Oh, that's all well and good, Miss Price, but we haven't come here to rob you – we've come to have some fun – and then kill you!"

Robert wasn't quite fast enough and the first millisecond of Melanie's scream escaped before he covered her mouth again.

Outside, the two police officers were struggling.

"Which one is it, sarge?"

"I'm not sure; they all look the bloody same in the dark." Sharp hesitated and pointed. "There, look two Minis. That's it!"

Then they heard a stifled scream.

"Back up!" yelled Sharp and she hurtled up the drive. She banged on the front door with a clenched fist. "Armed police!" she shouted. "Open up!"

Dawson joined her, still trying to get a breathless message to HQ. Apart from the PC's voice, everything was quiet until she heard distinctive clicks on the other side of the door – distinctive to anyone who had practised with a handgun!

Sharp realised her mistake. 'Armed police' had raised the stakes. "Down," she yelled and spun round to make a grab at the front of Dawson's uniform.

The bullet came through the uPVC door, through Sharp's forearm, through Dawson's stab vest and lodged in his sternum. Both officers fell in a single heap.

The door opened and out stepped a cautious Mr Jones. He studied the scene. The two coppers were in a weird lovers' embrace. The uniform was completely out of it – probably dead but that didn't worry Jones – except that the murder of a policeman tended to make his colleagues rather angry. The woman in civvies, who'd done the shouting, was moaning but she was no threat, her face buried in the other bloke's armpit.

Jones glanced around, looking for outside interference but all was quiet. The shouting and the thud as the silenced bullet passed through the door had attracted no attention. 'Sunday night TV in suburbia', he thought, 'you've just got to love it'.

He looked back inside and hissed, "Bring the woman, we'll need an insurance policy!"

Robert Jones dragged Melanie outside and pushed her into her Mini. Both men climbed in after her and Robert started the engine and backed off the drive. "Where to?" he asked.

"Just drive away from here, I have to think!" After ten minutes of considering very limited options, Jones senior said, "Go to Millthorpe, we can hide out for a couple of days then bugger off and never come back to this shithole ever again. If Wilbourn wants to have fun with this bitch himself, he'll probably give us a bonus."

In the rear seat, an almost terminally shocked Melanie Price thought, 'They don't know they're heading towards Dom and some of his mates at Millthorpe – maybe I've got a chance?'

191

Back on the doorstep, DS Sharp became aware of voices. It was Dawson's radio – demanding to know what was happening. Through the pain, she managed to reach it. She looked up and saw the house number. Mumbling the address, she just had time to add, "Two officers down – shot!" before she fainted.

Chapter Twenty-Six

9pm

Although the detectives arrived precisely on time, Andy Grainger still had to put up with the indignity of getting out of the car to ask for the gates to be opened.

"Good evening, sir, how many vehicles are in your party?"

"Just two," Grainger replied tersely to the pointless question.

"Please return to your vehicle."

The gates opened and O'Neil drove the Vauxhall through. The black crew bus, its seven armed officers hidden behind heavily tinted windows, followed on but stopped immediately it cleared the gates. It took just four seconds for a man in black to jump out before the bus sped off after the detectives' car. The man was carrying a substantial long pole which he wedged between the rapidly closing gates leaving a gap wide enough for more cars to follow. Another of Day's insurance policies sorted.

As they pulled onto the gravel in front of the Hall, DC Rutherford whistled. "Wow! Look at the cars – there must be a million quid's worth!" It was no exaggeration, Coy's immaculate E-type must have been worth £100,000.

Henderson was on the steps outside the Hall, backlit by powerful lights shining through the inviting open door. A good start.

As the five detectives exited the Vauxhall, Henderson studied the crew bus, obviously waiting for its passengers to follow suit. They didn't.

The butler turned to Day. "Good evening, Chief Inspector, are your colleagues joining us?"

Day pointed his thumb back at the bus. "Not yet – they've come on the off chance that Mr Wilbourn will permit a search of the grounds," he lied. "They'll stay in the van otherwise."

"Indeed," said Henderson, turning his back and stepping up. "Please follow me, gentlemen – and lady."

Day and his team entered the familiar ante-room and continued through to the scene of the fake lecture. The room

193

was entirely different; a dozen leather sofas were casually unarranged around the room. Day counted thirteen men in groups of three or four. Most were smoking and all had crystal glasses of expensive-looking liquids in front of them. Day thought it might be a good idea to have some uniforms with breathalysers waiting outside after he'd finished. Four of the men were wearing Jean Vincent denims but the others were more randomly dressed - except Simon Coy, who was wearing an immaculate suit. Upon the detectives' arrival, they all stopped chatting and looked up. None looked pleased to be there and the welcome was cold to say the least.

Henderson announced to the gathering, "Mr Wilbourn will be joining us in a few moments, gentlemen. He asks that you make our detective friends welcome and introduce yourselves." He turned to face Day. "You will, of course, recognise the famous DCI Day, but I'm afraid I'm unable to name his colleagues."

Day took the hint. "Detective Sergeant Grainger and Detective Constables Rutherford, O'Neil and Malysz."

"Thank you, Chief Inspector. Ah, here is Mr Wilbourn now."

An invisible door had opened and there stood the master of the house. There was no smoke or fanfare but it was still an impressive entrance. To Day's amazement, everyone in the room got to their feet.

Day had seen photos of Wilbourn but they had been taken years previously during his city trader days. Yes, he looked a little older but wasn't anything out of the ordinary. Not ugly or dashingly handsome, average size, fit with no excess weight – the sort you would pass in the street without noticing. Apart from the suit, that is. The fabulously tasteful garment made Coy look as though he'd bought his from a charity shop. And Day's No1 work suit looked decidedly shabby.

Wilbourn gave a smile that didn't quite work and strode towards Day. "Do be seated gentlemen please," he announced – and they all did – except the detectives, who hadn't yet been offered seats or anything else for that matter.

194

Wilbourn held out his hand and Day shook it. He'd expected wet fish, but Wilbourn's grip was firm and confident.

"Chief Inspector, what a pleasure at last. I see that Henderson hasn't yet offered you refreshments; I apologise for his oversight."

"Not a problem, Mr Wilbourn, this isn't a social visit," said Day formally.

"Indeed not, Mr Day. Let's get down to business. All our members have agreed to cooperate and answer your questions. How would you like to organise this?"

"Individual interviews, please," said Day. He looked around the spacious room. "Perhaps in the quieter corners?"

"Of course, but please don't detain any members longer than absolutely necessary, they all have homes to go to and some will have to be up early tomorrow to go to work!" The Jean Vincents all laughed.

Day forced a smile. "I have a search team outside, sir. I wonder if you would give permission for them to have a look around the premises?" Worth a try.

Wilbourn shook his head. "Oh dear, how embarrassing. The search warrant you had last night is no longer valid, is it Chief Inspector?" He didn't wait for a reply. "I'm afraid I must decline your request. We have nothing to hide but I do value my privacy! If I knew what you were looking for, it might help. Henderson will organise some refreshments for your chaps outside, though."

Day had been firmly put in his place. "Not necessary, sir. I'm sure they've brought more than enough drinks and snacks. Let's get on with the interviews, shall we?"

Furniture was reorganised and the detectives got down to work. It took all of them just a few seconds to realise that Day's suspicions had been confirmed – all the answers had been carefully rehearsed.

Between the second and third interview, Day's mobile vibrated. He was annoyed because he'd left strict instructions he wasn't to be interrupted. However, he took it out of his pocket and looked at the screen. Jill Halfpenny; a call he could not refuse.

Chapter Twenty-Seven

At first, the civilian operator in Communications thought it was a hoax. As far as he knew, Dawson was out on his own and that shaky voice was definitely a woman. He tried calling again but there was no response. He called the Duty Inspector.

Inspector MacColl was newly promoted and keen; she didn't hesitate. "Send ARV and paramedics!" she ordered - and reached for her jacket.

As often happens, the paramedics were first on scene. Despite the potential danger, both rushed to the aid of the two prone police officers. While one confirmed that gunshots were involved, the other set about saving lives. Within minutes the whole of Walton was smothered in blue lights.

-

"Ma'am?" he said.

"Derek, are you in company?"

"Yes, ma'am."

"Well, get somewhere private, quick!"

This was serious, he could definitely hear a shake in Jill's voice. He made his apologies and walked out into the ante-room. "Go ahead, ma'am."

DSupt Halfpenny wasn't famous for subtlety. "There's been a shooting. Two officers wounded. Young Dawson and your mate Sharp. What the fuck was she doing on duty, Derek?"

Day's brain went into a shocked spin and he couldn't find the words to respond.

"I asked you a question, Derek!"

"Sorry ma'am," he stuttered, "I've genuinely no idea – she was sent home, I'd refused her permission to come on this job and she was a bit peeved… badly hurt, either of them?"

"Don't know yet, they're on the way to A & E. Sharp's got an arm wound but Dawson got it in the chest."

Day closed his eyes. He liked Dawson and thought he had the potential to make detective one day. Sharp was a friend – a friend he owed everything to.

"It gets worse, Derek!"

"How the fuck can it get worse?" he almost yelled. "Sorry ma'am." It was the first time DCI Derek Day had ever used the f word aloud.

"Civilian in the same incident is missing – believed killed or kidnapped – her car's been stolen."

"Where was this?"

"Walton."

"Details?"

"Nothing more, yet."

The bad feeling that had enveloped Day took a very dark turn. 'Why am I here wasting my time?' he thought. 'Alibi! They wanted a perfect alibi! They knew this was going to happen.'

"They knew this was going to happen, ma'am!" he said.

"Who knew what?"

"Wilbourn and his cronies – they wanted me here for an alibi! Someone's told the Jean Vincents that Melanie Price has been helping us. It's got to be her – she's Dom O'Neil's girlfriend – he's inside doing interviews."

Not much of that made sense to the Super. "You making any progress at all over there?"

"No ma'am, we're not."

"I want you back here. Break off the interviews and take over at HQ. I'm going to the hospital." Halfpenny disconnected.

Day bashed his phone against his forehead and cursed silently. He needed a five second breath of fresh air and opened the outer door a fraction. As he inhaled, he noticed a set of headlights coming fast up the drive. A white Mini turned sharp right, drove through the car park, round the East Wing and disappeared in the direction of the blocks of outbuildings.

A white Mini – Melanie Price always drove light-coloured Minis.

197

Day didn't need to hunt the shooters – they'd found him! Better still, they'd firmly implicated Wilbourn and his group in their crimes.

He called the station and asked for reinforcements. "No blue lights and no sirens; tell them to take it steady coming up the drive, too," he ordered.

-

Prone in the back of her own car, Melanie Price was practising deep breathing and repeating 'you've got a chance' to herself. The two men in the front hadn't spoken for a good ten minutes when the car braked hard. She heard the older man say, "Gate's open, that's handy!" The car took a sudden right turn – immediately followed by a vicious crack. "What the fuck was that?"

"Lump of wood near the gate – don't panic, we're still going," replied Robert.

Half a minute later Robert yelled, "Fucking hell, look at all the cars – they must be having another fucking party!"

"Don't stop! Turn right and go round the back to the workshop; we'll stash the car there until all the visitors have fucked off!" instructed Mr Jones senior.

-

Day sprinted to the crew bus. "That Mini's just been involved in a shooting! Two police officers down. Call your man at the gate and tell him to let it close in case they try to do a runner. Then get round the back – find it and take cover. No action, there might well be a hostage inside!"

"Gate's already shut, boss. Got a report - that car smashed the pole when it went through. Everybody out, lads, you heard the Chief Inspector!"

As the armed officers disappeared into the dark, Day made his way back to the big room. Wilbourn and Henderson weren't there and the Jean Vincents were looking decidedly restless.

"Mr Coy," Day ordered, "will you please ask your colleagues to sit down? There's a situation developing

198

outside that confirms for me Mr Wilbourn's involvement in serious crimes. It remains to be seen whether you lot are involved. Until that's cleared up, none of you are going anywhere – except possibly to the police station, so I would advise total cooperation." Day produced a pair of handcuffs and waved them for emphasis. "No one is to leave – anyone who tries to do so will be arrested! No one is to use a phone!"

He turned to his colleagues. "I need to be outside, contain this lot. Anyone gets iffy in any way whatsoever cuff them together. If you run out of cuffs you can tie them to their chairs for all I care. If Henderson and Wilbourn return, cuff them immediately. In a few minutes the cavalry will be here then you can start a search of the house and find the two of them. I'll send a couple of the armed lads in, just in case." He glanced over at Dom O'Neil – who was now smiling. After listening to carefully prepared lies for thirty minutes, he could now be a proper policeman again. Day decided there was nothing to be gained for anyone by telling Dom his girlfriend was either dead or in deep, deep trouble.

There was a cry of anger and Henry Boston QC stood up and launched himself at Day. "This is an outrage!" he yelled. "We are all here voluntarily – this is illegal detention and I for one am leaving!" Then he made a mistake – he pushed Day.

The QC was a big man and Day retreated backwards into the ante-room with Boston continuing to poke him in the chest. Five seconds after the pair were out of sight of the others, a very puzzled Boston found himself on the floor – wearing handcuffs. Day stepped back into the big room and waved Andy Grainger across. "Take this person back in and sit him down. He's under arrest for assaulting a police officer. Check him for bruises, he tripped and had a nasty fall."

Day exited by the main door and ran to the left. He stopped as he reached the front corner of the East Wing and peered round. He could see the long, open-fronted vehicle storage building but nothing more. He advanced silently along the wall of the Hall until he could see around the back corner.

The Mini was parked close to the steps up to the accommodation above the garage. Both doors were open and the car appeared empty. Day spotted the feet of an armed officer protruding from a small clump of bushes and crawled over to join him. "What have we got, Mr Barry?"

"It's definitely them, sir. They were sitting in the car – arguing I think – when we took position. Then two blokes got out and dragged a woman up the steps and an old bloke opened the door and let 'em in. I could have shot all three of the bastards if I'd known exactly what was going on, sir."

"I wouldn't have blamed you but you did the right thing. Did you see any weapons?" asked Day.

"No, sir."

"Have they seen you – do they know they're surrounded?"

"Not sure, but don't think so. Only thing that's happened since they disappeared inside is some of the blinds came down."

"Right. The cavalry will be here any minute now, so you'll soon have plenty of help but, if you can spare one of your team to go inside and back up my lot, I'd appreciate it. I'm going round the front to meet the reinforcements and get them deployed." He pointed to the flat over the garage. "If they come out shooting, you'll have my full backing if you put them down but otherwise, just wait." Day crawled away until it was safe for him to stand and then proceeded to the top of the drive to await the arrival of the cars he could hear crunching up the gravel.

A thousand confused thoughts raced through his brain. What was going on here? This was a hostage situation of some uncertainty. The two kidnappers must have at least one firearm but was it a three kidnappers/one hostage event or two kidnappers/two hostages. Day was uncertain of the role of the elderly mechanic; was he capable of involvement in a serious crime? When he had been seen making tea for the Jones family, he had seemed detached – giving no real indication of being Mrs Jones' father. Still, it was always best to assume the worst.

The two thugs had brought their victim into a situation crowded with police. He couldn't believe that had been pre-planned. Surely Wilbourn wouldn't have invited detectives to his home then ordered criminals to join them? No, it had to have been a last-minute decision by the kidnappers when they realised they'd screwed up. They couldn't have been told Wilbourn was creating a rock-solid alibi by entertaining the SIO and his team at the precise time the crime was planned. The shooters had come here for protection after their attack got out of control. Did Wilbourn even know they were here? How was Henderson involved and where had the two of them disappeared to? When sufficient numbers of officers arrived, a search would need organising. The crime was baffling enough – and then, for some reason as yet unbeknown to the DCI, police officers had intruded into the abduction and it had gone badly. And Mandy – what the hell was she doing there – getting involved and shot? He was terrified for her; for her physical and mental condition - thinking she probably wasn't even insured and legally protected. His own career was in tatters – just when Jess was getting really excited about the house. The new Chief Constable hated his guts so, there was no doubt in Day's mind that this action would be his last hurrah – better make it a good one!

The first group consisted of two Chesterfield response cars and an Armed Response Vehicle. Day explained the situation in a couple of concise sentences. He ordered three of the local officers to go inside to support the outnumbered detectives. "Go through the main door and report to DS Grainger; there's a dozen or so men in there and as yet we've no idea if they're criminals or just unpleasant people." He introduced himself to the two armed officers. "Go left, around the West Wing and position yourself to monitor as many exits as you can. We're missing two men and I don't want them to leave the building. As soon as some more arrive, I'll send you some help." PC Rouse was ordered to take over traffic direction. Day was pleased to note that none of the officers hesitated and all immediately dispersed to their briefly explained duties. Police officers always achieve an enhanced focus when colleagues are gunned down.

Day was just about to jog back towards the garage when a fourth car arrived. It was Sergeant Davies.

He wound the window down. "Where do you want me, Derek?" Day had never seen his oldest police friend look so grim.

"Come with me, Pug; we've got potential for a siege round the corner and I need to be there directing stuff until the Negotiator gets here." He set off past the East Wing.

"Last I heard, he's about ten minutes behind me and, you should be warned, Carruthers is with him!" The contempt for the Chief Constable was evident in Pug's tone. Anyone giving Derek Day a hard time was no friend of Pug Davies.

"Just when I thought it couldn't get any worse!" said Day and both men laughed humourlessly.

-

Wilbourn and Henderson were locked inside their safe room and both were furious. Mr Jones had phoned them from Murphy's flat and told them what had happened. "Sorry, we didn't realise you were having another party," he said glibly.

"It's not a party, you cretin – the place is full of fucking coppers!" yelled Henderson.

Wilbourn was silently considering his options. At first glance, those idiots had brought confirmation of his involvement to his front door and this was going to take some serious sorting. They were secure for now; no one knew how to access the safe room except the two people inside.

"We thought Mr Wilbourn would like to play with Miss Price!" said Jones in a vain attempt to curry favour. It didn't work and merely earned more abuse from Henderson.

Wilbourn took the phone. "Sorry about that, Mr Jones – you know Henderson can be a little over-emotional. Your situation is difficult but I'm fairly sure the police aren't aware you're in the garage flat. Also, as far as I know, none of the policemen here are armed. My suggestion is that you

202

immediately get back to your car and make an escape. Henderson will make sure the gates are open. If any police try to stop you, just fire a couple of warning shots and they'll dive for cover. Once you're somewhere secure, let me know and I'll see you have sufficient funds to leave the country for a while."

Mr Jones hadn't survived for so long in the world's most dangerous game by doing anything in a rush, but he could see the advantage of speed in this unprecedented situation. Before the action began, he felt the need to call Mrs Jones and explain his predicament; backup was always handy. He pointed to the mechanic. "You, go down and suss out what's happening, have a smoke, wander around, see if there's any coppers about then come back and report – or else!" A little wave of his Glock 17 emphasised the meaning of 'else'.

The old fellow was too frightened of Jones to tell him he didn't smoke, so he opened the door and obeyed.

On reaching ground level, he pretended to stretch then walked to the Mini and shut both doors. He kicked some gravel and wandered, apparently aimlessly, up and down until he closed on a small clump of bushes. A sudden flash of movement near his feet and he was toppled. The hand gripping his right ankle gave a mighty heave and the unfortunate old chap was dragged into the undergrowth. Another firm hand covered his face and, before he even had time to think, he was handcuffed and face down in the dirt. A sinister voice whispered in his ear, "One move, one sound – and you're dead as a doornail!"

He felt himself being dragged further under cover, into almost total darkness, then rolled over onto his back.

"It's an old guy!" whispered one of the two black-uniformed men leaning just above him.

"Must be the mechanic! Are you the mechanic?"

The old man, too terrified to speak, nodded vigorously.

Another man appeared, this one wearing a scruffy suit. "Bring him!" he commanded. One of the uniforms dragged Murphy through the dirt and gravel until they were out of sight of the garage. He was propped up against a wall and enough of the panic subsided for him to recognise the senior policeman he'd seen the day before.

"Thank God," said the mechanic. "I thought I was a gonner; I thought they were going to kill me!"

"Who's they?" asked Day.

"Mr Jones and his boy – they're psychos! They dragged this girl in, made some phone calls then sent me out to see if the coast was clear for them to do a runner!" Day guessed the old man was only minutes from a heart attack but questions had to follow.

"Just two men and one woman inside now?"

"Yes."

"Is the woman okay?"

"Some bruises and she's tied up. Am I helping you, sir?"

"Yes. Guns?" Day needed information fast.

"Mr Jones had an automatic pistol – don't know what kind."

"And the younger man?"

"Didn't see a gun on him. He's the one who uses a crossbow but he doesn't have it with him – it's too big to hide under clothes." Murphy was getting his breath and senses back and knew his only chance of not spending the rest of his life in prison was to become the world's most helpful witness.

Crossbow – even more confirmation. Day turned to the armed officer, "Go back to Sergeant Barry, please – tell him what you've just heard – it looks like they're going to break out at any time."

"Sir!" and he was gone.

-

In the safe room, Wilbourn and Henderson were watching a screen showing the front of the garage. The Mini was clearly visible and they watched the mechanic shut the doors and then wander over towards the bushes. The sudden movement as he collapsed and mysteriously slid into the greenery confirmed that the police were indeed surrounding the place.

"Henderson, I think there are sufficient policemen on the premises, please shut the gates," ordered Wilbourn. He phoned again. "Mr Jones," he said, "I've managed to get a

204

camera on your car outside and the area around it. No sign of police and Henderson's opened the gates. You're good to go!"

"Armed police anywhere?" asked Jones.

"No, all the detectives are in here with us. Go now, it's your only chance!"

"Where's the old guy?"

"Murphy's done a runner; he's terrified of you two!"

Mr Jones went to the kitchen drawer and took out a menacing-looking knife. He threw it to Robert. "Cut the tie at the front and fit a new one round the back so I can use her as cover."

Melanie Price was barely able to stand and didn't resist the painful reorganisation of her bonds.

Mr Jones took the magazine from his pistol and checked it. He grabbed Melanie's tied wrists and whispered, "Any sound and you get a bullet, clear?"

Quite unable to speak, Melanie nodded.

Mr Jones called his 'wife', "Wilbourn says we're good to go so we're heading out now – I'll call you as soon as we're clear of the Hall grounds." He switched off the lights. "You first," he said to Robert – who opened the door a couple of inches and peered outside into the semi-darkness.

"Right," said Jones senior, "quiet as you can, off you go."

Still carrying the knife, Robert placed a cautious foot on the top step. Two more steps down and a trembling Melanie Price appeared in the doorway. Only a thin sliver of Mr Jones behind her but the silenced pistol was clearly visible – pointing into her right ear.

A hundred and fifty metres away, two men were lying prone in the bushes. Sergeant Barry whispered to Day. "What do you think, sir?"

This was a hideous position. Day's instinct told him that Melanie Price would be killed only if there was a botched rescue attempt – the kidnappers needed her as a bargaining chip – but that wasn't guaranteed. Also, these two men were going to be his best way of convicting Wilbourn – but only if they were alive!

Price was pushed forward and stumbled onto the top step, two steps above the younger kidnapper.

To give himself thinking time, Day whispered, "The man with the gun to the girl's head - chances of one-shot kill?"

Sergeant Barry's head stayed perfectly still, his eye to the telescopic sight. "One hundred percent," he said in a composed, flat tone.

Day closed his eyes and pressed his face into the soil. The three people on the staircase took another step down.

"Sir?" said Barry, still without emotion.

Day hesitated – this was playing God.

Another step down.

"Sir?" said Barry, with a microscopic tremor in his voice.

Day looked up. "You'll have my backing whatever your decision!"

At that precise second, from behind Day and Barry, a stage whisper in a strong Scottish accent said, "What the hell's going on, Day? Are you deliberately disobeying my orders – trying to make me look a fool?"

Mr Jones must have had very good hearing because he instantly swivelled his pistol and took a shot in the Chief Constable's general direction. The bullet cracked off the wall and ricocheted into the trees beyond.

"Fuck me!" yelled the Chief Constable - but no one heard it over the snap of Barry's sniper rifle.

On the steps, Mr Jones' head exploded and the rest of him collapsed like jelly. An off-balance Melanie Price screamed and fell forward onto Robert Jones. Entwined, both rolled to the bottom of the steps and landed in a single, dazed heap.

Nothing happened for the first full ten seconds when everyone was paralysed with shock. Then, Robert Jones began to feel around, obviously searching for the knife. Day looked at Barry. The Sergeant had let the rifle drop and he was quietly sobbing; the expert marksman had never killed before.

Jones saw his knife just a couple of metres away and lurched for it.

'No choice', thought Day and he leapt up and began the fastest sprint of his life.

-

Watching from the safe room, Wilbourn was delighted to see the demise of a major witness against him. He watched the slow-motion tumble down the steps and hoped, for a few moments, that the other witness and the interfering bitch had broken their necks. He was disappointed when he saw Price twitch then try to roll over but much happier when Jones went for the knife. Perhaps he'd slit her throat before the coppers shot him? Three down for no extra charge – thinking of the savings made his eyes water!

-

Day was a long-distance runner not a sprinter but he would have given Usain Bolt a close race in that fifteen-second dash. He arrived just as Jones grabbed the cable tie around Melanie's wrists with one hand and the knife with the other. There was no sophisticated connection – Day didn't slow down, he just ran, shoulder-down, straight into the younger man. Completely winded, Jones was unable to use the knife before Day spun round, grabbed an outstretched arm and snapped Jones' wrist. Five seconds later the young assassin was pinned to the ground by four more coppers. Game over.
"You okay, Melanie?" asked Day between gasps for air.
She didn't reply but the violent sobbing told him she was probably going to be alright. "Someone send for Dom O'Neil!" he ordered of no one in particular.

Chapter Twenty-Seven

Mrs Jones, blissfully unaware of what was happening to her 'husband' and 'son', ordered a minicab.

The chatty young Asian driver was very prompt and laughed when she gave the name of a pub in Barlow village.

Middle-aged woman – alone – pub – nearly closing time? "It's getting a bit late for a night out, luv?" he joked.

She laughed, "It's never too late, darling!"

"You're not from round here?" he asked, marvelling at her southern accent.

"No, Londoner born and bred – and proud of it!"

"D'you know – I've never been to London – daft innit?"

"Yes it is; you'd love it. You must go." A brief hesitation. "Would you pull into that garage, please, I'm feeling a little bit queasy?"

"Of course," said the driver. "My driving's not been bad, has it?" He had two worries – she might complain to his boss and, even worse, throw up in his cab.

"No, not your fault and don't worry, I won't be sick," she said, reading his mind. "I'll put my head down and relax a minute."

"That's fine, take your…" …were the last words he ever spoke. The speed of movement and the enormous pressure of the garrotte gave him no chance.

She's guessed the road downhill towards Barlow would be very quiet this late on a Sunday but she had a good look round before climbing out. Opening the driver's door, she pulled out the corpse and dragged it behind a car parked on the forecourt. She returned to the driver's seat and studied the taxi equipment. She calculated she had the car for ten minutes before the despatcher became curious. Just enough time to get to Millthorpe – where she intended to put the gun in her handbag to good use.

-

After the adrenalin rush, Day was exhausted. He lay on his back in the gravel and listened to the cacophony around him.

208

Robert Jones was screaming in agony as unsympathetic officers struggled to get handcuffs onto his broken wrist; someone was reading him his rights; Melanie Price was still sobbing uncontrollably and several police radios were active simultaneously.

A face wearing a dark green uniform appeared above him. "Where you hurt, mate?" asked the paramedic.

"I'm not. See to the woman," he stuttered, "please."

"Don't worry, we've got her. Don't think she's too badly hurt – judging by the noise she's making."

Another face appeared next to the paramedic's.

It was Pug Davies. "Nice turn of speed that, Derek!" he said with a grin.

Day wasn't amused. "How's Barry?" he asked.

"Pretty shaken. They've put him in a car and are trying to reassure him he did a good job but, anyway you look at it, killing someone is going to make anyone sane feel pretty rotten."

"Chief Constable?"

Pug laughed. "Mr Carruthers has left the premises. He said, and I quote, 'everything seems to be under control, here – I'll head back to Beetwell Street to assume overall control'! Actually, I think he was crapping himself after that shot didn't miss him by much!"

"Show a bit of respect, please, Detective Sergeant Davies!" ordered Day – and then they both burst out laughing. But the mirth was just pretend.

-

Watching, but unable to hear the events outside the garage, Wilbourn and Henderson realised their plan had only been half successful. "Jones the Younger appears to be alive – that is very unsatisfactory," said the owner.

The Butler nodded rather sagely. "I think, sir, that it may be time to put your plan 'e' into operation."

"I'm afraid you're right, my dear chap. Firstly, we'd better dress more appropriately, then we'll go for a short walk. Are the cases packed?"

209

"As always, sir – as always."

-

"Anything from the hospital on Mandy and Mr Dawson?" asked Day as Pug Davies pulled him to his feet.
"Just had a text from Jill – said 'neither wound life threatening'. Brief and to the point, typical Jill – but that's all we know, so far."
Dom O'Neil came running. "Dom, go to hospital with your girl. Do not let her out of your sight until I'm able to interview her – clear?" Day ordered.
"Yes sir, thank you sir!"
Day turned to Pug. "Come on, let's get inside, I can't wait to have a long chat with Mr Wilbourn."

-

The taxi continued past the closed gates of Millthorpe Hall, earning only a cursory glance from the police officers who were trying to get their vehicles inside. Two hundred metres further on, the boundary wall took a right-angle turn away from the road and disappeared into the dark countryside. Another fifty metres and Mrs Jones took an almost imperceptible track to the right, flicking off the headlights as she turned. The treacherous surface suggested that the last vehicle to travel that way was a heavy tractor during a period of persistent rainfall. The past week's unseasonably dry weather had turned the churned-up mud to rock. The Skoda Superb's suspension was protesting with a symphony of bangs and squeaks but Mrs Jones didn't care – it wasn't her car.
The track meandered left and right, sometimes almost touching the great wall then veering sharply back into dense undergrowth. She ignored the many collisions with branches and stones along the way; the thin moonlight wasn't really adequate for the task in hand. After almost a kilometre of this rough treatment, she was able to follow the wall sharp right along the rear wall of the rectangular grounds. According to her information, the secret entrance was only

210

about one hundred metres from the corner. She slowed to walking pace and studied the shrubs growing hard against the wall. There it was – her torch reflected from some metal fittings through the foliage. With no small amount of damage to the bodywork, she turned the car around to face the way she'd come.

Her call to Mr Jones went unanswered. Same result for the call to Robert. This was bad – but instinct told her it would be good to wait.

Chapter Twenty-Eight

Mr Wilbourn was walking calmly a couple of metres behind his faithful manservant down a feebly-lit tunnel. The escape route had been discovered by workmen during the restoration but they had been instructed to cap it off. Only when all the work on the Hall had been completed, did Henderson reopen the tunnel and explore its full length. It ended inside an ancient underground ice-house about half way to the northern boundary wall.

As the two men entered the larger space they were met by a disappointing sight; the exit up towards the fresh air was entirely blocked by a blue BMW. Swear words were exchanged.

"So that's where the idiot hid the car – he said no one would ever find it!" exclaimed Henderson.

"But how did he get out? There's not an inch to open the doors!" Wilbourn was bemused.

"Or over the top." But the butler's torch showed them the answer. "Through the tailgate; we can do the same if we can get inside."

Breaking the windscreen of a modern car is not as easy as most people think and, not wanting to risk using his old revolver, it took Henderson some time to find the right implement in the long-deserted ice-house.

Once out into the undergrowth, not daring to use their torches, progress was further slowed. The moonlight cast confusing shadows and both men tripped several times. At last they found a break between the packed bushes and followed the path north until they reached the butler's secret. The large lean-to against the boundary wall was entirely covered in climbing plants and Henderson donned heavy gloves and began tearing them away.

Wilbourn used the time to make a phone call. "Good evening, Miss Thomson, Paul speaking. Thank you for being sensible and not cooperating with the police, you will be well rewarded. More important, if you continue to follow my advice, neither you nor your mother will come to any harm.

Your brother's top-class defence will be financed and I will ensure he is protected throughout his, hopefully short, prison sentence. Now, just above the primary school on Church Street, there is a vehicle turning space. One hour from now you should evade the police, who I assume are still watching your house, and walk to this space. Stay out of sight and you will be picked up. Bring an overnight bag. Do you understand?"

Gina Thomson gulped. "I do," she said, relieved that the police outside her house had vanished a little while ago.

Neither Will Thomson nor Robert Jones would spend any time in prison and Wilbourn said as much to a disbelieving Henderson.

Wilbourn's second call was to an old friend who kept a Piper PA46 Malibu at Retford Gamston Airport. Yes, the plane would be refuelled and ready just after dawn. It had the range to take them pretty much anywhere in northern Europe.

As he put the phone back in his pocket, Wilbourn marvelled as a pair of wooden doors came into view. Another ten minutes work and the butler was able to force them open, revealing an older model Landrover Defender.

"Henderson, you really are a genius – but how do we get through the wall?" asked Wilbourn.

"All will become clear, sir." Henderson walked a few metres to another patch of dense greenery and began to tug at it. It took longer this time but eventually a gate was revealed. Henderson turned and bowed. "Ta-da!" he said.

"Excellent!" said Wilbourn. "Let's get moving!"

Henderson removed the iron bar that was securing the gate and opened it a fraction. There was an equal amount of shrubbery on the other side but he knew the Defender would make short work of that. He pulled the gate a little more and peered through the gaps in the foliage.

"What the fu…!" he said. The flash, loud bang and sharp pain on the side of his head was something of a shock for Butler Henderson.

213

"Give me a minute," said Day to the paramedics tending to Jones. He kneeled by the stretcher and got very close. "I'm in a bit of a hurry and I need some info. Where's your mother?"

Through bloodstained teeth, Jones replied, "Gone back to London," with such promptness and certainty it was clearly a lie.

"Wilbourn and Henderson?"

"In hell, I hope - those bastards set us up!" The truth this time.

"There's nothing to be gained here, Pug – let's get back inside." As they jogged round to the front of the Hall, Day asked his friend, "Situation report, please."

"Only thing I'm up to date with is gates have closed again and more of our lads can't get in and the ambulances can't get out. I've sent for a heavy recovery truck to break 'em open but it'll be another half hour yet."

On entering the big room, Day asked the same of Andy Grainger.

The Acting DS replied enthusiastically, "No sign of the owner and butler. Three of the Vincents have been prats, sir – hence the handcuffs. We've tracked down the servants and a couple are cooperating and guiding searches. They've shown Tara the control room but none of them knew how to operate the gates. Apparently only the butler knows how. Tara's still up there pressing every button she can find. All this lot are protesting their innocence, sir." He indicated the now-subdued Vincents.

It's amazing the calming effect the threat of handcuffs and the crack of a sniper rifle can have.

"A couple of them have admitted they get up to some funny stuff, sir – but they insist it's not illegal," continued Andy. "Any more news on Sharp and Dawson, sir?"

"Only that neither has got life-threatening injuries, but I guess you already know that?"

"Sir."

214

There was a fuss by the entrance and one of Sergeant Barry's team rushed in. "Gunshots, sir!" she shouted.

"Where?"

"To the north, sir. Quite far away, I'd guess!"

North? Near the boundary wall? The mysterious hidden entrance? Escape route? Vehicle? Thoughts flashed through Day's brain too quickly to be properly processed but he was able to give an order to the young constable. "Collect the rest of Barry's team and head off in the general direction; see what you can find. Take your time and be careful!"

She was so thrilled to be given responsibility, she actually saluted and said, "Aye, aye sir!" before she rushed to the door. Her excitement didn't last more than a couple of seconds, though; Sergeant Barry had reappeared.

Day called over, "You okay, Mr Barry?"

"I'll do, sir," he said flatly.

Day had never seen anyone look so disappointed as the young PC but had to smile as the sergeant put his hand on her shoulder and said, "Don't worry, Tina, you'll get your chance!"

Day was proud to be surrounded by such good people. "Where's the chopper?" he asked of anyone near enough to listen.

"Mechanical trouble, sir. Couple of hours, minimum!"

That caused a spark. "Where's the mechanic – Wilbourn's mechanic. Murphy is it? Where is he?" asked Day.

"He'll still be in one of the cars stuck at the gate, sir," said Pug.

"Get him back here quick, will you, Pug, please? If they keep a vehicle near their secret escape, he must be the one who keeps it serviced!"

Five minutes later the still-handcuffed mechanic was cowering in front of DCI Day.

"Murphy, you said you'd do anything to help, okay?"

"Yes sir."

"Where's the secret rear entrance to the Hall grounds?"

The man looked blank for a few moments then said, "I don't know, sir."

215

Day cursed under his breath and was just about to dismiss Murphy when the old man suddenly said, "But I do know where Mr Henderson keeps his Landrover! At least, I think I could find it."

"Explain!" demanded Day.

"He keeps an old Defender in a shed near the north-west corner of the estate. God knows how he got it in there in the first place, it's all overgrown. I reckon he's always serviced it himself because he used to take the quad bike and some tools from my garage every couple of months but, once last year, he couldn't get it going so took me up to start it for him."

"And did you?" asked Day, realising he'd been tricked again – not the north-east!

"Yes – I can start anything," he replied with professional pride.

"Could you find it again?"

"I reckon so – ninety percent sure!"

"How old are you, Mr Murphy?"

Mr? Mr Murphy now knew he had a slight chance to get into this detective's good books. "Seventy-two, sir."

"Can you still ride a quad?"

"Me? Of course! Fit as a flea, me"

"Andy, uncuff Mr Murphy and take him round to the garage to fetch his quad bike. Bring him back here to pick me up."

At last, Day thought he could do something positive. He turned to one of the armed officers and held out his hand. "Pistol and torch," he demanded. The shocked officer hesitated but then handed over his powerful torch.

"You know better than anyone I can't hand over my weapon, sir. That would qualify as an illegal order, sir!" said the PC with rather shaky conviction. "I'll come with you on the quad, though."

Day realised immediately he was in the wrong, apologised and thanked the officer for the offer.

When Murphy returned, his face was set like a young cavalry officer about to lead his first charge. Day climbed on but there was no chance of an additional passenger. "Pug, contact Barry's team and tell them to listen for us coming and fall in behind us. Right Mr Murphy, show me what this thing can do!"

-

Henderson had fallen with his back against the wall with the shock. Although he was holding what remained of his right ear as blood streamed down his neck, he felt rather pleased with himself. The glimpse of the gun barrel through the shrubs had been enough to reinstate his old reactions; he'd dived, drawn his revolver and fired two shots in the blink of an eye.

Wilbourn crawled up to him. "Good God, Henderson – you're covered in blood!"

"Oh, very fucking observant, your majesty," hissed the butler, clearly not pleased. "There's a first aid kit in the Landrover – go and get it. Then put the bags inside but do not start the engine!"

Wilbourn was horrified. Had the servant become the master? He left.

Their one-sided conversation was interrupted by a thin voice from the other side of the wall. "Oh, you're still alive then, Henderson?"

"Mrs Jones," replied the butler, "I thought it might be you."

"Shoot first and ask questions afterwards, hey? We're both the same," she stammered.

"It appears so. Did I hit you?"

"Yes," she said, "twice!"

"If it's any consolation, you took my ear off."

"Oh good. I was impressed by the speed of your reactions – ex-professional?"

"Indeed."

"What's happened to Bob and Marcus?"

"Who?"

"The people you know as Mr and Robert Jones – Bob and Marcus." She gurgled a wet cough.

"They made a terrible error of judgement and both ended up in police custody, I'm afraid," he lied.

217

"Oh dear, then we're all fucked!" She sounded almost relieved.

"Not so, Mrs Jones. If Wilbourn could get his arse in gear, we've all got a chance of getting away."

"Not me, unless you've got the world's best paramedic handy?"

"Afraid not."

"Could I just ask, did you shoot me to stop me giving evidence against you?" She was really breathless now.

"No, not really – just an automatic reaction to you shooting me."

"Good effort. I shot because I thought you were Wilbourn and that twat really gives me the creeps. I bet he did the dirty on Bob and Marcus, didn't he?"

"I'm afraid that's exactly what he did."

"Would you mind shooting him for me, please?" she whimpered.

"I'm sorry I can't do that!"

"How about telling him to look through the gate so I can shoot him myself?"

"Not that, either – he's the key to all the money and he's promised me a fortune if I get him to his bolt-hole in the Caribbean!"

"Damn!" She gave a blood-curling moan. "Still, I expect that detective'll get him. Bye Henderson!"

The single gunshot startled the butler.

Chapter Twenty-Eight

Day didn't consciously hear the gunshot over the roar of the quad-bike's motor but he ordered his driver to stop. They'd left the armed unit way behind and Murphy was getting decidedly nervous.

A few silent seconds and Day whispered unnecessarily, "How far?" Murphy had done a remarkable job, feeling his way through what looked like impenetrable undergrowth.

"Close enough to stop here and wait for your lads to catch up!" he said.

Day agreed; although he'd faced a man with a gun before, it was not a prospect he wished to repeat so he climbed off the quad, walked around then stretched and massaged his sore rear end. A few more seconds wouldn't hurt. Suddenly, he heard the roar of a big diesel and saw a blue cloud emerge over the tree tops. DCI Day took off at a run.

-

Wilbourn returned with a big wad of bandage and thrust it on to Henderson's ear. The butler yelled and snatched the bandage to wind it around his head like an ancient cartoon of a toothache sufferer.

"It's gone quiet – did you get the shooter?" whispered Wilbourn.

"She shot herself…"

"She? Mrs Jones?"

"I'm guessing she was in agony and knew she was done for! I really shouldn't have told her my little secret."

Wilbourn didn't notice that Henderson actually seemed quite reflective and he blurted out, "Good riddance – one less witness if we ever get caught!"

'Bastard!' thought Henderson. "Help me up, I'm going to get the Landrover, you get that gate open. Don't worry, she can't hurt you, she's dead!" 'You bastard!' Again.

Wilbourn was about to object to being given orders but went towards the gate anyway. There was just a little bit more foliage to remove before it could be fully released. He heard the Landrover start at the third attempt and was immediately aware of the smell of exhaust. Two more minutes, in which he worked harder than he ever had before, and he was ready to pull open the gate. The Landrover approached painfully slowly, lurching from rock to tree stump - but the old warrior was up to the task.

"Open up," shouted Henderson, "and jump in!"

Wilbourn pulled the gate wide open and saw a barrier of shrubbery. He turned to Henderson, looking horrified.

"Don't worry, we'll shove our way through that! Get in!"

Henderson was confident that, in its lowest gear, the Landrover would have no difficulty in pushing aside the foliage. He was probably right – but he hadn't allowed for the battered Skoda Superb wedged into gap behind. Mrs Jones had been determined to have the last laugh.

-

Day's hands and face were lacerated by a hundred flicking branches by the time he got his first glimpse of the vehicle. The Landrover was struggling; its bonnet almost buried in foliage and all four wheels spinning on the grass. The engine was revving high in a very low gear and the whole scene was in danger of being obscured by blue smoke.

Day was no expert on vehicle traction but it didn't look as though this one was going anywhere. He circled to the left, under cover of trees, until he could get a clear view into the passenger side front window. Wilbourn was there, holding onto the dashboard and shouting silently at whatever was blocking their exit. Beyond was a comic figure in the driving seat. Henderson had a huge, crude bandage wrapped around his head. What had happened to him? In any other circumstances, Day would have difficulty controlling his sense of humour. Not now – there was too much he didn't know.

It was one man onto two. Okay, one member of the opposition was injured but the way he was attempting to drive suggested a negligible loss of strength. The main factor was, of course, guns. Day didn't have one and, for all he

220

knew, the two men in the Landrover could be armed to the proverbial teeth. How far away was the armed support? It could be seconds or five minutes but the noise and smoke would definitely lead them here. Every instinct told Day to wait.

The revs dropped. The blue cloud blew away. Both men inside slumped forward in frustration. There was an argument. A crash of gears and the vehicle reversed as far as it was possible within the limited clearing. More revs and smoke.

Day knew what was going to happen and, able to see the massive bull bars on the front of the Landrover for the first time, he thought they might just get away with it.

As the Landrover surged forward, Day left cover and made a dash calculated to intercept the passenger side door. He missed. Whatever had been blocking the vehicle's progress gave way a couple of metres and Day hit the rear panel. He bounced back and fell in the dirt. As the Landrover reversed to make a second run, an open-mouthed Paul Wilbourn stared at the figure below staring back at him. Wilbourn turned away and there was suddenly only one thing on Day's mind – 'he's reaching for a gun!'. That was sufficient motivation to get the detective to his feet and run like hell.

What saved him was the lack of electric windows on the Landrover. By the time Wilbourn had picked up the gun and wound the window down his potential target was back amongst the trees. He fired a couple of speculative shots anyway but they flew well above Day's prone body.

Day risked a quick look. Would they get out and hunt him down or make another attempt to get free? Neither option was much to Day's liking but, hopefully, the gunshots would give his armed support more incentive to get a move on. He put his head back down and listened – hard.

The decision was made. Henderson and Wilbourn were more interested in escaping than killing an irritating cop. The Landrover reversed.

Day had only the sketchiest idea of what could be on the other side of that gap in the wall. He'd seen several aerial views of the Hall grounds and knew there wasn't a main road in the vicinity. It couldn't just be fields and forest, though – there had to be some kind of rough, little-used track that would lead eventually to a road to somewhere. He had to stop them!

It was a really daft plan. As the Landrover charged the wall, he ran to its rear to make an attempt to climb on. He made a grab for the spare wheel attached to the tailgate but failed to connect and fell flat on his face - again.

They say fortune favours the brave and it certainly did in those few electric moments. Wilbourn had twisted in the front seat and, gun in hand, leaned out of the side window for an easy shot. Day glanced up into the barrel of the automatic.

At that moment, the front of the accelerating vehicle collided with the side of the abandoned Skoda. Without warning, the Landrover ricocheted to the left and its passenger door impacted the sturdy gate post.

For Mr Wilbourn, the timing was very unfortunate. His right elbow was crushed, his arm rendered useless and the gun dropped to the ground. None of which really mattered to him because a microsecond later he was in a deep faint.

Unperturbed, Henderson turned the wheels hard left and reversed, forcing Day to roll out of the way. As the Landrover attacked the Skoda for the third time, DCI Day saw the gun and made a determined grab for it. Too late! This time the Landrover struck the Skoda on its front wheel and brushed it aside. Henderson and Wilbourn (sort of) were free.

The Landrover was much better suited to this vague track than the Skoda had been and Henderson was more familiar with the route than the late Mrs Jones but progress was still slow. Henderson took a second to reach over to pull Wilbourn round in the seat and was horrified by the sight of the shattered elbow. It would be months before Wilbourn could sign the paperwork he had promised would make his butler a rich man.

Even worse, a look in the mirror caught the briefest glimpse of a man running in pursuit. He couldn't be sure but guessed it must be DCI fucking Day! Henderson accelerated to a speed well in excess of the vehicle's capability on that kind of hidden surface.

Day had found Wilbourn's gun but, in the process, had lost his torch and smashed his radio. He could hear the armed officers thrashing about in the undergrowth but decided not to wait. He yelled at the top of his voice, "Two armed men in a Landrover – gone through a gap in the wall and turned left – am in foot pursuit – order roadblocks everywhere!"

Sergeant Barry, not far away but out of sight, stopped and thought, 'Oh, fuck! Senior officers are just not supposed to be this reckless'. Barry radioed in his limited understanding of the situation and led his team after three crazy men.

-

As instructed, Gina Thomson packed an overnight bag, checked that her police protection had indeed vanished and set off down Church Street in the direction of the designated meeting point. She knew that Wilbourn had the power to destroy her family and had already demonstrated the ruthlessness to use that power. The bastard obviously had an army of assassins in tow so, even if she got him arrested, there was no guarantee her family would be safe.

Will had been unbelievably stupid! He'd helped in the killing of her boyfriend just to curry favour with a group of perverted millionaires. She'd never forgive him and suspected a long jail sentence awaited him but also knew he was too soft to survive for years in any maximum-security prison. Every aspect of her family's future depended on her keeping Mr Wilbourn happy; the prospect horrified her.

Hiding in the shadows was not a natural state for a popular young woman and the time passed slowly. She didn't want to have to explain her presence in this odd place late at night and only narrowly avoided encounters with two late-night dog walkers.

223

The clock on her phone indicated it was way beyond the time she was supposed to be picked up. Gina couldn't identify her strongest emotion. Was it fear, loathing, anger, heartbreak – or a combination of them all? On top of all that she was getting bloody cold.

Frustration set in and she began to analyse her situation. Some way into her internal argument she realised her only solid, dire problem was her mother's safety. Will had been stupid, yes – but all his troubles were self-imposed; her limited sympathy for his situation was evaporating.

Concern for her own safety also began to wane; it was her beauty that had set this whole chilling tale in motion – Gary's murder was her fault! Her face had been a curse since her early teenage years. She'd enjoyed the attention and flattery at first but it quickly became tedious. Boys, and even a few girls, following her round making comments. The jealous ones employed low-level bullying. Trying to make herself look plain in a dowdy school uniform just made it worse. Then the pressure to be a model – she couldn't think of anything worse. Then Gary – what a lovely man - inside. He was an ugly bugger and knew it; he brought her down to earth and, she believed, he genuinely didn't care what she looked like. It was her fault he was dead! She slapped her own face – no it bloody wasn't – it was Wilbourn – that despicable piece of shit! There was no way he was having her!

She looked at the time again. Far too late. She walked back up the hill and made a decision. There was a train to Newcastle at seven the next morning and her aunt lived there. Mother would be going on a short break with a ticket bought for cash. Only two problems – how to persuade her to go – and where to hide her for the next few hours?

But as soon as mother was on that train, Gina would head up to Beetwell Street Police Station.

-

Derek Day ran half-marathons for fun. His best time was only two minutes outside the world record. In better

224

conditions, he would have found it possible to keep up with the struggling vehicle in front but now he was losing it.

Wearing his now destroyed No1 work suit and No2 work shoes didn't make for speed. The path was treacherous and the light not far from non-existent. He could hear the Landrover wallowing in low gear but only caught the odd glimpse when Henderson put a nervous touch on the brakes.

Day was hoping the armed response officers were following on but had heard no sounds behind and was in no mood to slow down to listen.

The Landrover couldn't be far from a road by now? Presumably, Henderson knew the area well and had practised this very escape plan? Day had no idea where this narrow, overgrown track came out – would the officers at the Hall be able to find the exit in time to put in a road block?

Running around a dense collection of small trees, Day almost collided with the back of the Landrover. He instinctively dived for cover and froze.

The engine wasn't running and the clicking of the exhaust was the only sound. No obvious movement inside so Day felt confident to manoeuvre to a better vantage point. There was the reason – the front off-side wheel was wedged against a substantial tree stump. They must have come to a shockingly abrupt stop.

He checked the automatic pistol he'd recovered yet again and eased up to get a view inside the cab. No driver – but there was a figure slumped in the passenger seat. It could only be Wilbourn – but where was Henderson? Could he be waiting for Day to present an easy target? Anyone with an ounce of common sense would wait for backup to arrive.

That didn't include Day. He fired a shot into the soft earth by his feet. The gun worked! He hoped it would bring Henderson out into the open and stimulate his armed officers to greater speed.

Nothing! Although he did hear swearing in the far distance as one or more of his potential backup tripped and fell.

Day tried to give his night-vision chance to steady and then took stock of his location. The Landrover had come to a halt where the track was quite close to the Hall wall. The huge structure was there, just a dark shadow, disappearing in both directions. Behind him were vague outlines of fields bordered by dry-stone walls and interspersed with clumps of shrubbery. Henderson had a thousand places to hide; he might even be hiding in the back of his vehicle. His shout of, "Armed police – show yourself," met with no response. Only one way to speed things up – Day put a bullet through the rear side panel. The figure in the passenger seat twitched but there were no shouts of pain from the back or, better still, a cry of, "Don't shoot, I surrender!"

Day opened the driver's side door. No sign of Henderson. Wilbourn was there but he was no threat. His right arm was at a very strange angle and the immense pain must have been blurring every sense.

"Where's Henderson?" asked Day in the gentlest voice he could contrive.

The reply was an indecipherable grunt.

Day felt confident to creep silently all around the vehicle. Still nothing. He explored towards the wall and got lucky. A freshly broken branch right against the stonework – someone had climbed the wall here very, very recently. Henderson was heading back home – and that meant there would almost certainly be more prepared hiding places. Anyone who was willing to keep a fully-serviced Landrover available for escape 'just in case' was certain to have made other arrangements. Henderson would go to ground and it might take days or weeks to find him. But only if he had time to reach a hideout! Day decided to follow.

He pulled himself up the tree and very carefully looked over the wall. The half-expected shot didn't materialise and he took a breath of relief. It was dark out there and he rated his chances of finding Henderson at just above zero but that wasn't the point, he had to unsettle the butler – keep him moving to distract him from any pre-determined route to a bolt-hole. Day had a dozen or more lacerations on his face and hands but the man he was pursuing had a head injury. Day had a gun – did Henderson? It was a risk worth taking.

226

Day began shouting orders to the hordes of fictional officers who had climbed over the wall with him – even though the real half-dozen were still hundreds of metres behind. "Fan out! A-Team head in the direction of the Hall. B-Team head towards the Landrover storage shed. C-Team – down the middle with me!" No one obeyed, although Sergeant Barry's keen ears picked up the shout and he realised what was happening.

"Christ – he's gone over the wall in pursuit! Come on lads, the silly bugger's gonna get himself killed!" The armed officers turned towards the wall and began to climb. Unfortunately, they were in the wrong place.

Despite his injury, Henderson was making good time. The sky had become clearer and the moonlight stronger. Only a couple of minutes after scaling the wall he had realised where he was. This part of the grounds had been kept fairly wild but there were well-tended paths – Mr Wilbourn liked to relax in his hides to watch the wildlife and it had been the butler's job to make sure refreshments were always to hand. The path he was on now would get him back to the abandoned ice-house in ten minutes if he could keep up a reasonable pace. His damaged ear hurt like hell but he'd been lucky, the injury was entirely superficial. The shouting behind gave him all the motivation he needed.

Day was lucky, too - he stumbled on the same path just a couple of minutes after his quarry – but then he was unlucky – he chose the wrong direction! Two hundred metres and the path ended at an elaborate hide; Day wasted another minute confirming it was empty. He reversed his tracks and accelerated.

Henderson was nowhere near as fit as he had been when he left the army. He knew the ice-house was only five minutes away but he had to rest. To the left of the winding path was a clump of bushes that would give excellent cover. He crawled inside, took deep breaths and checked his automatic pistol. He didn't have long to wait.

A man, gun in hand, and wearing battered civvies jogged past at impressive speed. DCI Day! Henderson waited

227

patiently for uniformed officers to follow but there were none. Two minutes later, he set off stealthily after the detective. Now who was doing the hunting?

Chapter Twenty-Nine

Detective Superintendent Jill Halfpenny had left the Royal Hospital as soon as she had been reassured that her two officers would survive their injuries. She arrived at Millthorpe Hall after a maniacal drive and took command.

Pug Davies' report did nothing to calm her down. "We don't know where Derek is, ma'am – he's out of contact. Last we heard, he was chasing Wilbourn and the butler when they made a break for it out of the north wall. They were in a vehicle but he chased them on foot. Sergeant Barry's team are after him but they lost him after he climbed back into the grounds, presumably in pursuit. We know he's somewhere in the north-west corner of the gardens but that's it!"

"He can be such a bloody idiot!" hissed Halfpenny, and Pug was surprised at the mildness of that response. She began issuing orders to send every available officer in that direction, until Pug assured her it had already been done.

"Ma'am!" shouted a breathless officer as he ran inside. "A couple of our lads have found a dead woman near an opening in the north wall – three gunshot wounds – no ID! Also, a smashed-up taxi, reported stolen."

"Fuck me!" exclaimed Halfpenny. That was more like it.

Pug Davies' radio buzzed and he listened intently. "PC Rouse and crew have found a Landrover! There's a badly injured man inside; they're trying to direct paramedics to the place but they're not sure exactly where they are!"

Halfpenny snatched the radio. "Sod that!" she shouted, "Get over the wall and find DCI Day – he's chasing a bloke who's almost certainly armed! Go now! …and be careful."

For the first time, Halfpenny gave her attention to the sullen group of Jean Vincents. "Which one's in charge?" she asked of Andy Grainger.

"Him – Simon Coy!" The Acting DS was agitated – he desperately wanted to be outside supporting his mentor.

Halfpenny ignored the lack of respect and waggled a finger at Coy. "Over here… please, sir," in that reverse global warming tone she was well known for.

229

Coy reluctantly obeyed. She led him to the whiteboard he'd been writing on the previous evening. "You look like an intelligent chap," she said. "Draw me a diagram of the grounds."

He started to protest. "I don't live here, you know – I only visit…"

"Do it," she demanded. "There are multiple deaths around here and if you don't help, you'll be up to your neck in it!"

Within five minutes, Coy had drawn a creditable sketch of the site showing the Hall, the outbuildings and various other features.

"Where's the gate in the north wall?" Halfpenny demanded.

"I've never been but my understanding is it's about here." He pointed to the top left-hand corner.

"All these spots – what are they?"

"Hides – Mr Wilbourn is a great nature lover; he's had hides constructed all over this wooded area."

"Oh, that's bloody great!" said Halfpenny.

She hadn't noticed that Phil Johnstone had arrived and set up his laptop on a side table. "Here ma'am," he called over. "Drone images of the whole area from earlier."

She rushed over. "Can't you get a drone up now?"

"No point. The posh one with heat-seeking was written off!"

"Where's that fucking helicopter!" she demanded of nobody in particular.

"Replacement's just set off from Derby," offered Pug Davies.

"Mr Coy," said Halfpenny rather more politely this time. "Come here, please and tell us what some of these shapes are."

"Not sure, not sure," he repeated as she pointed to images on the screen. "Oh that – I think that might be the old ice-house; not been used for a hundred years."

-

DCI Day was marvelling at the blue BMW wedged tightly in the entrance to some obscure underground structure. Even a cursory glance would tell an observer that the way only inside was through the open boot of the car – and that explained the smashed windscreen. Was this the way Henderson and Wilbourn had evaded capture inside the Hall; the proverbial hidden escape tunnel every stately home should have?

The car would no doubt provide a mountain of evidence but had Henderson gone back through? That question was about to be answered.

The voice that came from behind was quietly respectful with an almost indiscernible edge of threat. "Good evening, Chief Inspector, I wonder if you would be kind enough to place Mr Wilbourn's gun on the ground?"

Day began a slow-motion turn.

"No, don't do that! Place the gun on the ground!" The threat was clearer this time.

Day placed the gun close to his right foot.

"Kick it away!"

Day kicked the gun under the boot of the BMW – where he could make a grab for it should the opportunity arise.

"Now you may turn around."

Day did and, despite the seriousness of his predicament, almost laughed.

Henderson spotted the emotion and actually did laugh. Not the sinister movie-villain laugh you would expect, but one of genuine, twisted amusement. "I know what you're thinking, Mr Day, I had time to admire myself in the mirror. I do look like the popular image of Vincent Van Gogh. Ironic, isn't it – I have the look of a Vincent but, thanks to you, I'll never be rich enough to join their hideous club!" He laughed again, this time without humour. "To business, Chief Inspector, I'm guessing many of your colleagues aren't far away?"

"You guess correctly, one shout should do it!"

"And that would prove fatal! Despite your unfortunate interventions, I wish you no harm, Mr Day. Like me, you are just a man doing a difficult job to the best of his ability. Now, I have limited choices: the first would be to kill you and go into secure hiding until your colleagues tire of looking for me. The second – to simply give myself up – in which case I'll need an extremely expensive lawyer. But there is a third; Mr Wilbourn is seriously injured and is now presumably in police custody. I know all his dirty secrets, including where the bulk of his wealth is hidden. I was aiding his escape in return for a great deal of cash…" Henderson paused and reflected sadly, "…but I expect he would have cheated me in the same way he cheated the Jones family. Mr Wilbourn is not a nice man and, if I could have made use of that knowledge myself, I would have been long gone. If I passed on all that information to the financial authorities, do you think a certain senior police officer might drop all the charges against me?"

Day shook his head. "That would depend on exactly which of Wilbourn's crimes you've been involved in. If you tell us everything, I'll do my…"

He was interrupted by a crash from behind Henderson as two armed officers burst through the undergrowth. The butler instinctively swivelled to face the sound, meaning his gun was pointing in the vague direction of the newcomers.

Day could see what was about to happen. "Don't shoot!" he screamed – and he dived a perfect rugby tackle at the back of Henderson's legs. It didn't save the butler.

Armed officers are trained not to muck about when someone points a gun at them and two bullets hit Henderson squarely in the upper chest.

"Shit!" hissed Day again – rather uncharacteristically.

Derek Day arrived home at dawn. His attempt not to disturb his wife was unsuccessful and she sat up in bed rubbing her eyes.

"What the hell?" she exclaimed, studying the multiple cuts on his face and the state of his No1 work suit.

"I had an argument with some serious shrubbery," he replied, trying to make light of his situation.

Jess picked up the bedside phone. "I'm getting Carol round to babysit; I'm taking you to the hospital!"

"I've just come from there. You should have seen me before the nurse cleaned me up!"

"Bloody hell, Derek, what's happened!" The Sunday name – only used when she was truly anxious.

He sat on the bed and took his shoes off. "We've had a couple of officers hurt, so I've paid them a visit and one of the nurses took pity on me while I was with them. Mandy Sharp was one of them."

"Oh no – how is she?" There was genuine panic in her voice.

"She'll live – that's the best they can say at the moment. Sorry love, I need a few hours sleep, I've had a difficult night." He collapsed on the bed and his wife undressed him. "Don't let me go beyond ten!" and he was asleep.

'Difficult' was the understatement of the century. Stopping the more serious of Henderson's two wounds from pumping blood for the twenty minutes it took the paramedics to get to them was bad enough but then the fun really started. Day insisted on making the lengthy walk to see Mrs Jones' body before it was taken away. He questioned the officer standing guard about the battered taxi and its driver. No one knew anything but everyone assumed the worst. He was about to set off back when fortunately, Pug Davies arrived at the scene in a borrowed 4X4 to pick him up.

It was a much easier route with headlights on main beam. On the way back to civilisation, they stopped to examine the abandoned Landrover under floodlights. By that time, Wilbourn had been carried off to hospital; word was he'd probably lose the use of his arm. Given that he was in the act of pointing a gun at Day's head when his accident happened, the DCI didn't feel too much sympathy.

By the time the two old friends arrived back at the Hall, almost everyone had gone. The few officers still there gathering evidence were horrified at Day's appearance. His clothes were torn and covered in blood – fortunately only a tiny proportion was his own. A constable Day didn't know handed him a piece of paper torn from his notebook. The message read, 'Report to Chief Constable's office, Ripley, 1pm Monday'. A kick in the teeth.

On Halfpenny's orders, all the Jean Vincents had been carted off to Beetwell Street for questioning. Wilbourn's four remaining servants were in the lounge looking totally bewildered. All had been ordered to remain on the premises and they stared at Day as if he were from outer space.

"Go and get some sleep," he ordered. "Be up and ready for interview at 8am."

After checking everyone was doing what they should be, he asked Pug to drive him to the hospital.

"About time," said Davies, "you need some treatment!"

"Not for me, I want to see Mandy and Mr Dawson."

On the way to Pug's car, Day called the station and asked them to find a number for the Military Police Holding Centre. It didn't take long and, as Pug drove, Day called and asked for Captain Church. There was lots of clicking on the other end of the line before a very sleepy voice said, "Yes?"

"Good morning, Caroline," said Day, in the most artificially cheerful voice he could muster, "Derek Day here, you remember, Chesterfield police. I just…"

"Fucking hell, Inspector, have you any idea what time it is!"

"I know exactly what time it is, thank you. I thought you'd want to be the first to know – we've made several arrests and I can confirm that Marines Martin and Hamilton were not victims of terror attacks. Indeed, no Muslims were involved – certainly not Tahir Abbas. Please pass on my best wishes

234

to Sergeants Bryant and Vernon. Goodnight, Captain. Oh, and it's Chief Inspector." Day hung up and allowed himself a spiteful grin.

"You know, Derek Day, you've got a vicious streak!" laughed Pug.

Day ignored him and dialled another number. Much to his surprise, the call was answered immediately.

"Abbas!"

"Good morning, Mr Abbas, DCI Day here. Sorry to call at this disgraceful hour but, I thought you'd like to know immediately – I've just called the MPs holding Tahir and told them we've arrested the real murderers and they've got the wrong man!"

"Thank you, Chief Inspector." The response was alarmingly flat.

"I was just thinking that you're the right person to start applying pressure to get him released. Their number is…"

Day was interrupted before he could pass on the information.

"You're a good man, Mr Day, goodnight." The call was disconnected.

Pug had heard most of the brief conversation and raised his eyebrows. "That didn't sound good," he said.

Indeed, it wasn't good. Alone in his study, Mr Abbas was thinking about the lies he had been told and the truths he'd discovered. Did he even have a son?

The journey to the Royal Hospital was easy in the early hours and, unsurprisingly, both injured officers were sedated and fast asleep. Day didn't mind, he just wanted to see for himself they were alive and likely to stay in that condition. He sent Pug down to the station to prepare for a day of very intense detective work.

Day cross-examined a doctor at length and was repeatedly assured his colleagues' lives were not in danger.

He'd already learned it was one bullet – through a uPVC door – through a detective's forearm – and through a PC's stab vest. It must have hit Dawson's sternum like a sledgehammer but, thank Heavens, it had penetrated no further. Sharp's condition was more problematic. The bullet, already knocked out of shape by its passage through the door, had done considerable tissue damage.

"We can only think she'd grabbed the constable's vest and was trying to pull him out of the line of fire. Brave woman!" said the doctor. "She's going to need some pretty extensive reconstruction work but my guess is she'll not lose her arm." The doctor gave a reassuring smile and added, "It's amazing what our lot can do these days!"

Henderson was still in surgery and there was no hint which way it would go. When he enquired after Wilbourn, Day discovered he wasn't there; after DSupt Halfpenny had declared a Major Incident, ambulances had arrived from every direction and, very inconveniently, Wilbourn had been transported to the Hallamshire Hospital in Sheffield.

Day asked after Melanie Price and was told she wasn't seriously hurt. He was escorted along some eerily quiet corridors until he spotted a uniformed constable sitting on a bench reading a book. The youngster leapt a foot in the air when he saw Day but was relieved when the DCI gently waved him back down again. The doctor opened the door to the private room without a sound and there was Miss Price sleeping soundly in bed. On a chair next to her was DC Dom O'Neil, also sleeping soundly. They were holding hands – in any other setting, it would have been a scene of domestic bliss.

The doctor took Day back in the direction of A&E and led him to a cubicle.

Ten seconds later a nurse appeared and began to treat his abrasions. It was another painful experience but the big mug of tea helped. "We always try a little bit harder for police officers," she said.

"Much appreciated," he replied. But he wondered how long he would fit that description.

-

Home matters…
There was definitely a man's voice in the house. At first, he thought he was in some dark corner of Millthorpe Hall but,

as sleep receded, he realised he was safe in bed at home. There it was again – Jess and a strange man, conversing in whispers – what was she up to?

The bedside clock said 9.30am and he tried to sit up. A hundred aches and pains shot through his battered body and he groaned loudly.

The bedroom door opened and in came Jess and a man in a suit. "Ah, Dee, you're awake. This is Mr Allen, from Purple Bricks, he's come to value the house."

She opened the blinds at the precise moment Day made his second attempt to sit up, exposing a face full of steri-strips and a torso covered in bruises.

"Arghh!" he said.

"Jesus Christ!" The estate agent took two steps back.

"No, no," said Jess cheerfully, "he's a police officer – bit of a rough night apparently. You can see it's a good-sized room; and that's the en-suite through there."

Day collapsed back flat on the bed, taking a split second's delight in his wife's barmy sense of humour.

Jess whisked Mr Allen out of the bedroom and Day heard her say, "Help yourself to a good look round. Forgive me for a minute or two – I need to talk to the fuzz."

She came back in full of apologies. "I'm so sorry, with you coming home in such a state, I'd totally forgotten he was coming this morning; there's another one this afternoon."

"Don't worry, I'll be out of your hair in half an hour. Today's going to be frantic!"

"You can't be serious! You're going in, in that state! You're bloody bonkers!"

"Frantic!" he repeated.

She surrendered just as quickly as she always did. "Loose ends, eh? Found out who murdered those marines? You make an arrest?"

"Lots of arrests – and dozens of witnesses to interview…"

"Witnesses? Oh, crikey, I almost forgot. Someone rang from the station. A woman called Gina walked in at seven this morning and said she wanted to tell Mr Day everything.

237

Sorry." A grin appeared on Jess' face. "Everything, eh? Is she pretty?"

"Very," said Day. This was good news; with Gina's statement he could tie up most of the case before Carruthers sent him off to run security at Lidl – if he was lucky.

He rang the station and asked to be put through to his own office. To his delight, Andy Grainger answered after six rings. The DS sounded alert and positive. "Everybody's turned up, sir – except Dom that is, I've told him to stay with his girl for a couple more hours. We've started taking statements from the motorbike lot and the Super's told us to send them away unless they incriminate themselves or each other. Tara's talking to Gina Thomson and getting lots of useful stuff but her brother's still clammed up. Word from the hospital is mixed: DS Sharp's going into surgery anytime now; Dawson's not too bad but they're keeping him in for a couple of days just in case; Henderson's out of surgery and hanging on by a thread, apparently, and Robert Jones, or whatever his real name is, has just been discharged and is on his way down here under considerable escort." Andy paused for breath. "Wilbourn's at the Hallamshire under guard but we haven't heard anything about his condition, yet." There was a gulp. "Oh shit!"

"Andy! What's up?" shouted Day down the phone.

"They've just found a body on the forecourt of that garage near Cutthorpe crossroads! It's got to be the missing taxi driver."

Day groaned again but for a different reason. Poor devil – wrong place, wrong time. More broken hearts for no good reason. This was all down to Wilbourn!

"I'll be with you in half an hour. Organise a briefing for eleven, will you, Andy? And thank everyone for coming in; you must all be exhausted!"

"Excited, sir! We all feel we're winning now – at least we did, until this latest news!"

238

"Agreed! But it's got to be that Jones woman; she must have driven the taxi to Millthorpe – we'll have to collect the evidence but she won't be needing a trial!"

When Day arrived at the station, he received a request from Henry Boston QC for an immediate audience.

"Has he been behaving himself?" asked Day before deciding whether to grant the request.

"Model visitor, sir," confirmed the Custody Sergeant. "Says he wants to apologise in person."

Day looked at his watch. "Let's do it!" he said.

The man brought into Interview Room Three looked pretty shocking after a bad night in the cells – interrupted by a comprehensive medical examination.

He held out his hand and Day graciously shook it.

"Chief Inspector," he began, "I have been very, very silly and I want to apologise most sincerely. I should not have pushed you and you had every right to restrain me. If the charges go ahead, you can be assured I will plead guilty and take the consequences."

He seemed genuine enough and Day had enough to do without spending hours on a pointless prosecution. "Okay. Mr Boston, I understand it was a very fraught situation for all of us; I'm prepared to forget the incident provided you'll return, after you'd had chance to clean up, and make a full statement about your involvement with Mr Wilbourn and his club."

"Agreed, Mr Day. Thank you!"

Day had never seen anyone so eager to leave the station.

Next business was to phone the senior doctor treating Wilbourn and, much to Day's relief, he was tracked down pretty quickly. "Thanks for talking to me, doctor. What's the situation with our Mr Wilbourn?"

"Not good, I'm afraid. In layman's terms, the right elbow and the bones twenty centimetres above and below are completely shattered. If he wasn't heavily sedated, he'd be screaming in agony."

"Prognosis?"

"The arm needs to come off, but that's the problem – in his lucid moments, he's most insistent that we don't amputate!"

"And if you don't?"

"Massive infection and death – only a matter of time."

"Any point in me coming over to interview him?"

Day actually heard the doctor shrug. "You might get some sense out of him. Depends how patient you can be."

Day thanked the doctor and said he'd ring again later.

Chapter Thirty-One

11.00 Briefing

Andy Grainger had organised the briefing Day had requested but he wasn't present; he'd gone off to Cutthorpe to take charge of the crime scene where the taxi driver's body had been discovered. DSupt Halfpenny had sent her apologies; she'd gone off to Ripley HQ on some important mission or other. Day knew he'd have to follow her not later than 12.15 to guarantee being on time – not that that would make any difference to the Chief's overpowering desire to sack him. In fairness, Day had broken more rules and protocols in the last 24 hours than most officers broke in a career but, in his defence, he would argue that the end justified the means. That wouldn't wash, though – the Chief was a stickler for rules.

The team gathered and, despite the positive atmosphere, most looked shattered. There was plenty of coffee but not the bucketloads of refreshments he had expected to see.

"Where's DS Davies?" Day asked of the crowd.

"Think he went off with the Super, sir," answered Kam.

"Right," said Day, "time is limited, so make me happy with lots of useful reports!"

Day already knew most of what followed but it was important the whole team was kept up to date.

Details of the condition of the two wounded police officers came first, closely followed by information about the injured people who'd been arrested.

Henderson in Intensive Care with two bullet wounds; Jones with bruises and a broken wrist had just arrived in the cells, soon to be interviewed and Wilbourn under sedation while doctors discussed what they could do with his shattered elbow.

Will Thomson was also still in the cells but simply kept repeating 'No comment' to every question. Gina Thomson, however, was an entirely different story. Her statement given to DC Rutherford had opened the case completely. That alone, when corroborated, would mean lengthy jail sentences for a number of suspects.

Day selfishly hoped it would be enough to get the Chief Constable off his back.

The deceased Mr and Mrs Jones had not yet been identified but all present were quietly confident that DNA and/or fingerprints would reveal their true identities.

"These three Jones people have the look of killers for hire brought in by Wilbourn. That's the confirmation I need from Robert 'whatever-his-name-is' Jones," said Day. "It really is crazy – Wilbourn was so obsessed with Gina Thomson, he actually had her boyfriend bumped off just to free her up. He went to a lot of trouble to make it look like Islamic terrorists, including having another guy killed for no other reason! He's going to pay!"

There were nods of agreement all around the room.

"What do you think Will Thomson's involvement was in all this, boss?" asked Kam.

"His solicitor said he'd make a statement today, so all will be revealed but, my guess is he helped set up Gary Martin just to get in Wilbourn's good books – insane!"

Reports on the interviews with lesser members of the Jean Vincents followed and in every case except two, the detectives thought the interviewees unpleasant but not guilty of involvement in the major crimes being investigated. Boston and Coy, though were regarded with some suspicion.

Realising that the end of this briefing would probably be the end of his involvement in the case and possibly the end of his career, DCI Day organised a detailed list of duties and interviews for his team to conduct throughout the next twenty-four hours.

At noon he retired to his office and packed his briefcase. He had a last look around and headed down to the car park. At 12.15, just as he was about to start the engine, his mobile rang.

"DCI Day? Helen Sparks."

The Chief's PA! 'What now?' thought Day.

"Go ahead, Helen."

"You have an appointment with the Chief scheduled for 1pm – it's been cancelled."

"Cancelled?"

"Cancelled, correct."

"Cancelled, not postponed?"

"Am I not being clear, Mr Day?"

"Sorry, Helen, you are being very clear. Thank you." He hung up. 'What's all that about?' he thought.

Mightily puzzled by the unexpected stay of execution, he wandered back into the station, re-entered his office, sat down and, for the first time ever, put his feet up on the desk. After five minutes contemplation, he went out into the main department. There wasn't a detective in sight so he found a comfortable chair and began making phone calls.

In the first call, Andy Grainger confirmed that it was the taxi driver who'd been found dead on the garage forecourt. First examination suggested a garrotte was the murder weapon. The DS was now on his way to break a young family's heart.

The second call was to Chesterfield Royal for an update on Mandy Sharp's condition. He was told the surgery went well but more operations would be required in the coming months.

Dawson was sitting up in bed, chatting up nurses and showing off the massive bruise on his chest to anyone prepared to look.

Henderson had been moved to HDU and doctors seemed confident he'd make a good recovery.

Another call to MP Captain Church was more frustrating. They still hadn't agreed to release Tahir Abbas even though Day had sent through written reports about the arrests made after the revelations of the previous night.

"We accept your evidence for charging others with the two murders, bet we're still not convinced by his explanations for his conduct in Afghanistan," she said.

Equally frustrating and for some reason Day didn't understand, Will Thomson's solicitor insisted his client wouldn't make a statement before 5pm.

The cancelled meeting with the Chief Constable had given Day some time to play with and he was just about to go to sit in on the Robert Jones' interview when in walked Dipa Sindhu, obviously off duty.

"Ms Sindhu, what can I do for you?"

"Nothing, thank you, sir. I was just looking for Andy... DS Grainger. I know it's cheeky but I was hoping he could be spared for a while on a personal issue?" Looking around, she added, "I'm guessing that's impossible?"

"Afraid so, sorry. I think we're all going to be booked solid for the next seventy-two hours!"

"No surprise there then. See you later, sir."

"Hang on a minute; if you're at a loose end, do you fancy doing a bit of detective work with me?"

"Love to, sir," she said. 'Mission accomplished,' she thought.

-

"Ah Derek, glad I've caught you," said DSupt Halfpenny as they crossed on the car park stairs. "Miss Sindhu taking you on a trip?" She grinned at her own joke. "Let's find a quiet corner – I need to talk to you for two minutes."

Not easy in Chesterfield Police Station but an empty room was discovered.

"Did you have anything to do with my appointment being cancelled, ma'am?" he asked.

"I was a small contributor," she admitted modestly. "It was a group effort. Your friend Pug and Sergeant Barry both helped. The main candidate, though, was the rumour-mill. Someone started telling stories about the Chief's unfortunate intervention in the hostage situation and his reaction to being shot at. You know what it's like, Derek – by the time the story had done the rounds of HQ, our noble Chief was being presented as a complete tosser who nearly got the hostage killed – not to mention the soiled underwear!" Halfpenny

244

couldn't hold it in any longer and burst into almost hysterical laughter. "The silly sod's gone off sick! He'll not be back for weeks – if at all. I think you'll be in the clear!"

The weight of a thousand misdemeanours were lifted from his shoulders and he began to stammer his thanks.

"Oh, bugger off, Derek. Take Sindhu on your excursion!"

Day never ceased to be impressed by Sindhu's driving. She'd offered to take her own car and she understood the elderly BMW's performance and foibles intimately.

It was always pretty miraculous to find a parking space at the Royal Hallamshire Hospital in Sheffield – one of his reasons for wanting a chauffeur – but today luck was on their side.

Following directions to the appropriate department, Day was surprised to see no police officers on duty.

When Day and Sindhu introduced themselves to the Ward Sister, she laughed out loud. "We're popular with the police today, I've never seen so many!"

Day wasn't amused. "Where's Wilbourn?" he asked.

The nurse was a little peeved that her bonhomie had fallen on stony ground and she replied tersely, "Gone!"

"Gone? What do you mean? Gone where?" Day's instinct had turned his stomach into a knot.

"A lawyer came with a doctor and some policemen and a court order. They told us they were transferring him to the Royal National Orthopaedic Hospital in London. They've got some hotshot surgeon who reckons he can save the arm. One rule for millionaires, eh?" But the senior nurse was now looking more than a little anxious.

"Did you see the court order?"

"No, but the officers guarding Mr Wilbourn seemed satisfied with it."

"When? How long ago?"

"Only a few minutes." She looked at her watch. "Less than fifteen, I reckon. It'll take that long to get him into the ambulance. If you run, you'll probably catch them."

Day and Sindhu ran.

There was a queue for the lifts so they took off down ten flights of stairs.

"What are the odds, sir?" Sindhu panted.

"Can't be good. Court order in that time? No wonder Boston wanted out of the cells so urgently!"

They rushed out onto the access road to see nothing out of the ordinary.

There was, however, a security man on duty. Seeing Day's credentials, he immediately became Mr Helpful.

"Yes sir. There was a private ambulance parked here for best part of thirty minutes. I tried to move him on but one of your lot got out of a car behind and told me to mind my own business."

"One of my lot?"

"Detective, sir. He showed me his badge. Sounded a bit foreign."

"Police car?" asked Sindhu.

"No miss. Civvy. Blue Subaru."

"Any uniforms?"

"No miss, all in civvies."

This was bad. Very, very bad.

"Describe the ambulance."

"Silver Renault – with 'PRIVATE AMBULANCE' written on the side! Blue light on top."

"How long ago did they leave?" demanded Day.

"Five minutes, tops. Have I done something wrong, sir?"

"No, not at all!"

As they set off running towards Sindhu's car, he chased after them waving a slip of paper. "Would you like the registration numbers?" he shouted helpfully.

Day had been tempted to kiss the security man but sensibly refrained.

As Sindhu started the car, Day sent the registrations of the two relevant vehicles to Beetwell Street and instructed them to be distributed nationally.

"Which way?" said Sindhu.

"No idea yet," replied Day. "Tell you what – head off in the general direction of the M1, we might get lucky!"

The tiny element of hope both officers felt that the hospital transfer might be legitimate was dashed when it was confirmed that ambulance and Subaru had been stolen hours earlier.

This was some slick organisation; Wilbourn had been in hospital for only fourteen hours. Could this possibly be the work of a bunch of rich degenerates like the Jean Vincents?

Day issued a stop and detain order but stressed, after the near-misses of the previous night, that the people in both stolen vehicles might be armed. Extreme caution required!

They drove steadily through heavy city traffic waiting, impatiently, for a bit of ANPR magic to come through.

There was a breakthrough but it came from a most unexpected source.

DC Tara Rutherford was just parking her car at Chesterfield Royal Hospital, on her way to do a report on the conditions of the two police officers and Henderson, when she heard of the Wilbourn disappearance on the radio. Not knowing what else to do, she continued on her mission to DS Sharp's room first.

Mandy was awake and alert and immediately demanded an account of progress in the investigation. On hearing about Wilbourn, Sharp exploded into action. "Wheelchair! Find me one quick!"

Despite her misgivings, Rutherford went out and returned two minutes later suitably equipped.

"Take me to Henderson!" demanded the DS.

Rutherford objected again but was forcibly overruled.

The two sped along crowded corridors causing consternation amongst staff, visitors and patients. They were refused admission to HDU until Sharp made ambiguous threats about obstruction and wasting police time.

Henderson appeared to be unconscious but Sharp insisted on being pushed up close. She whispered to him in the softest of sing-song voices, "Mr Henderson, Wilbourn is on the run – where will he go?"

Nothing.

She repeated the question just as a posse of senior doctors burst in and ordered the detectives out. But Henderson's lips were moving and he said a single word that no one heard clearly.

As they were escorted back to Mandy's room, the detectives debated what they had heard.

"Gamston? What the hell is Gamston!"

Rutherford's iPhone gave the answer at the second attempt. "Village near Nottingham... Bloody hell – it's an airport near Retford!"

"Tell the boss – now!" ordered Sharp.

A dozen calls later, armed police were on their way to Retford Gamston Airport but Day wanted to be in on the action and set the satnav on his phone to give Sindhu directions. "Step on it, Dipa!" he ordered in a passable imitation of a deep-south sheriff. "According to this, it's only forty-seven minutes from the Hallamshire to the airport – they'll be there by now!"

But they weren't.

The driver of the private ambulance was in no hurry. Like his colleagues in the Subaru, he'd no idea the police were already looking for them and even had an idea where they might be heading.

The airport was indeed one possible destination but they didn't want to create suspicion by arriving in an ambulance. The A57 took them through a heavily wooded area and they pulled off the road to make modifications. The magnetic signs were removed and one man climbed up to detach the roof lights as the recently struck-off doctor inside did his best to make Wilbourn more comfortable. Injections of drugs designed to make the multi-millionaire calm and talkative had been administered. Even so, PW was sufficiently alert to be aware the only way to stay alive was to avoid divulging the codes for his secret offshore bank accounts.

His 'rescuers' would be on the A1 heading south soon and that's where they had been told to make the decision: if they had the required information early enough for verification, they should kill him and find somewhere convenient to

248

dump the body. Without verification they should deliver Wilbourn and a one-man escort to his pilot chum and then get back on the motorway to London. No account numbers at all meant the same trip to the airport but with a much larger escort for the very illegal pre-booked flight into Europe – probably followed by some rather sophisticated torture. When the information was verified, Mr Wilbourn would become an ex-millionaire and, shortly afterwards, an ex-human being.

-

Tahir Abbas was released by the Military Police at 4pm. By 6pm, he had made it to his parents' house and received a frosty reception. As he entered the lounge, his father got up and left the room. It was up to his mother to act as peacemaker.

"He's found out about you and Lianna. Why didn't you tell us you weren't happy, we could have helped? What's really upset him is that you lied and kept up a sham. He came back from Lianna's…"

"What? He went to Lianna's flat?"

"Yes. He said she explained that you were good friends – brother and sister – I think she said, but not in love. He wondered about that flatmate of hers – they seem very close. Do Lianna's parents know she likes girls?"

"I doubt it; it wouldn't go down too well!"

"You need to make it up with your father, Tahir. As I said, it's the lying that's upset him. I think he'll eventually forgive that you don't want to go through with the match we made for you. Talk to him; tell him how you feel."

"I will, mother but first I must have some sleep. Forgive me, I'm going to bed."

-

Sindhu was driving well above the speed limit down a long, straight road surrounded by trees, when a blue Subaru pulled out in front of her. With superb reactions she managed to execute a perfect slide to avoid a collision but, to her disgust,

249

the other driver just drove off with no acknowledgement of his dangerous driving.

Day had closed his eyes a split second before the impact that didn't come. When he looked up, Sindhu's BMW was stationary and the other car was disappearing into the distance. "That's them!" he shouted.

As Sindhu engaged gear to give chase, Day caught a glimpse of silver amongst the trees in the extreme left of his peripheral vision. "Stop, I'm getting out. You follow the Subaru – but don't engage!" He jumped out and ran into the trees before she had chance to argue.

He doubled back and approached the stationary van from the front near side. The driver was concentrating on his phone screen. Another man was on the roof pulling at the array of emergency lights. As he threw it to the ground, he noticed Day walking casually towards him.

"Who the fuck are you?" shouted the man. "And what are you looking at?"

"Hitchhiker!" said Day, "Any chance of a lift to Lincoln?" He hoped his eccentric response would create another second's confusion to allow him to close in. He needn't have worried, the over-confident man jumped down right in front of him presenting a perfect target.

Not knowing the number he was up against, Day had no time for niceties, the man had to go down - no introduction necessary. Day didn't wait for him to regain his balance; a perfectly timed right cross broke the man's nose and he staggered against the side of the van. Day kept up the momentum by cracking the dazed man's head against the metalwork. One down.

He heard the rear doors and driver's door open simultaneously and an instant decision was made – back end first. Day ran around and hit the door hard with his shoulder, smashing it into the head of the first to exit. Day grabbed his collar and yanked him to the ground. His head hit the gravel with a crunch and Day guessed he was out of the fight for a couple of minutes. Long enough.

Day risked a glance inside. Wilbourn strapped to a gurney with an older man bent over him, hypodermic in hand.

"Police!" yelled Day. "Don't move, you're under arrest!"

That actually seemed to amuse the man and he came towards Day with the obvious intention of using the syringe as a weapon.

Day had never cared for injections but other things were on his mind. The driver had approached stealthily down the off-side of the vehicle and now attempted to slam the half-door into this nuisance policeman.

More by instinct than judgement, Day took a half-step to his left and grabbed the outstretched hand of the distracted syringe wielder, pulling him out into the open and, using his weight to reopen the door and knock the driver off balance. It worked – but Day now faced two startled, but not incapacitated enemies - and the driver had a gun!

The gun took priority. Day leapt onto the gunman and knocked him to the ground. They wrestled for possession of the pistol for a few seconds before Day managed to get in a decisive head-butt. As the driver groaned and melted into the gravel, Day felt a scratch on the back of his neck. He instinctively swung his right elbow back hard and made contact with the face of his assailant.

How relaxed he felt! Day laid on the oh-so-soft gravel and stared up at the azure, cloudless sky. For the first time that day he noticed the warm autumn colours enhancing the sparse foliage above and the trilling of a thousand birds. He floated weightlessly from the ground and began rotating smoothly around the layby surrounded by the drifting rabbits, foxes, badgers and garden gnomes that had emerged to watch his gentle odyssey. Gnomes? One of the gnomes was shaking him.

Focus! It wasn't a gnome; it was a bobble-hatted football supporter. The man's lips were moving but Day couldn't make out what he was saying.

He had to explain the situation to this potential good Samaritan. "Crawl da plees," he said. "Iza plees offitzer."

Three more bobble hats came into view. "What did he say, Len?"

"I think he's a copper – but he's out of it!"

"See if he's got ID."

Day felt his jacket being rearranged and then heard a triumphant shout.

"He is a copper! Chief Inspector!"

"Wow! Dial 999! Tie the others up with your scarves!"

"Goon – where's the glun?" slurred Day.

"What's he say?"

"Does he mean 'gun'?" said the supporter in the most extravagant hat. He held up the automatic. "Does he mean this?"

"Is it real?"

"I don't think it's real." He pointed it in the air and pulled the trigger. The result changed the mood considerably. "Oh shit, it's real!" he yelled.

Day vaguely remembered he had always disliked bad language – and then everything went black.

EPILOGUE

The four London gangsters followed by PC Sindhu were arrested at Retford Gamston Airport but there was never enough evidence for successful prosecutions. When they returned to London without the keys to Wilbourn's fortune, their boss had them tied up and thrown into the Thames.

The four London gangsters found injured by the side of the A57 were found guilty of several offences and would serve lengthy prison sentences. Lucky them.

Henderson made a full recovery. When told by his doctors that the detective's desperate rugby tackle had undoubtedly saved his life, the butler became very helpful and enabled Fraud Squad officers to confiscate most of Wilbourn's ill-gotten gains.

Wilbourn lost all his wealth and his arm – but that was just the good news. Three days after he was transferred from hospital to remand, he was stabbed - on the orders of his former friend from London. RIP.

Millthorpe Hall was sold to a close friend of Vladimir Putin. He employed an experienced, one-eared butler named Henderson.

Robert Jones (real name Marcus Blackshaw) took detectives to find Gary Martin's body but was still sentenced to life imprisonment for murder. He escaped six weeks after his trial and now lives in Switzerland – where he is Assistant Curator of the William Tell Museum.

Will Thomson got ten years for his part in Shiner's murder. His sister would never forgive him.

No charges were ever brought against other members of The Jean Vincent 1000 Motorcycle Club but it was disbanded by Simon Coy three months after graphic descriptions of their orgies were reported in 'The Sun' – he couldn't handle the flood of membership requests.

Tahir Abbas was exonerated of all charges and eventually made peace with his father. He qualified as a paramedic and went to live with his real girlfriend, Lisa. He sold his medal and donated the money to the International Red Crescent. Tahir's former fiancée, Lianna emigrated to Canada with her partner.

Gina Thomson and Angie Lake also agreed to sell their boyfriends' medals. They used the proceeds to set up a helpline for bereaved partners of armed forces personnel.

Murphy the mechanic mends motorbikes in Melton Mowbray.

Chief Constable Carruthers took early retirement and now runs security in Chesterfield Lidl.

PC Dawson was featured in the 'Best Bruise Compilation' on YouTube and returned to work three weeks after leaving hospital.

DS Amanda Sharp had two more surgeries but eventually would make a full recovery and return to Derbyshire Police as Detective Inspector.

DS Andy Grainger proposed to Detective Constable Sindhu but she turned him down – wanting to concentrate on her new career.

Melanie Price invited DC Dom O'Neil to move in with her. After four seconds of careful consideration, he agreed.

DSupt Halfpenny is still going on posh dates with the same bloke – she can't decide if he's a 'keeper'.

Home matters…
Jessica Day was horrified when there was a difference of
£9,000 between the lowest and highest valuations of the
house on Holme Park Avenue. She wanted to offer the lower
but her husband said they should definitely pay the higher
valuation. When Jimmy and Sally Hammond found out –
they insisted that the lower price was fair. The deal was
done. Happy Days.

-

It was 4.30am on a cold November morning. Outside Angie
Lake's house in Brampton, a man dressed in running gear
was doing warm up exercises. Appearing satisfied with his
preparation, he set his stopwatch and began his run. At this
time in the morning there would be no difficulty in crossing
the many roads that might have otherwise delayed his
progress, so he accelerated to a blistering speed and followed
Steve Hamilton's challenging route without variation.
He arrived back outside Angie's house and checked his time.
Very satisfactory. After some cooling down exercises, he
climbed back into his car and drove home. DCI Derek Day
had completed his personal tribute to two dead heroes.

End

By the same author:

'ONE DEAD HEAD' – DCI Derek Day's first outing. At last, a senior detective who's normal! Happily married, good at his job and well respected – with only one tiny, dark flaw (that everyone knows about).

In One Dead Head, the killing of a popular young headteacher is a shock to all the families involved with his successful school. Until, that is, Day discovers the real motive for his death and identifies dozens of suspects. But, every time the DCI gets close to the truth, another suspect vanishes!

Coming in 2021 – 'Three Dead Tourists'

Writing as George Ian Stuart:

THE TREBIAN TRILOGY
Book 1 Trool's Rules
Book 2 Cruel Trool?
Book 3 Trool's Fools

The human race is almost wiped out by a plague (not Covid19)! The few survivors gather in the English Lake District. Soon Britain is occupied by a race of super-intelligent aliens who allow the rest of the planet to return to nature. The newcomers appear friendly and provide support for the struggling humans – but do the humans deserve that support? Only the great Trebian Mindminder, Si Trool thinks so...

Dark comedy satires with laugh-out-loud moments, these three novels will set you thinking about the human condition. Recommended for 16+ only.

Available:

As ebook on Kindle

In paperback direct from publishers **feedaread.com** or contact the author direct on **ian.s.mccollum@gmail.com**

9 781839 455735